'Exactly how m[uch does] it take to convi[nce you you're in] danger?'

'Fine. I'll hire a bodyguard,' Amanda stated coolly.

Midsummer heat flowed over them like lava, and David's temper was firing on all eight cylinders. 'There's not a man on earth who can protect you better than I can.'

'Oh, really? Do you have gun?'

'Don't need one.'

'Do you know karate?'

'I know you,' David said.

Amanda planted her fists on her hips and scowled up at him. 'What difference does that make?'

'I know when you're tired, when you're angry, when you're pleased. I know you pretend to be efficient when you feel out of control. I know you sometimes say "no" when you mean "yes." For example, if I asked you right now to kiss me, you'd say no...' He slipped his hand behind her neck and slowly moved towards her. 'But I know you want to...'

Dear Reader,

What a month May is! With four gripping tales of mystery, Silhouette Intrigue® will have you on the edge of your seats!

Gayle Wilson's SECRET WARRIORS trilogy comes to an end this month with *Her Baby, His Secret*, where Griff Cabot comes back from the dead and has to save the baby daughter he never knew he had—it's romantic suspense at its best! But don't be too disappointed by the loss of the warriors, we have more than a sneaking suspicion that they'll be back and, meanwhile, we have a new trilogy beginning— CAPTIVE HEARTS. Three women go from hostages during a crime to prisoners of passion… That's *Father, Lover, Bodyguard* from Cassie Miles now and, next month, Patricia Werner's *His To Protect*.

In Tina Vasilos's *In Her Lover's Eyes* nurse Abby Chance becomes involved with sexy murder suspect Zach Andros. And in Saranne Dawson's *Lawman Lover* Michael Quinn is reunited with old flame Amanda Sturdevant in their quest to find a killer. We're sure you'll find them all quite breathtaking!

Look after yourselves and come back next month when there'll also be new books from Rebecca York, Shawna Delacorte and Charlotte Douglas.

The Editors

Father, Lover, Bodyguard

CASSIE MILES

SILHOUETTE

INTRIGUE

Silhouette and Colophon are registered trademarks of
Harlequin Books S.A., used under licence.

First published in Great Britain 2000
Silhouette Books, Eton House, 18-24 Paradise Road,
Richmond, Surrey TW9 1SR

© Kay Bergstrom 1999

ISBN 0 373 22521 0

46-0005

Printed and bound in Spain
by Litografia Rosés S.A., Barcelona

Dear Reader,

While researching CAPTIVE HEARTS, Pat Werner and I took an insider tour of a bank in Denver in order to check out the vaults, safe-deposit boxes and security procedures. We asked the security guards so many questions that they began exchanging suspicious glances. Perhaps they wondered whether we were—as we claimed—wide-eyed, innocent romance writers or whether we were plotting the next big heist.

I have to admit that the idea of bank robbery flitted across my mind, but I was more intrigued by the possibility of being held hostage. Such a terrifying and intense situation would be like drowning. My life would flash before my eyes. I'd regret the mistakes and promise that if I got out alive I would be a better person.

In *Father, Lover, Bodyguard*, Amanda has a chance to heal the mistakes of her past and reconcile with the most important man in her life.

I hope you'll enjoy reading this and the other CAPTIVE HEARTS stories, *His To Protect* and *The Safe Hostage*.

Happy reading!

Cassie Miles

To Matt and Jackie

Prologue

The windowless conference room on the lower level at Empire Bank of Colorado was conveniently near the safe-deposit boxes, but it was small—claustrophobically small. The beige wall seemed too close to Amanda Fielding's back. She felt crowded at the square laminated wood table with the two other women, Tracy Meyer and Carrie Lamb.

Amanda's discomfort was underlined by the difficult subject of this nine-o'clock meeting on July 1. In short, Tracy Meyer needed ready cash to care for her stepdaughter, and Amanda opposed dipping into the stepdaughter's trust fund.

Closing the manila file folder on the table, Amanda stated, "I'm not completely heartless."

"I know," Tracy whispered in a shy voice. "I appreciate that you would take the time to meet with me."

"That's my job." Amanda was president at this midsize branch of Empire Bank. "As I see it, we need to consider the big picture. Your stepdaughter is seven years old, and we must consider her best interests in the long run. I understand your attachment to the child, but—"

"Do you?" Tracy Meyer softly interrupted. "I don't think of Jennifer as my stepdaughter. She's as much a part of me as my hands and my eyes. I've raised her since she was four. Jennifer and I went through her father's death together.''

A tear spilled down her cheek, and Carrie Lamb reached over to pat her arm and murmur comforting words.

This meeting had been Carrie's idea, and Amanda was glad that she was here. Carrie was a teller at the bank with a personal connection to the Meyer family. She was Jennifer's tutor whenever the child, afflicted with a severe pulmonary disorder, couldn't attend public school.

More important in this situation, Carrie had an innate ability to comfort others, a talent Amanda lacked. Not even motherhood had softened her in this respect. Her philosophy could be summed up in three words: "Get over it!" Amanda worked hard to attain her goals, and she expected similar discipline from others.

Impatiently, she peered across the table at gentle Tracy Meyer with her long auburn curls and at kindhearted Carrie Lamb with her adorable, short black hair. In contrast, Amanda felt like the blond ice princess, dressed in a wheat Armani pantsuit with black piping.

"Tracy," she said, "let's start by reviewing the facts."

"You're right," Tracy said. "I'm sorry."

"After your husband, Scott, was killed in the line of duty, a trust fund was set up for Jennifer. The Denver Police League has made significant contributions, as have several citizens. The amount in that fund is close to seventy thousand dollars."

"I need to use some of that money," Tracy said. "I've had to quit my job to stay home with Jennifer. She's sick. She needs me."

"What about your insurance?"

"It doesn't even cover all the medical costs, much less living expenses." Tracy unlatched the lid on her metal safe-deposit box and opened it. "I have the papers right here.

I'm Jennifer's legal guardian. And I'm the trustee for that fund."

When Tracy removed a stainless-steel revolver from the box, the beige walls of the small conference room seemed to shrink even more. "My God, Tracy. Why do you have a gun?"

"It's Scott's service revolver," Tracy explained.

An odd memento. Amanda would've assumed the gun would be confiscated by the police department. Did Tracy have a license for that thing? "Not loaded, is it?"

Startled, Tracy blinked. "I don't know. I hate guns. I wouldn't even know how to check."

Carrie took the revolver from the tabletop and expertly unlatched the barrel cylinder, removing five bullets and dropping them into the box. "It was loaded, but not anymore."

Tracy thrust the documents toward Amanda. "Here."

"I have copies. I know what they say. Legally, you have the right to access the trust. However, as the overseer of this fund, I advise against it. The money should be used for Jennifer's college, possibly for special schooling right now."

"She's keeping up with her class. With Carrie tutoring her, Jennifer reads well beyond her grade level."

"I'm not criticizing."

"It sure sounded like you were."

Amanda flashed a glance at Carrie, seeking her support. But Carrie shrugged, unwilling to take sides as Amanda struggled with her recurring claustrophobia and a tense situation. Hoping for a quick finish to this situation, she was blunt. "Your problem, Tracy, is more than immediate cash flow. You need to think of how it looks to a judge before you start using money from the trust fund. As you know, Jennifer's grandfather has initiated a suit for custody. He's a biological relation. And he's a wealthy man who could offer certain advantages."

"But he doesn't even know Jennifer," Tracy said with surprising vehemence. "His daughter died when Jennifer was two years old. During the four years I've taken care of her, he's only seen her six times. He hated Scott."

"Sounds like a hard man," Carrie said. "Surely, he doesn't have a chance of winning custody. Does he?"

"I'm afraid so." Amanda had a law degree and had practiced for a few years before going into banking. She was not prone to sugarcoat the facts. "After all, Jennifer's grandfather can afford the best attorneys."

"And I can't." Tracy cringed. "I can see how it would look bad if I started using the trust fund."

Finally, they were making headway. "Tracy, you need to find another way to support yourself and Jennifer. A job with flexible hours. Possible loans from your family or—"

Before Amanda could dole out more painful advice, the door handle jiggled and she called out, "We're busy in here."

The door crashed open, kicked in by a heavy boot. The man who stepped inside was dressed all in black, wearing a black ski mask and carrying a semiautomatic weapon. "Let's go. Now!"

"What's happening?" Tracy asked.

Amanda knew exactly what was happening. A nightmare. "Bank robbery."

The man yanked her arm. "You're Amanda. The lady bank president, right? You know the combination to the vault."

She nodded. This couldn't be happening! It couldn't! But it was. This really was a robbery at Empire Bank. My God, what would happen to her employees? To herself? If

Amanda were injured or worse, who would care for her baby? Nine-month-old Laurel Fielding was her life.

Roughly, the bank robber shoved Amanda and Tracy through the conference room door. "Move it! All of you!" he ordered, turning to push Carrie out the door.

The shock of being physically threatened exploded in an all-consuming, suffocating rage. Amanda literally saw red. Her throat constricted, and she couldn't speak. *Get over it!* She had to get a grip. This was her bank. These people were her responsibility. Stiffly, she marched up the stairs to the main level.

On the main floor, two other masked men with guns stormed back and forth between the teller counter and the desks. The early-morning customers and employees lay facedown, not moving. The security guard, Harry Hoffman, sprawled motionless on the marble floor. The back of his head was bloody.

She prayed he wasn't dead. Gritting her teeth against her disabling anger, she spoke to the robber who stood behind them. "We'll do anything you say. Please don't hurt anyone else."

"Move fast. We need you to open the vault."

Amanda walked steadily past the teller counter. Her only thought was to get this over with quickly before there were any more injuries. Standing before the walk-in Remington vault, she halted. "It's a dual lock. It needs the combination and a key."

"Who's got the key?"

Amanda pointed to the head teller, Jane Borelli, who lay facedown, trembling. Her shoulders heaved with silent sobbing. When another of the robbers grabbed her, she curled into a tight little ball. He drew back his boot to kick her.

"Stop it," Amanda ordered. "Can't you see she's too frightened to move?"

Carrie stepped forward. "I'll get the key from her."

Quickly, she knelt beside the other woman, retrieved the key and held it up.

A burst of semiautomatic gunfire shattered the air. The largest of the three men barked, "Quit playing games! Get the goddamned vault open. Now!"

Side by side with Carrie, Amanda faced the main door of the vault, three feet of tempered steel that automatically unlocked from eight in the morning to five-thirty in the afternoon. If Amanda closed it now, the system would activate and the vault would be inaccessible. There was over a million dollars in cash and bearer bonds inside, since the Wells Fargo armored truck had made a drop this morning. With a shove of the door, she could protect the money.

But the cash was insignificant compared with the lives of her employees and customers. She approached the combination lock beside the heavily barred safety door. Working the combination from memory, she twisted until she heard the final click, then she nodded to Carrie, who turned the key.

The vault was open.

While one robber stood watch, the other two went inside.

Amanda, Carrie and Tracy stepped back, huddled together. Though none of them spoke, they communicated by touch, sharing their fear, their helplessness, their frustration. These two women—Tracy Meyer and Carrie Lamb—might be the last people Amanda ever saw. They might die together.

Amanda swallowed that thought. She had to survive. She had to take care of Laurel. Touching Tracy's arm, Amanda felt a bond between them that went deeper than logic or words or what would look good to a judge. If they got out of here alive, she'd make things right for Tracy Meyer.

Amanda's gaze turned toward the windows overlooking

Speer Boulevard. Across the street, she saw a man holding a cell phone. Before he turned away, she recognized him. What was he doing here? Why was he—?

"You!" The shout came from the robber who patrolled outside the vault. "Get away from the windows. Now!"

But before she turned away, Amanda saw a sight that quickened her heart and, at the same time, filled her with dread. Police cars.

The robber saw them, too.

He yelled to the others. "We got company!"

At that moment, one of the customers changed position. He was gray haired, but moved with the agility of youth as he whipped a handgun from beneath his sports jacket and fired three times.

The masked robber screamed with pain, then aimed his weapon and let loose with a prolonged blast that echoed deafeningly. Bullets ricocheted. There was the hot smell of cordite, gunpowder and death.

Amanda ducked and covered her head. She heard screaming as if from a distance. Then there was a whimpering stillness.

When she looked up, the gray-haired customer had fallen in a disjointed heap. His arm stretched out toward her in mute appeal. His blood seeped across the marble floor. "Oh, God. This is my fault."

"There was nothing you could do," Carrie whispered.

"I have to do something."

The need for resolute action burned within her. But what? How could she stop them? She was dimly aware of a telephone ringing and brusque conversation. The robbers must be negotiating with the police. Decisions were being made; their fate was being determined.

One of the robbers announced, "We're going to let you people go."

"An ambulance," she said to him. "Tell the police we need an ambulance."

He gestured toward her, Carrie and Tracy. "You three stand over there."

Quickly, he organized their retreat, using the male executives to carry the injured bodies of the bank guard and the customer with the gun. The others followed one by one, and Amanda watched gratefully as her employees and customers reached safety.

Finally, it was their turn. Amanda and her two companions started toward the door, toward freedom.

"Not you three," said the big man. "We need hostages."

"Not them," Amanda argued, nodding toward Carrie and Tracy.

"Sorry, honey. By yourself, you're not enough."

Imperiously, she drew herself up. Amanda was president of this bank, damn it. She had a reputation in this town. "Do you know who I am?"

"Yeah," he sneered. "You're a hostage."

Idiot! "You have to let these other women go."

"Don't push me. Or you're going to be a dead hostage."

She turned to Tracy, the guardian for a sickly seven-year-old who had already lost her natural mother and father. Why had Amanda been so hard on her? "Tracy, I'm so sorry."

"I know."

She wouldn't let them hurt this woman. Or Carrie. My God, Carrie had already been through too much pain in her life.

Whirling, Amanda confronted the robbers. "Listen to me. I insist—"

From the corner of her eye, she saw the butt of an automatic rifle swinging toward her. Before she could dodge, she heard an explosion inside her head. Her vision distorted in nightmarish images of blood and terror. Then her world went dark.

Chapter One

Amanda lay flat on her back, arms at her sides. Intense pain roared inside her head, and she squeezed her eyes shut, fighting the agony that threatened to sweep her more deeply into clouded slumber. Why did it hurt so much? She didn't remember being sick, didn't remember anything.

Through the haze, her mind emptied into a surreal desert, uninhabited by thought or sound. She stood alone beneath a blank gray canvas of sky. All around her, as far as the eye could see, the desert plains stretched toward a desolate horizon.

She needed to regain consciousness and find her way home, but she didn't know which way to go. The cracked brown earth beneath her feet gave no indication. There were no signposts. Not a path or roadway. Forward or back?

"Amanda!" A deep baritone voice called to her, "Amanda, wake up!"

I'm trying. But she couldn't move. A great heaviness sat upon her chest, weighting her limbs. In her condition— whatever that was—she considered the mere fact that she was breathing a major accomplishment.

"Wake up now."

Why wouldn't he leave her be? She inhaled, exhaled and

inhaled again. The blankness began to clear. Behind closed eyelids, she saw shapeless flashes of neon. Her aching brain ordered her arm to move, but she only managed to twitch her fingers.

"Amanda!"

"Stop it!" Her eyelids snapped open. Blurred images sorted into a glaring light in the middle of a white acoustic-tile ceiling. Where was she?

"Good," the voice said. "You're going to be all right."

Easy for him to say. He wasn't lying here, helpless. In a hospital? Was she in a hospital? Her ears became aware of steady bleeps, buzzes and an undercurrent of faraway voices.

Cautiously, she squinted and looked around. She found herself in a square cubicle. The wall in front of her was a white, sheetlike curtain. Though she still wore her black silk blouse, a hideous yellow blanket covered the legs of her Armani pantsuit. All around her were machines with dials and screens. The sleeve of her blouse was pushed up to the shoulder, and an IV was attached to her arm.

A hand stroked her cheek, and she gazed at the man standing beside her bed. His thick black hair was trimmed short. A cleft marked his chin. He smiled as she gazed into his hazel eyes. She knew those eyes. She'd seen them flare with stormy turbulence and glisten with pleasure.

"David," she said.

"You remember me. That's good. I was concerned about possible memory loss."

"There's nothing wrong with my memory," she snapped. What was David Haines doing here? He was the last person on earth she wanted to see.

A fury, disconnected from logic, churned inside her mind, making it difficult to recall exactly why she was so angry with him. "Damn you, David."

With her free arm, she slapped his face. The sudden movement was more exertion than she could handle. With a groan, Amanda closed her eyes again.

Oh, God, that was the wrong thing to do. She and David were engaged to be married. He'd bought her the most magnificent diamond.

But her ring finger was bare.

She gazed up at him again. Redness from her slap colored his jaw beneath the high cheekbone, but she wasn't sorry she'd hit him. He deserved a punch in the mouth, even though she couldn't remember why.

A tight smile twisted his lips. "You haven't changed, Amanda."

Oh, but she had. She wasn't the same hapless twit who'd fallen in love with him and forgiven him a hundred times. Forgiven him for what? God, she was confused.

Her eyes narrowed to slits as she glared. David wore a white lab coat with a name badge and had a stethoscope in his pocket. Underneath were shapeless blue hospital scrubs. "Why are you dressed like that?"

"I'm a doctor. A second-year resident."

None of this made any sense. She was absolutely sure that he'd never completed his medical training. He'd graduated from med school, but hadn't gone on to do his internship. How could he possibly be a doctor? David Haines was an irresponsible playboy, a man about town who drove a sleek black Porsche. He had taken her love and torn it to shreds. A succession of wild parties and drunken brawls had made a mockery of her sincere commitment.

And what had happened to their engagement? "We didn't get married, did we?"

"You dumped me. Twice."

She remembered. The decision to end their engagement had been more agonizing than the stabbing pain inside her skull. It was a long time ago. Five years ago. That miserable tragedy was far behind her now.

She turned her head toward the loudly bleeping machine beside her. "Where am I?"

"Denver General Hospital," he said. "You're in the E.R. In an examination room."

"The emergency room? Why am I here?"

"You don't remember?"

Her defenses rose. Instinctively, she knew better than to admit that her mind was a blank, desolate landscape. Hadn't he said he was looking for memory loss? She didn't want to stay here and be examined, poked and prodded. Especially not by David. "It's the, um, details," she stammered. "They're a little vague."

His eyebrows lowered in concern. For a moment, she almost believed he was a real doctor, practicing his bedside manner.

"Can you sit up?" he asked.

"Of course I can. What a ridiculous question!"

But when she propped herself up on her elbows, the room began to spin like a rushing carousel. The inside of her head exploded in brilliant Technicolor pain.

Get over it! She forced herself to sit upright on the hard hospital bed. The dizziness accelerated. She was caught on the carnival ride, unable to dismount. Faster and faster she whirled. She was going to faint again.

A terrible panic overwhelmed her. Amanda could cope with the pain. She could face this bizarre confusion, but she couldn't stand being out of control. "David, help me."

He wrapped his arm around her. "You're going to be okay."

Grateful for his support, she leaned against his chest and closed her eyes, drawing on his masculine strength for solace. Even when David behaved irresponsibly—which he did quite often—he was strong. In his arms, she felt secure. His cotton scrubs chafed the side of her face, and she inhaled his familiar clean scent. It had been a long time since he'd held her. Over a year, a bittersweet year. Pressed against him, she heard his steady heartbeat as he held her firmly, rescuing her from the storm of pain.

"Amanda, don't go back to sleep again." His deep voice vibrated inside his chest. "Amanda?"

She shifted within the shelter of his arms, not wanting to leave his embrace. But she had to resist him. David wasn't the right man for her.

She pushed away from him. Being too close was dangerous to her mental health. Sitting on her own with her legs dangling over the edge of the rock-hard bed, she said, "I'm fine."

"If you say so."

"I do."

"Okay." He took a spoon-sized instrument with a light on the end from a drawer. "Hold still. I need to look in your eyes."

"Why?"

"Just do as I say." He held up the stainless-steel instrument. "I want you to follow the light with your eyes. Don't move your head."

Though she had no idea why she should pay any attention to David Haines, she did as he instructed.

"Good," he said. "Your eyes are tracking."

"With all due respect," she said sarcastically, "what, exactly, is supposed to be wrong with me?"

"Concussion," he explained. "You haven't been in a coma, but you've been floating in and out of consciousness. You took a severe blow to the head."

He held up his hand. "How many fingers?"

"Three."

Weakly, she batted his hand out of the way. This was absurd! She had absolutely no recollection of being beaten. This joke had gone too far, and she wasn't laughing.

She needed to get off this hard bed. She had a very full agenda. Things to do, places to go. At nine o'clock this morning, she had a meeting scheduled with Tracy Meyer and Carrie. "It's been nice to see you again, David. But I really must—"

"You're not going anywhere."

"Excuse me?" The nerve of him! "Don't even try to tell me what to do, David. Those days are over."

"If you want another doctor, fine. But you're not getting released from the hospital until we're sure you don't have serious brain damage."

Though she didn't entirely believe him, his words had a sobering effect. "Explain."

"Severe bruising or swelling inside your skull. A blood clot, an aneurysm. If you're lucky, the only symptoms will be a bad headache and some dizziness. Maybe a slight loss of coordination. Ocular irregularities, like seeing double. You might have short-term memory loss."

"Amnesia? But this can't be amnesia. I remember my name and my address."

"Yeah? Tell me what you had for breakfast this morning."

She started to say that she'd had cereal and coffee, but that was another day. Yesterday? This morning was a foggy haze. Obviously, she'd gotten dressed in this wheat-colored pantsuit that went with her Gucci pumps. But she couldn't remember. "I don't know."

"Short-term memory loss is a temporary disorientation," he said. "You can remember the distant past. More-recent events are unclear, but they'll probably come back to you.

Typically, the last thing you'll remember are the circumstances immediately surrounding the trauma to your brain.''

"This condition goes away, doesn't it?"

He shrugged. "Some people never recall the actual events leading up to the injury."

Amanda wasn't *some people*. She did not intend to walk around with a memory hole, a lack of cognizance. "Tell me exactly what happened to me, David. Exactly."

"It's not important. You need to relax and concentrate on feeling better."

She was alert enough to know that he was avoiding an explanation. What had happened to her? A mugging? A car accident? Sudden panic stiffened her spine. A fierce tremor shook her body. "Laurel."

"Calm down, Amanda."

What if something had happened to her baby? "My daughter. She's not hurt, is she?"

"Your daughter?"

"Laurel. My baby." She clutched desperately at the lapels of his white lab coat, searching his eyes for an answer. "Please, David. Tell me nothing's happened to my baby."

His eyes darkened. "I didn't even know you had a child."

A scream rose in her throat. "Is she all right?"

"Your child wasn't involved."

"Thank God." Relief opened a door in her mind as she visualized Laurel's beautiful cherub face and soft blond curls. Amanda could endure an injury to herself, even brain damage. But to Laurel? She couldn't stand it.

"How old is your child?"

"Nine months. She's the most wonderful baby. A little blonde. And I just know she's gifted. I guess every mother says that, but she's so bright." Something in his face warned her to stop talking about Laurel. An unformed memory teased at the corners of her mind, and she winced. "David, you have to tell me how I was injured. I can't relax until I know what happened."

"There was an attempted bank robbery at Empire Bank."

At her bank? "Was anyone else hurt?"

"Three adult males were brought to emergency. A bank guard, a customer and one of the men who tried to rob your bank."

"Are they all right?"

"I don't know."

"Have the police apprehended the robbers?"

"I don't know that, either."

Her shoulders slumped. Why the hell couldn't she remember something so important? The bank was her responsibility, and she'd failed. A customer had been injured.

Amanda reached up and touched the side of her head. The temple above her left eye felt painfully tender. There was a large bandage. "Oh, my God, they didn't shave my head, did they?"

"I was tempted." David stepped back a pace and folded his arms across his chest. "I thought you might be cute with a punk hairdo. But it wasn't necessary to shave. The cut was superficial, right at the hairline. You only needed five stitches."

"You put stitches in my head?"

"That's what I do, Amanda. I'm a doctor. A second-year resident."

"Sure, you are. And I just won the Nobel Peace Prize." She plucked at the IV. "Please take this out of me. I have to go now. There's a lot to do."

Gingerly, she inched toward the edge of the bed, but when she looked down, the tile floor seemed as deep as the

Grand Canyon. She closed her eyes against the strange distortion.

"Vertigo," David said. "You won't be able to walk three paces without falling down."

"I can. I know I can."

He stood in front of her, keeping her on the bed. "Here's the story, Amanda. The IV drip is giving you a nonnarcotic drug to relieve the pain. Without it, you're going to be in a world of hurt. Another symptom of concussion is that you're going to be dizzy. It'll take you a while to get your bearings."

"How long?"

"Stay here overnight for observation."

"Out of the question," she said determinedly. "Where's my purse?"

He rested one hand firmly on her shoulder. With the other, he tilted her chin up and stared into her eyes. "Tonight you should stay in the intensive-care unit so someone can monitor you. Also, I'm recommending an MRI and a CT scan."

"A CAT scan, right? An X ray of my brain?"

"It's standard procedure."

"Not for me." She'd heard about the CT scan. X rays bombarded the head of the patient while they were completely enclosed in a huge machine. "Don't you remember, David? I'm claustrophobic. There's no way I'm going through with a scan."

"They've made improvements in the equipment. We don't have the latest machine here, but we can transport you to another hospital. You'd only need to have your head inside the machine. This is important, Amanda. We need a picture of your brain to make sure you don't have a clot or an aneurysm."

"I won't do it. I want to get out of here."

"Lie down." There was steel in his voice. "Now."

She glared defiance. She would've loved to leap off the bed and storm out of there, but she was too faint headed and confused. And her head hurt. Reluctantly, she stretched out her legs and sank into a recumbent position. "Can you find my purse? There's a cell phone in there and—"

"Forget it," he said.

"I've got to find out what happened. I need to check on the condition of the people who were injured."

"I can do that for you." He tucked the ugly yellow blanket around her. "A nurse will be in momentarily to take some information, and there'll be a neurologist in to examine you."

"Promise me, David. You'll find out about the bank guard and the customer who were injured."

"Okay." David gritted his teeth. Frustration was building inside him. "I'll be back. Don't go anywhere."

"I know my rights," she muttered. "You can't keep me in the hospital if I refuse treatment."

"I swear, Amanda, if you try to get up, I will personally handcuff you to the bed frame."

David stepped into the hallway and yanked the curtain closed behind him. With his thumb, he massaged his jaw where she'd slapped him. She hadn't changed. Not at all. Amanda Fielding was the most stubborn, infuriating woman he'd ever known.

A year and a half ago, when they'd gotten together for a one-night reunion that had rocked the foundations of his world, he'd thought she might be different. He'd hoped for her forgiveness, but it hadn't happened. She'd shoved him out the door of her high-rise condo like yesterday's newspaper. David wouldn't make the mistake of trusting her again.

A year and a half ago, she'd been childless. And now she had a baby daughter. Eighteen months ago.

The timing was right. The child might be David's.

No way, he argued with himself. She would've told him that he was going to be a father. Not even Amanda the ice princess could be so selfish and cold.

At the time, she hadn't mentioned another man, but there must have been someone. Obviously, there was another man, the father of her child. That was the reason she'd refused to see David again, hadn't returned his phone calls.

Though she hadn't mentioned a husband, she might be married by now. His gut twisted when he thought of Amanda with somebody else. Settled down. Married.

Eighteen months? He couldn't ignore the coincidence. Biology was no respecter of wedding vows. Even if she was married or engaged to another man, the child might be David's. He might be a father.

Taking a moment, he allowed the thought to sink in. Was he the father of a blond baby girl? If he'd still been a drinking man, he would now be headed for the nearest tavern, about to order several double shots to dull the edge of his regret. No way would David be an absentee father. He loved children.

Silently, he swore not to let Amanda out of his sight until he had a chance to confront her. He needed to know the truth about baby Laurel.

AFTER ARRANGING for a consultation with one of the neurologists, David instructed an E.R. nurse to talk with Amanda about insurance and health information while keeping an eye on her to make sure she didn't bolt from her bed.

Then he approached Stella, the administrative nurse who manned the central desk in E.R. Through her Coke-bottle eyeglasses, Stella saw everything. She knew every detail about the comings and goings at Denver General. Consulting with Stella would be the most efficient way to get information about the other people who had been injured in the robbery.

She glanced up from the glowing green computer screen as David approached the waist-high counter that surrounded her workstation. Briskly, she said, "You're treating Amanda Fielding, right?"

He nodded.

"She's a popular gal. A bunch of people want to see her."

"Like who?"

"Like that television news reporter, Elaine Montero." Stella pursed her lips. "Honestly, Ms. Montero knows better. We never allow news crews in E.R., but here comes Ms. La-di-da Elaine Montero asking if I can arrange a special interview."

Media interest was to be expected in a bank robbery. "Who else?"

"Some real persistent guy. Stefan Phillips. He says he's Ms. Fielding's fiancé. I've got to tell you, he's a babe."

"Her fiancé?" A knot tightened in David's belly. "She's not wearing an engagement ring."

Stella's eyes widened with curiosity. "What's going on, Dr. Haines? Do you know this Amanda Fielding?"

"We were friends. A long time ago." And that was all he intended to say. Confiding in Stella was like making an announcement over the public-address system. "How's the bank guard doing? I think his name is Hoffman."

"A sprained wrist and a concussion," she said. "He's regained consciousness, and we've already got him in ICU for observation. The other two guys weren't so lucky. The bank robber who took a bullet in the leg ran into complications in the operating room. He's going to be here a couple of days, under police guard, of course.''

"And the third victim?"

She tapped the keys on her computer. "His name is Nyland. Gunshot wounds to the chest and abdomen. It doesn't look good. He's still in O.R."

David made an instantaneous decision to avoid discussing Nyland's condition with Amanda. She was suffering enough guilt.

"Anyway," Stella said, "I need to know if Ms. Fielding is able to talk. The FBI wants to see her."

"The FBI?"

"They investigate bank robberies, Doc." She snapped her fingers. "Get with the program."

David was never good at keeping the various law-enforcement agencies straight. A lot of uniforms came and went in E.R. His concern was dealing with the patients. "What can you tell me about the bank robbery, Stella?"

"I'll tell you one thing for sure, Doc." Her expression brightened at the opportunity for gossip. "The cops messed up."

"How so?"

"The robbers let all the hostages go, except for Ms. Fielding and two other women. The way I heard it, the robbers were about to surrender. They were in the middle of negotiations when, pow!—the SWAT team busted in the windows."

"Major snafu," David agreed.

"Not only that, but one of the robbers made a getaway using a hostage for a shield. Her picture is on the news. Carrie Lamb is her name. Looks like a nice girl."

"I can see why Elaine Montero wants a piece of this action."

"Wait, there's more. At the same time every cop in Denver and the ace SWAT team with all their firepower were at Empire Bank, a federal prisoner who was being taken to the courthouse escaped.''

''Who?''

''Jax Schaffer. A big-time crime boss. He never would've gotten away if the SWAT team had been able to respond.''

David frowned. Here was another bit of information he wouldn't share with Amanda. She was already too confused to be burdened with the escape of a crime boss. With her overdeveloped sense of responsibility, she'd probably take the blame for the victims, the escape and the lousy timing of Denver's SWAT team.

A blond man in a business suit with a maroon silk handkerchief in the breast pocket stepped up to the counter beside David and addressed Stella. ''Pardon me, I wondered if you could give me some information about Amanda Fielding.''

Her magnified eyes surveyed him and made a snap judgment. ''You don't belong back here. What's your name?''

''Frank Weathers. I'm a close associate of Ms. Fielding.''

''How close?'' David asked.

''We work together.'' Frank Weathers pivoted so quickly that the tassels on his loafers flip-flopped. To David, he said, ''I'm an executive at Empire Bank. And you are...?''

''Amanda's doctor.'' Though Frank Weathers didn't seem like Amanda's type, David wasn't sure how well he really knew Amanda anymore. After all, the woman had gone off and had a baby without even informing him.

''Well, Doctor, can you tell me how she's doing?''

''She has a concussion and some superficial bruising,'' David said. ''Her condition is fair.''

''Marvelous,'' he said.

And David breathed a sigh of relief. No way would Amanda allow a man who said "marvelous" to father her baby.

Frank continued, "I'll be sure to tell the other employees that our Amanda is in no real danger. They've all been detained, you see. For questioning by the FBI. It was just my luck that I didn't happen to be at work this morning. Dentist appointment, you know. So, I'm free to—"

When Stella's hand slapped down on the counter, Frank jumped. "You'll have to leave," she said. "Hospital policy doesn't allow a patient's associates to hang around in E.R."

"Of course," he replied. "I'll be in the waiting room. Please keep me informed regarding Amanda's progress."

"Hold on," David said. If he were smart, he wouldn't get involved. He would treat Amanda like any other patient and forget about her. But he needed to find out the truth about Laurel. "Do you know Stefan Phillips?"

"Indeed, I do. As a matter of fact, I saw him in the waiting room."

"Introduce me," David said as he directed Frank through the E.R. to the waiting area, where rows of uncomfortable leatherette chairs faced the desk. A television mounted near the ceiling broadcast a talk show.

After a quick survey of the room, David easily picked out Stefan, who stood out from the crowd. Tall, athletic and blond, he looked like the kind of guy who carried himself with a sense of entitlement. Bitterly, David realized Stefan and Amanda would make a handsome couple. Both fair haired. Both wealthy. Both successful.

When Stefan shook his hand, David noted the muscular grip, which only served to arouse his competitive instincts.

"Is she all right?" Stefan asked.

"Apart from a killer headache, she'll probably be fine. I'd like to do some tests. A CT scan."

"Good luck." Stefan grinned. "Amanda is severely claustrophobic."

"I know." Fighting his jealousy, David peered into Stefan's green-brown eyes. "I heard you were Amanda's fiancé."

"Not really." He had the good grace to look embarrassed over his slight deception. "I thought if I said we were engaged, I could get in to see her. We've been friends for a long time. Our families knew each other back in Chicago."

"So you're the boy next door," David said. He couldn't keep the sneer from his voice. His hostility was way out of line. "Are you her boyfriend?"

Taken aback, Stefan eyed him curiously. "I don't think that's any of your business."

His response was thoroughly appropriate. Actually, he seemed like a decent enough guy, and David was beginning to feel like a rabid jerk. Why did Amanda always have this effect on him?

"If Amanda is all right," Stefan said, "I'd like to take her home."

"Would that home be her condo?" David couldn't help asking. He was behaving badly, but he couldn't help himself. "Do you live with her?"

"Amanda lives alone. Except for Laurel and the nanny."

Good! David permitted himself a smirk. She wasn't married or engaged or living with anyone. She might have dumped him twice, but she hadn't found another suitable mate. For some reason, he found that information deeply satisfying.

"Doctor?" Stefan regarded him warily. "Can you tell me when Amanda will be released from the hospital?"

Frank Weathers appeared at Stefan's shoulder. "Yes, when?"

David glanced back and forth between the two blond men. Though their coloring was similar, they were a contrast. Stefan matched David's height of six foot one. He was outdoorsy with a deep tan. Wiry little Frank had a prissy air about him. And neither one of them was going to get his hands on Amanda while David was still in control. He needed time alone with her to talk.

"If she refuses to stay at the hospital overnight for observation," he said, "I'll arrange for an ambulance. She needs special electrode monitoring equipment."

More than a little white lie, David had just told a whopper. Electrode equipment? That sounded as though she was Frankenstein's bride. He turned on his heel and headed back toward E.R.

"Doctor," Frank called after him. "Will you keep us posted on developments?"

"Yeah, sure."

David would provide the next update just about the same time that hell opened a ski run. If he never saw those two guys again, it would be fine with him.

Back in E.R., David went directly to the curtained room where he'd left Amanda. The neurologist, Dr. Loretta Spangler, was there, looming like another rain cloud on David's horizon. A tall woman with black hair pulled tight in a bun, Dr. Spangler wasn't one of David's greatest fans and took a dim view of his tendency toward practical jokes.

But right now Loretta Spangler directed her glaring disapproval at Amanda, who sat upright on the bed, trying to look imperious in spite of the IV in her arm and the bandage on her head. Her complexion was pale, except for feverish spots of crimson in each cheek.

As soon as she saw David, she appealed to him, "Tell this woman, David. I'm not going to be put inside an X-ray machine."

"Be reasonable," Dr. Spangler said curtly. "For an accurate diagnosis, we need to see what's going on inside your brain."

"I'm fine," Amanda insisted. "All I need right now is my purse and my shoes."

"Dr. Haines?" Using her clipboard, Dr. Spangler pushed the curtain aside and motioned David into the hallway with her. "I can't believe her attitude. Who does Ms. Fielding think she is?"

"A former lawyer," David said. "There's no point in pushing her. She knows we can't treat her without permission."

"Doesn't she understand the risks? Why is she objecting?"

"She's claustrophobic. The idea of being confined for a CT scan frightens her. I'd advise you to give it up, Loretta."

"Let's get one thing straight, Haines." She scowled. "When I need advice from a second-year resident, I'll ask for it."

He wasn't in the mood for her snippy little reprimand. "What the hell do you suggest, Loretta? You can't force a patient to take tests."

"Are you challenging me?"

"Amanda's vital signs are good. She's coping with the pain. She has some short-term memory loss. Some vertigo. But that's all. People get clunked on the head all the time, and they survive. Probability says she's going to be okay."

"Without a scan or an MRI, I won't venture a guess." She tapped furiously on her clipboard with her pencil. "I won't recommend discharging this patient."

"You don't have a choice," he said simply. "Amanda Fielding isn't going to give permission for further treatment."

"I'm writing you up, Haines."

"Fine. You do that."

He returned to the room where Amanda was lying down. She popped up on the bed like a jack-in-the-box. "Well?" she demanded. "Did you get my purse? Do I have my cell phone?"

"Why stop with a phone? How about a fax machine and a computer? Hell, you could bring your whole office in here and pretend like you didn't have a life-threatening injury."

"You don't have to be so cranky."

Her blond hair stuck out at crazy angles. Her mascara was smudged around her eyes like a raccoon. She was a mess. So why did he still think she was the most beautiful woman he'd ever known? What was it about her?

As he stared, he wanted to kiss her until her intense blue eyes took on a dazed expression of willing sensuality. He wanted to make love to her. Damn it, she made him crazy.

He took the stethoscope from his pocket. "Unbutton your blouse."

Her graceful hand flew protectively to her throat. "Why?"

"I need to listen to your heart."

David tried to act like a doctor, but he couldn't help being a man. When she unfastened the top two buttons on her black silk blouse, he experienced a fierce yearning.

Sitting on the bed beside her, he gently pushed aside the material, revealing the intricate black lace of her bra. When he placed the stethoscope on the silky skin of her breast, she trembled in response.

The sound of her heartbeat, steady and slightly accelerated, resounded through the tubing to the earpiece. Suddenly, he remembered what it was like to be inside her. When he looked into her eyes, observing the dilation of the pupils, he saw the past they'd shared. "Breathe deeply, Amanda."

Her breasts rose and fell. He watched, mesmerized by the silky texture of her skin.

"David, did you find out anything about the security guard from the bank?"

"He's in intensive care for observation. He has a sprained wrist and a concussion, like you. He'll be fine."

"What about the other man? The customer."

"His name is Nyland." Tersely, he said, "I don't have an update on his condition."

"Is it bad?"

David hesitated. He couldn't lie to her. "He's still being operated on. He was shot in the stomach and chest."

"Shot?" Stark fear shimmered in her eyes before her defenses rose and she was, once again, distant and in control. "I want to go home. I'm not having the scan. I'll sign whatever waivers are necessary."

But he wasn't ready for her to leave him. He needed to know about the baby. "Here's the deal. I'll discharge you from the hospital, but you can't stay alone tonight. You need to be observed and wakened every three or four hours to make sure you don't lapse into coma."

She nodded. "I can find someone to do that."

"Not just someone," he said emphatically. "Me. I'll go with you as soon as I finish my shift."

"Wait a minute," she said. "What makes you think you're invited to spend the night at my condo?"

"It wouldn't be the first time," he said. "Do you remember? It was a year and a half ago."

"Don't ask me to think. It makes my brain hurt." All she wanted was to go home. She needed desperately to cuddle Laurel in her arms.

"Amanda?"

"I don't want to talk about it, David."

"Eighteen months ago," he persisted. "We met by chance in the Cherry Creek Mall."

She visualized the stores in the mall and a bronze sculpture of geese in flight. "We had coffee."

At first, they'd talked like civilized human beings. She vividly recalled the resonance of his deep laughter. Slowly, the memories became clear. "That was when you told me you were an intern and going to be a resident," she said. "I was happy for you."

And proud. She remembered looking at David and feeling gratified that he'd pulled his life together. He was on his way to fulfilling his dream of becoming a doctor.

Though Amanda could never take him back after their broken engagement five years prior, she had found him irresistible that night.

Her brain flashed on a disjointed montage of images. She saw David lying beside her on primrose-patterned sheets. She remembered him striding naked to the glass doors that led to the balcony in her fourteenth-floor condo. His muscular body was silhouetted against the dawn light.

Startled, she remembered the most important thing. David Haines was the father of her baby.

Chapter Two

They called him the Iceman. He was known for being cool.

But not today. His throat was dry. He sucked down a breath to quench the burning in his lungs. The hospital air smelled like antiseptic, sweat and failed dreams.

Stupid mistakes! The Iceman still couldn't believe it. The robbery should have been a slick operation with three professionals: Temple, Sarge and Dallas. Dallas was the electronics expert who did the override on security systems. Temple plotted the getaway. Sarge was the muscle.

And the Iceman coordinated the three. Every detail had been planned. He should have gotten his payoff and been done with it.

Instead, Amanda Fielding had survived.

Shielding the telephone from the undercurrent of background noise at Denver General, he spoke quietly into the receiver. "She's recovering."

"Bad luck for you."

"This isn't my fault," he said. "Sarge didn't do his job. He was supposed to take care of her."

"It doesn't matter. She's your problem now, Iceman."

And he knew what that meant. He could get caught. Amanda could put the details together and realize that he was involved. She was a witness.

Though he'd learned that she had memory loss from the concussion, her condition was most likely temporary. It was only a matter of time before she'd figure it out and point an accusing finger directly at him. And when she did…

"What should I do?" he asked. "What's the plan?"

"Kill her."

He'd never committed murder before. He didn't even own a gun. "That's not my thing. Get somebody else."

"You kill her," the voice repeated.

The phone went dead in his hand.

He was isolated, on his own. He had to take care of Amanda by himself. To kill her.

He centered that thought in his mind. Her death would be ironic. The Iceman would kill the ice princess.

Mental preparation was necessary. He needed to believe that eliminating Amanda Fielding was nothing more significant than the next step on his path. He could do it.

The Iceman could commit murder.

DAVID PUSHED ASIDE the curtain and entered Amanda's cubicle where she sat on the bed, waiting impatiently. The IV had been disconnected from her arm.

"When do I get to leave, David?"

"Now." He reached into the hall and whipped a shiny, stainless-steel wheelchair into the cubicle. "Hop aboard."

"I can walk," she said.

"No doubt. You're in great shape. Hell, you could run a marathon, but let's do it my way. I have a plan."

She eased herself off the bed. When her feet touched the floor, she wobbled. Her complexion was ashen beneath her summer tan, and he knew the pain hadn't left her.

David took her arm, directing her toward the wheelchair. "Are you still dizzy?"

"A little." She clung to his forearm with a death grip,

refusing to sit down. "Before we go anywhere, explain your plan."

"Why?"

"Because you're one of the most notorious practical jokers on the planet. You always used to get me into embarrassing situations."

"Did I?"

"I seem to remember almost being arrested for wading in the Civic Center fountain."

"You were the one who insisted on stripping down to your underwear," he pointed out.

"I was wearing a silk Versace. I wasn't about to ruin it with that water."

He'd always enjoyed putting her in spontaneous situations. Her sense of adventure was an incredible contrast to the cool facade. "This time, I'm not joking," he promised. "You get in the wheelchair, and I'll take you through the hospital to the front entrance. We'll get in my car and drive to your condominium."

"Why the front entrance? Isn't the back more convenient?"

"Here's the deal. The bank robbery is big news in town. Half the media in Denver are swarming the hospital. They'll expect you to leave through the emergency exit."

"Don't you have security?"

"Sure, but the photographers have telephoto lenses. If I take you out the front and treat you like a regular patient, we might get away without anybody noticing. That's my plan. Unless you want to see yourself on the evening news."

"I think not." A delicate shudder rippled across her shoulders. "I certainly don't want my picture taken with this ridiculous bandage. Even if I can't remember what happened at the bank, I need to keep up appearances."

He didn't point out that her sterling reputation was grossly tarnished after this morning's events. Apparently, bank robberies and brain damage paled in comparison to a woman's vanity. "Also, the FBI wants a statement. If we want to avoid them, I should sneak you out of here."

"Sneak? That doesn't sound sensible." She was gaining strength. Her backbone straightened by perceptible degrees. "I want to do the responsible thing, David. I don't have anything to hide."

"Okay," he said. "The sensible, sane thing is to let me admit you to the hospital for an MRI and a CT scan. Then you should talk to the feds. After that, you might want to issue a statement to the media. On the other hand, if you want to go home, we should sneak out of here right now. Take your pick."

Her blue-eyed gaze steadied as she considered. Then she climbed into the wheelchair. "Let's roll."

Amanda might be a bank president, but she had an endless supply of spunk. It was one of the things he liked about her. "That's my girl."

"I'm certainly not a girl. And I don't belong to you or anybody else."

"Never give an inch, Amanda."

David tucked a blanket over her legs and wrapped another around her shoulders and head, hiding the bandage. He completed her disguise by placing his aviator sunglasses on her nose.

Sarcastically, she said, "This is subtle."

"Keep in mind that this is the city hospital. We get a lot of unusual-looking people here. Try to act like a bag lady."

"Shouldn't you change out of your scrubs?"

"Nope. This way it looks like I'm just another resident, wheeling his patient outside to enjoy the July sunshine."

"My shoes, David. Where are my shoes?"

He glanced around the cubicle. "Don't see them."

"They'd better not be lost. Those are three-hundred-dollar Italian-leather Guccis. Bone-white with a black half-inch platform sole and a sling-back."

"That's what I call selective amnesia," he teased. "You don't remember anything about the bank robbery, but you can describe the soles on your shoes."

"It's no great deduction. I always wear those shoes with this pantsuit."

"Well, they don't seem to be here. We'll find something else for you to wear on your feet."

He pushed the wheelchair through the curtains and into the emergency-care area. Though it was only one o'clock on a Wednesday, there was a lot of activity. The dying wail of an ambulance undercut the sound of people talking, people groaning, people coughing. A harried mother dragged one child by his hand and held another on her hip. Interns wheeled patients on gurneys and in wheelchairs. A uniformed policeman accompanied a manacled prisoner wearing the standard bright orange jumpsuit of county jail. Emergency wasn't David's favorite rotation, but it was never dull.

He approached Stella's counter. Knowing that he could never slip past her without notice, he'd informed her earlier about his escape plans. "Stella," he said, "I'd like for you to meet Amanda Fielding. She seems to have lost her shoes."

"Hello, Stella," Amanda said. "And my purse. I still haven't found my purse."

Critically, Stella stared through her magnifying eyeglasses. "Not much of a disguise, David. She looks like a mummy."

"Thank you," Amanda said. "I told him this was an irresponsible plan."

"The plan's okay. But somebody could still recognize you, and we don't want that to happen." She went to a tall cabinet beside her workstation, opened it and pulled out a cardboard box. "Let's see what we've got in lost and found."

In moments, Amanda was decked out in a pair of cloth slippers and a pink mohair cardigan. A black cloche hat with a yellow daisy on the brim covered her bandage.

"There," Stella said, replacing the sunglasses on her nose. "Throw the blanket over your lap, and you'll blend right in."

"With the inpatients in the psychiatric ward?"

Her disguise was ludicrous. If she hadn't wanted to get home to Laurel so desperately, Amanda never would have considered David's scheme. It was typical for him to come up with something crazy. At one time, she'd thought his spontaneous ideas were charming. But now?

Before she knew it, he was propelling her through back hallways, past operating rooms and recovery areas. At the doorway leading into the front lobby, he leaned close to her ear. "It might help if you slouch down."

"Oh, here's a thought. Why don't I drool and flail my arms? That shouldn't attract any attention whatsoever."

"Whatever turns you on."

Muttering to herself, she humped her shoulders. There was still a dull throbbing in her head, but she ignored the pain. Her only thought was of Laurel.

Cautiously, Amanda peered out from beneath the ridiculous hat, keeping an eye on where they were going. The front lobby of Denver General was two stories with escalators on one end. The space was plain and clean with an information desk in the middle. Though Amanda's condominium was only a few miles away, she'd never been inside Denver General before. As David had said, this was the main city hospital facility. In addition to the regular patients, Denver General provided for accident victims, prison inmates and transients. Not that Amanda could look down her nose. In her pink mohair sweater and daisy hat, she was the queen of weird.

Peeping through the dark sunglasses, Amanda saw a well-dressed, black-haired woman making a beeline toward them.

"Dr. Haines!" the woman called out.

Silently, frantically, Amanda prayed that David would ignore her and keep going. But she felt the wheelchair come to a halt. No such luck.

David stepped in front of her, shielding her from view, as he spoke to the woman. "You're Elaine Montero," he said. "Network news."

"And you're the doctor who's treating—"

"We don't allow newspeople in the hospital, Elaine. Your presence tends to disrupt the patients."

"Is it true, Doctor, that Amanda Fielding is in a coma?"

"If you'll step out of the way, I need to take this nice little old lady outside for some sun."

When he gestured toward her, Amanda ducked, but Elaine Montero didn't give her a second glance. The newswoman was on the trail of a scoop, and it would take more than a bizarre lady in a wheelchair to distract her. She asked, "Does Amanda Fielding have amnesia?"

Behind David's back, Amanda grew more agitated. They needed to escape. Immediately. She reached out and yanked on the back of David's lab coat. When he turned, she clawed at his lapels, bringing his face to within inches of her own. "No comment," she whispered tightly. "Tell her no comment and get the hell out of here."

"What was that, Mrs. Higgenbottom?" His hazel eyes twinkled. She had the distinct impression that he was enjoying her embarrassment. "No compacts? I agree, Mrs. Higgenbottom. I prefer a bigger car myself."

He circled her chair and began to move. "Sorry, Elaine. We have to go."

"Come on, Doc," she said. "Give me a break."

Amanda slumped low in the wheelchair and hunched up her shoulders so the pink mohair covered the lower half of her face. Over and over in her mind, she repeated the two-word escape, *No comment. No comment. No comment.*

But David was blithely chatting as he pushed her toward the front exit. "Can't tell you anything about Ms. Fielding," he said, "but I had an interesting case yesterday. It seems that there was an old lady who swallowed a fly. I don't know why she swallowed the fly. Perhaps, she'll die."

They were almost to the front door, nearing the security guard's station.

"One question," Elaine Montero pleaded. "Just answer one question for me."

"How about if you answer one for me? Why aren't you in the back with all the other reporters?"

"Instinct. I have a gut feeling that the real action is right here." She persisted, "Is Amanda Fielding in police custody?"

"What?" The word flew from Amanda's lips. Had she really spoken?

"Now, now, Mrs. Higgenbottom," David said as he patted her shoulder and pulled the itchy mohair up farther on her face. "Don't get yourself all excited."

"Is Amanda Fielding under police guard?" Elaine asked. "I heard the attempted robbery was an inside job, and Amanda Fielding was involved."

"You heard wrong." Amanda was out of the chair, confronting the perfect makeup and immaculate coif of the network newswoman. "Amanda Fielding is a top-notch executive whose integrity is beyond reproach."

Dizzy again. She must have bounced to her feet too quickly. The catlike smirk of Elaine Montero blurred before her eyes.

The newswoman asked, "What was your name?"

"Higgenbottom." Amanda collapsed into the wheelchair. "And you can quote me."

Keeping her attention trained on the wheelchair, Elaine signalled vigorously. From the corner of her eye, Amanda saw a man with a video camera running toward them.

David called to the security guards. "Detain these people. They have no business here."

While Elaine and her cameraman were momentarily occupied, showing credentials, David charged through the automatic front door.

"Hang on tight," he warned.

Like a high-speed race car, he went from zero to sixty in five seconds. They flew along the sidewalk, scattering pedestrians and patients who'd come outside to relax in the July heat. Amanda shrieked as they careened around a cluster of nurses and made a sharp left on one wheel.

She saw his black Porsche up ahead.

From behind them, she heard Elaine Montero calling his name.

He halted the wheelchair by his car. "Passenger door's open. Get in."

She dived, flinging herself into the low-slung vehicle and squishing down in the leather bucket seat as David fired up the powerful engine. Tires squealing, they backed out of the parking lot, swerving maniacally to avoid a van. Then they were on the street, driving at a more sedate pace.

David gave an earsplitting whoop and thrust his arm through the open window. "We did it!"

"Why did I ever listen to you?" Her head was pounding as she yanked off the cloche hat and sunglasses. "That was the dumbest plan of all time. And then, you made it worse by talking to that horrible woman."

He laughed. "And I betrayed a patient confidence."

"What patient?"

"The old woman and the fly. 'She swallowed a spider to catch the fly, but I don't know why'"

"You're so crazy!" Didn't he understand how serious this was? "Nuts!"

"Come on, Amanda. That was a grown-up game of hide-and-seek. Just for a minute there, you were having fun. Admit it."

"I worked hard to build my career. Do you think I could be a bank president if there were photographs of me impersonating a bag lady?"

"You want my opinion as a doctor? We should go back to the hospital and remove that Popsicle stick from your—"

"You're the one who's sick. You're terminally irresponsible." She'd been right to break off their engagement five years ago. Her reasoning had been correct when she'd decided not to tell him about Laurel. David wasn't good father material. "You haven't changed a bit."

"Not in the important ways. I still like to have fun." He stopped at a light and turned toward her. "The difference now is that I'm doing it sober."

"Immature. Childish. Dangerously immature." She leaned against the soft leather seat that molded around her body like a glove. It was hot. Her head hurt. Terrible things had happened this morning at the bank. But that still didn't excuse her lapse in judgment. "How could I have said those things to a reporter?"

"I thought you did a nice job of standing up for yourself, Mrs. Higgenbottom."

"Not funny." The situation was very worrying. Why had Elaine Montero asked David those questions? "Do the police really think the robbery was an inside job?"

"I don't know." He seemed to be staring intently at the rearview mirror. "And we've got a bigger problem right now. I think we're being followed."

"That's just swell!" Why not top off the day with a high-speed chase through the streets of Denver? She almost hoped for a confrontation, a way to let off steam. But when she glanced over her shoulder, Amanda laughed. "Not to worry, David. I know that car. It belongs to Stefan Phillips."

"Your fiancé?"

"Who told you that?"

"He told the administrative nurse in E.R. that you two were engaged."

"Well, he lied."

She couldn't imagine why he'd say they were engaged, but he probably had a decent reason. Stefan was a good guy, and she'd known him forever. His parents were friends of her parents, and they'd all travelled in the same circles when they were back in Chicago. It was only natural for Stefan to make contact with her when he'd moved to Denver.

"What kind of relationship do you have with him?" David asked.

"We're friends. Good friends. Old friends." Stefan was a willing escort for the many social events where Amanda needed a date. Unlike David, he never once embarrassed her. Stefan always looked impeccable and behaved properly.

"I don't like him," David said.

Surprised, she turned toward him. "I wasn't aware that you'd met."

"At the hospital, we talked long enough for me to know that I don't like him. He's too pretty. I bet he never gets his hands dirty."

"For your information, Stefan is an expert rock climber and ski instructor. He does all those sweaty macho things very well."

"Have you been to bed with him?"

"Shut up, David." What was wrong with him? He was acting like a jerk.

"It's a simple question, Amanda. Have you?"

The pain behind her eyes focused into a razor-edged outrage. She didn't have to put up with this rude behavior from David. Nor from anybody else. "You have no right to know anything about my personal life. No damned right at all. We shared something special in the past, but it's over, dead, finished. Don't ever presume you can treat me with disrespect."

They parked on the street in front of her nineteen-story condominium building. When Amanda got out, she slammed the car door. Storming up to the front entrance, she marched through the pain and dizziness. She'd rather fall flat on her face than lean on David.

Because she didn't have her purse or her keys, she buzzed the concierge to let them in. Now that she was standing still, the vertigo caught up to her. Waves of nausea washed over her, and she braced herself against the wall beside the house phone.

The security door opened. The concierge stared questioningly at Amanda's pink mohair sweater and cloth slippers.

"Don't ask," Amanda warned.

"I was terribly worried," the concierge said. "Are you all right, Amanda?"

"I'll be fine as soon as I lie down."

Stefan came into the foyer. Immediately, he slipped his arm around her waist. "Are you okay? I was worried."

Gratefully, she leaned on him. "Fine. I'm fine."

He helped her through the door to the elevator. "I thought you were going to be riding in an ambulance. David? Didn't you say she needed an ambulance?"

"Changed my mind," David said.

"Shut up, David." She hurled the comment over her shoulder. Why wouldn't he just go away? Her legs wobbled, and the throbbing in her head sounded like a timpani.

"Should I carry you?" Stefan asked.

"I can walk," she said.

She needed to regain her strength before she saw Laurel. Her baby might be frightened to see her mother faint. Amanda drew on her strength, the same determination that had propelled her career, the inner fire that had kept her sane while balancing single motherhood, work and social obligations.

On the fourteenth floor, she led the way down the hall. Her equilibrium had returned. Though she didn't move at her usual brisk pace, she was able to place one foot in front of another without collapsing. Outside her condo, she rang the bell.

The nanny—a red-haired college student named Vonnie—whipped the door open. "Amanda!"

Vonnie backpedaled into the living room, where she grabbed the remote and clicked off the television. "Are you okay?"

Later, she would discuss Vonnie's annoying television habit. Right now, she only had eyes for nine-month-old Laurel, who stood in her playpen, hanging on to the side and bouncing up and down to her own mysterious rhythm.

"Hi there, precious." When Amanda picked up her daughter, the waves of pain rolled back out to sea, and she smiled. It was impossible to look at Laurel without smiling. She was the most beautiful baby in the world. Her perfectly round head was covered with downy blond hair. Her blue eyes, fringed with thick lashes, were bright and lively.

"Amanda," Vonnie chirped, "there have been a gazillion phone calls from television people. I didn't know what to say, so I took the phone off the hook."

"Whatever." She held her baby close, absorbing her sweet innocence. No matter what else happened, her child was safe. And Laurel's well-being mattered more than careers, concussions and all the other craziness. Laurel was the center of her universe.

Unfortunately, her baby's usual fragrance was particularly pungent. "You need a diaper change," Amanda said.

"Let me," Vonnie offered. The skinny redhead darted forward with arms outstretched. "I've been watching on the TV news about the robbery. There were SWAT teams and everything. You should have called me, Amanda. I was real scared when they said you had to go to the hospital."

"I thought you had the phone off the hook."

"Oh, yeah." She managed to roll her eyes and toss her curls at the same time. "Duh! I guess I wouldn't have answered if you did call."

Amanda held her daughter closer. "I'll take care of Laurel. I want to spend a little time alone with my baby girl."

On her way to the nursery, she had to walk past David. Though she felt guilty about keeping Laurel from him, she was also proud. She wanted to show him their baby, to share the joy of this wonderful child. But not yet. Not while she was so furious that she couldn't stand to look at him.

In the nursery, Amanda closed the door behind her. She placed Laurel on the changing table. "Oh, sweetie. I've really made a mess of things this time."

Laurel cooed happily.

"And I love you, too," Amanda said with a fond smile.

As she went through the diaper-changing routine, her mind drifted back through time. Gradually, she sorted the memories punctuated by stabs of conscience.

She should have told David when she first discovered she was pregnant after their one-night reunion a year and a half ago. As soon as she read the result of her home pregnancy test, pure joy flooded her heart. A baby! At age thirty-five, with her biological alarm clock pealing madly, Amanda was going to have a baby!

"And that was you," she said to Laurel as she swabbed her incredibly smooth bottom. "You're my little miracle."

Laurel laughed uproariously, as if her mother had made a brilliant joke.

She remembered reaching for the phone, full of excitement, anxious to tell David the spectacular news. But she never completed the call.

She knew him too well. David would have insisted on doing the right thing. He would have wanted to be married.

But he wasn't the right man to be her husband or the father of her child. Their marriage would have been a disaster. She'd already decided that when she'd broken off their engagement five years ago. He was too wild and irresponsible. Completely untrustworthy, he stayed out too late and drank too much.

In too many ways, he reminded her of her own father, a charming man who always made her laugh...when she didn't think about the broken promises along the way.

She finished with the diaper and carried Laurel to the rocking chair. Her little girl had a lot of energy and liked to scoot around. But, for the moment, she seemed content to lie against her mother's breast as they rocked gently. And Amanda thought about her father.

Jack Fielding. A handsome man. Third generation of the

wealthy Chicago Fieldings. Jack was far different from his
father and grandfather. Earlier generations of Fieldings had
expanded the family fortunes, while Jack depleted it.
Though Amanda had inherited the powerful family name
and connections, there was no money behind her.

How odd that she was thinking about long-ago family
history! The concussion must have affected her brain.
Though recent, relevant events shimmered like vague ho-
lograms, the distant past seemed solid and clear.

"I'm going to tell you a story, Laurel." Her voice was
low and soft. "A long time ago, on my ninth birthday, my
daddy promised to take me for a sailboat ride on Lake
Michigan. Just the two of us."

Amanda had dressed in her Keds and windbreaker at one
o'clock in the afternoon, when the sun was high in the June
skies. She'd sat on the front porch, waiting anxiously for
her special day with Daddy. "But Daddy was late."

At three o'clock, her mom suggested an alternate plan.
A movie or a trip to the ice-cream parlor. But Amanda
refused to budge. Daddy was coming. If they left the house,
she'd miss him.

By dusk, Mom was angry. She told Amanda that she
was being too stubborn, ruining her own birthday. At the
very least, she should come inside and blow out the candles
on her birthday cake.

"I waited and waited."

When Daddy parked in the driveway at eight o'clock, he
picked an orange geranium from the border outside the garage. He brought the flower to her and held it out. He
smelled like booze. "For you, princess," he said. "Do you
love me?"

"Yes, Daddy."

When she went to bed on the night of her ninth birthday,
she lay very still, holding herself together. She never wept.

And she never told her father how hurt and disappointed she'd been. Her sadness was a secret.

She should have told him. Just as she should have told David. Though she didn't want to marry David, a man who was too much like her father, she should have told him when she got pregnant. It was his right as the father to know.

"There's a moral to this story, Laurel. But I'm not sure exactly what it is."

There was a tap on the nursery door.

"Come in," she said.

It was David. He squatted down beside the rocking chair so he could see Laurel more directly. "She's beautiful."

Amanda should tell him right now. She knew what he must be thinking. David could do the math. Laurel had been born almost nine months to the day from when they'd made love.

"May I hold her?"

She hesitated, but how could she refuse?

"Don't worry," he said. "Kids are my specialty. When I'm done with my residency, I'll be a pediatrician."

He took Laurel and held her. Unlike most men, he seemed completely comfortable with the baby. Not too cautious, but not at all careless.

When Laurel found the stethoscope in his pocket, he pulled it out so she could see it. "Can you say *stethoscope?*"

He held it to her tummy, and she giggled.

He laughed with her, and the sound of his baritone and Laurel's pealing laughter was musical.

A year and a half ago, he'd told Amanda that he had changed. But she hadn't really believed him. She didn't honestly think that people were capable of change. Certainly, her father wasn't. Even now, he was the same charming ne'er-do-well.

Still holding the baby, David sought her gaze. "I'm sorry, Amanda. I badgered you on the drive over here, and that wasn't right. I never meant any disrespect."

"Apology accepted."

When he smiled down at Laurel again, her heart melted. *Tell him. Tell him now.*

"You're wanted in the other room," David said.

"Why?"

"The FBI has some questions for you."

Chapter Three

"The FBI?" Amanda sank into the rocking chair. "What am I going to tell them?"

"I don't know." David rescued his stethoscope from the baby and distracted her by nuzzling at her tummy, a maneuver that produced a low chortle. "Hey, Laurel. Is that your tummy-tum-tum?"

"Please don't," Amanda chastised. "I try not to use baby talk with Laurel."

Purposely disregarding Amanda, he nuzzled again. "Woogie-woogie-woogie. Where's your tummy?"

Apparently, Laurel didn't care, because she grabbed his ear. With her other hand, she smacked his nose. When he reacted, she squealed with delight.

She waved her pudgy arms like a cheerleader, and her shining eyes beamed approval. Blue eyes, he noticed, like Amanda's. David had hoped Laurel's eyes would be the same odd hazel color as his own, which would have been some kind of genetic suggestion that she was his child. But no such luck.

More giggles. God, she was a beauty! If it turned out that Laurel was his daughter, he would never want to be apart from her.

"In spite of the goo-goo talk," Amanda said, "it looks like you're a hit with Laurel."

"I wish *everybody* was so easily amused."

"Meaning me?"

He didn't want to rake up old arguments about the importance of having fun and using laughter as an antidote for stress. But that was exactly what he meant. "Meaning you."

"Really," she said, bristling. "I seem to recall you went on wild binges, occasionally ending in blackouts. Is that considered amusing?"

"I was over-the-top," he admitted. "But I've changed."

"People don't change, David. You can't alter DNA. You can't erase environmental influences."

David settled Laurel into the walnut-frame crib with yellow flowered bumpers that echoed the bright yellow-and-white-plaid wallpaper in the nursery. She flipped to her stomach and swam across the sheets toward a stuffed pink dinosaur.

He marveled at her speedy progress. After working with the babies at the hospital, it was a treat to be around a normal, healthy child. But fun time with Laurel was over.

"I need to get back to Denver General," he declared. "I'll finish out my shift, then come back over here tonight so I can keep an eye on you."

"It's not necessary for you to return," she said coolly.

But it was. Not only was he concerned about her physical condition, but he also intended to discover the identity of Laurel's father.

"I took a risk in springing you from the hospital without the tests," he said. "I want to make sure you're okay. Just doing my job."

"All right."

"In fact, I think it's time for a little doctor-to-patient chat right now. I need for you to be honest with me about your memory loss, Amanda. Do you remember the distant past?''

''I just told Laurel a story about when I was nine years old.'' She leaned back in the rocker and closed her eyes. ''When I first woke up in the hospital, everything was foggy. But it's over. I'm perfectly fine.''

''Good. Tell me about this morning. Start with when you first woke up.''

''I must have gotten dressed in this outfit.'' She glanced down at the black silk blouse, which was looking much the worse for wear. ''And the Gucci shoes. And I must have—''

''Do you remember putting on your clothes?''

Frowning, she shook her head.

''What about yesterday?'' he asked. ''What did you do yesterday?''

''Vonnie had the night off. Laurel and I were alone, and I made popcorn. I played some Aretha Franklin music, and we danced around the kitchen. It's all very clear.''

He grinned as he imagined Amanda and Laurel and Aretha. He would have liked to have been there. ''And what happened at the bank yesterday?''

''I must have been busy. It's always that way. I probably signed some loan papers and—''

''Hold it.'' From the vagueness of her description, he suspected she wasn't remembering. She was guessing. ''What were you wearing?''

She concentrated for a moment, then shook her head. ''I don't know. Everything at the bank is a blur. Oh, David, what's wrong with me?''

Though he wasn't a brain surgeon or a psychiatrist, both disciplines interested him, and he was familiar with the symptoms associated with concussive injury. Without delving too deeply, he diagnosed her short-term memory loss as being highly topical, associated with the bank.

He tried to explain. "This morning, during the robbery attempt, you suffered a trauma at the bank. Your brain is blanking the whole thing out, trying to protect you from remembering how scared you were."

"I wasn't scared—I was angry."

"Okay, protecting you from your anger." Which, David knew, was a classic psychological mechanism to battle fear and pain. "It's possible that your memory loss will only pertain to the bank and incidents surrounding the bank."

"But it won't last forever, will it?"

"Probably not. However, as I said before, you might never remember the trauma."

"The robbery itself?"

He nodded. "That's a positive thing, Amanda. Why would you want to relive what happened at the bank? It's over. It's better to forget."

"But I want to remember."

Amanda needed to remember every second of the robbery, every detail, every sound. She wasn't sure why her recollection was so vital, but it was.

Never before in her life had she been so certain. If she didn't remember what happened at the bank, her world would come to an end.

From the crib, Laurel shouted.

And Amanda instinctively reacted to her cry. She leaned over the crib, immediately attentive to her daughter's needs. But Laurel was all right, just kicking up a ruckus.

"I should get out there and face the FBI," she said. "I only wish there was something useful I could talk about."

"I can send them away," he offered. "As your doctor, I can tell them you're physically unable to speak with them."

"It's okay." *Get over it, Amanda*. She reached up to straighten her hair and realized it was still a tangled mass. "I need to clean up first. Would you tell them I'll be out in five minutes?"

"Sure."

She caressed her daughter's cheek before standing erect and walking slowly toward the door. Her balance was supercautious. It felt as if she were walking on a frozen pond and needed to take care not to slip and slide.

"Dizzy?" he asked.

"I'm fine." With her hand on the doorknob, she turned back toward him. "I'd appreciate it if you would stay with me during the FBI interrogation."

"Interrogation? Come on, Amanda. That sounds like you're a suspect."

"Please, David." A slight tremble in her voice caught his attention.

"I'll be there for you, Amanda. You know that."

She left the nursery door open as she left, and David plucked Laurel from the crib. Staying at Amanda's condo hadn't been part of his plans. He'd intended to finish out the rest of his shift at Denver General emergency, then come back here tonight to monitor Amanda during the sleep hours.

Well, what the hell? It was only another twist on the downward spiral he'd taken at work. Dr. Loretta Spangler had probably already filed her complaints about his unprofessional conduct. Also, his high-speed charge across the front entrance with the wheelchair probably hadn't endeared him to the hospital staff.

They ought to understand by now that he might be unconventional, but he was basically a good doctor and didn't make mistakes on the important things. His work came first in his life. Except for now. He couldn't leave Amanda. Not when she needed him.

As he looked into Laurel's eyes, she beamed and babbled and wrinkled her nose. David couldn't help smiling back. This baby girl was going to be a heartbreaker someday.

"Just like your mama," he said.

IN THE BATHROOM, Amanda set about repairing the damage to her cool mask of competence. Why had she asked David to stay? Moments ago, she'd wanted him out of her life completely, erased and forgotten. Now her instincts told her to keep David by her side.

Quickly, she washed her arms and face. Though she didn't remove the bandage on her temple, she brushed her straight blond hair around it. Each stroke pulled her scalp painfully, but decent grooming was necessary. She didn't want to look like a victim when she spoke with the FBI.

After applying heavy-duty concealer beneath her eyes and a dash of lipstick, she dressed in turquoise slacks and a matching sleeveless tunic. She snipped the plastic hospital identification bracelet and replaced it with her gold Cartier wristwatch. Checking the time, she noted that it had taken ten instead of five minutes to pull herself together.

She slipped her feet into white sandals and went down the hall into the living room. Her decor, predominantly in grays and blues to complement a very good oil copy of Monet's water lilies, was neither masculine nor feminine. But the four men dispersed around the room seemed uncomfortable—too large for the furniture and too macho. They all stood as she entered.

Amanda sought David's gaze. "Where's Laurel?"

"Vonnie took her into the nursery."

A tidy gentleman in a gray summer-weight suit with a

white shirt and bland necktie stepped forward. "Ms. Fielding, I'm Special Agent John Metcalf, FBI."

She met his gaze and shook his hand. He looked more like an accountant than a federal officer, but his appearance didn't surprise her. A few years ago, the FBI investigated another incident at Empire Bank, and Amanda had been impressed with their calm, businesslike attitude.

"My partner," he said, "is Agent Greg Hess."

A lanky man, also conservatively dressed, Hess was clearly the junior officer.

"I'm pleased to meet both of you," she said. "Shall we get started?"

"Amanda, wait." Stefan came across the living room toward her. His thick blond hair was a rakish halo. Shoulders thrown back, he was the most muscular of the men present. "Maybe you shouldn't talk to the FBI without an attorney."

"Thanks for your concern, Stefan. But, as you might recall, I am an attorney." She faced Agent Metcalf and Agent Hess. "I want to do everything I can to help you. However, I must warn you that my memory of the robbery attempt is rather incomplete."

Metcalf glanced toward David. "The doctor told us that you were totally blank."

"I'll do what I can." She gestured toward the long cherry-wood table in the adjoining dining area. "Why don't we sit in here?"

The floor-to-ceiling window at the end of the table displayed a panorama of the Denver skyline and the foothills beyond. One of the reasons she loved this spacious, three-bedroom condo was the view. On the other side of the kitchen was an enclosed porch, all windows, where she could watch billowing clouds roll down from the mountains and spread across the high-rise buildings, the houses and the leafy treetops.

At night, there were a million stars. Under those twinkling celestial lights, she and David had made love. Was it only a year and a half ago? It seemed like an eternity. That night had brought her Laurel and changed her life.

As she moved toward the table, she couldn't help glancing toward him. Was he sharing her thoughts? A meeting with the FBI wasn't the appropriate time for sensual fantasy, but her mind rebelliously wandered. Would David ever make love to her again? Would he hold her in his arms and breathe kisses along the line of her throat? When she told him about Laurel, would he ever forgive her?

At the dining table, Amanda sat beside David, and Stefan claimed the head. Agents Metcalf and Hess remained standing.

Metcalf said, "Ms. Fielding, I prefer to interview you alone."

"As Amanda's doctor," David said, "it's best if I'm present."

Not wanting to be outdone, Stefan put in, "Amanda needs me here for emotional support."

"Nevertheless, gentlemen, we have procedures to follow."

"Amanda has been through a lot today." Stefan reached over and took her hand. "I'm staying right here to make sure you don't bully her."

Before she could inform him that she was perfectly capable of standing up for herself, David chimed in, "And I need to provide medical supervision. She's had a life-threatening injury."

He grasped her other hand.

Amanda's first impression of excessive macho attitude was confirmed. The men seemed to be posturing, pouncing upon opportunities to snarl at each other. She could almost smell the testosterone in the air. "Gentlemen, please. I—"

A loud pounding at the front door interrupted her.

From down the hall, she heard Laurel wailing from the nursery.

It was too much distraction, even without the residual ache and vertigo from the concussion.

When Vonnie opened the front door, Frank Weathers bounced into the living room. He came at her like a well-groomed, blond torpedo and hugged her shoulders. "Thank goodness you're all right."

"What are you doing here, Frank? How did you get past the concierge?"

"I have a friend in the building." With his hands still planted on her shoulders, he introduced himself to the FBI agents, then leaned over Amanda again. "You really should do something about security. If I could stroll right in here, so could the press."

"Enough!" Amanda disengaged each of her hands from the grasp of Stefan and David. She shrugged off Frank's hold on her shoulders and stood. It was well past time for her to take charge. Technically, Amanda was the least macho individual in this mix, yet she had no trouble asserting her authority. She hadn't gotten to be a bank president by simpering.

"Stefan and Frank, I insist that you leave. Immediately. This is an FBI investigation, not a tea party."

"I can take a hint," Frank said. He brushed an air kiss past her cheek. "I'm glad you're all right. When I talked to Bill Chessman, he sent his best wishes for a speedy recovery."

Chessman was the chairman of the board for Empire Bank. Of course, Frank wouldn't waste a moment calling

Chessman to offer his services while Amanda was on the mend. "Goodbye, Frank."

He held the door for Stefan, who was still dragging his feet. "Amanda, I should stay. There must be something else I can do."

"Actually, there is." One of the most dreadful tasks of all. "Would you call my parents in Chicago and tell them I'm all right?"

Grimly, he nodded. "Should I tell them you'll call?"

"Yes, and they won't be able to reach me here. Vonnie put the phone on the answering machine. Thank you."

He gave her a gentle pat on the shoulder. "If there's anything else, you know how to reach me."

When she closed the door behind Stefan and Frank, Amanda finally felt that the immediate situation was under control. Returning to the table, she sat beside David. "Agent Metcalf, shall we get started?"

He placed a small tape recorder on the tabletop as the two agents both sat down across from her. "Do you mind?" Metcalf asked.

"Not at all."

"First, I need to go over details about the security mechanisms at the bank. Let's start with the video-surveillance cameras."

"There are six of them," she said. The operational system was crystal clear in her mind. "Four are focused on the lobby. One is inside the vault. One is in the safe-deposit-box area. They record continuously on a forty-eight-hour loop. They're monitored at the bank and maintained by Summit Security Systems, a local firm. It's all computerized. If the transmission is interrupted, Summit is automatically notified."

"What happens when you need to shut down the cameras to do maintenance and change the videotape?"

"We have override computer codes to notify Summit that the cameras will not be operating for fifteen minutes."

"Who knows this procedure?"

"The security guard, Harry Hoffman, who works for Summit. And, of course, I keep a copy of the codes in a locked drawer in my desk."

She hesitated. A memory flickered in her mind like a vision seen in peripheral vision. "We've had some trouble with the cameras lately. In the past month, they've been shut down at least three times."

Or more? She couldn't remember. A technician from Summit had shown up with a work order. All of his credentials had been in order. "Why are you asking me about this? Were the surveillance cameras off during the robbery?"

"I'll ask the questions, Ms. Fielding. You said there were six cameras?"

From her former career as an attorney, she was familiar with interrogation techniques. By repeating himself and ignoring her questions, Metcalf subtly applied pressure. He seemed to be treating her like a hostile witness.

"We're on the same side," she reminded him. "In my position as president of this branch bank, I would appreciate if you leveled with me. Were the cameras off?"

"Don't tell me how to do my job, Ms. Fielding."

They locked gazes, and Amanda didn't like what she saw. Though Metcalf had been unfailingly polite, he was the aggressor, verbally stalking her. Why didn't he trust her?

When David leaned toward her, she was glad for his protective presence.

Agent Metcalf said, "Tell me about the silent-alarm system."

"There are buttons to activate the silent alarm at each

teller station and in the vault and the safe-deposit area. Also, we have alarms in several of the offices, including my own. When any of these buttons are pressed, it notifies the local police and Summit Security Systems.''

She wasn't telling him anything new. The silent alarm was standard equipment in financial institutions.

"During the robbery attempt," he said, "did you manage to press any of the alarms?"

She tried to think. Where had she been when the robbery was taking place? "Sorry, I can't recall what happened."

"But you would have tried," Metcalf said matter-of-factly. "As bank president, you would have tried to avert the robbery."

"Yes, of course."

"Suppose one of these alarms were accidentally pressed," Metcalf said. "What would happen?"

"We call Summit Security. They notify the police. Then the alarm is aborted. Afterward, however, a security person comes to the bank to make sure."

"Did you place such a call this morning?"

"I don't remember." What was he getting at? Amanda couldn't think of any good reason that she would have aborted an alarm. Certainly not when a robbery was in progress.

"Think hard, Ms. Fielding."

"She doesn't remember," David said. "Until she regains her short-term memory, there's no point in pushing."

Metcalf didn't take his eyes off her. His unrelenting scrutiny made Amanda worry that she might know more than she should about this robbery. But how? Amanda couldn't have been involved. And yet, Elaine Montero, the reporter at the hospital, suggested there might have been an inside contact at the bank.

Struggling to recall, she looked down at her hands folded

precisely on the cherry-wood tabletop. "My mind is blank. I'm sorry."

"Let's talk about Carrie Lamb," Agent Metcalf said. "What can you tell me about her?"

"She's a teller at Empire Bank and a trusted friend."

She and Carrie had confided in each other, shared silliness and tragedy. They knew each other's deepest secrets. Carrie was the only person who knew that David was the father of her child.

"When did you hire her?"

Amanda betrayed no signal of her internal tension, but warning bells pealed in her brain. Carrie's hiring had been highly irregular, but Carrie's secrets weren't something she could tell the FBI. "I must have hired Carrie about two years ago."

"Were you acquainted with her before you hired her?"

She couldn't lie, but she couldn't betray Carrie's friendship. "It seems like I've known her forever."

"Are you telling me that you don't remember?"

She saw suspicion in his cold accountant-like eyes. Aware of the tape recorder, Amanda avoided a direct falsehood. "I've had a concussion. My memory is faulty."

"Dr. Haines told us that you could recall your distant past. It's only the events of this morning that are unclear."

"But concussions are unpredictable," David said. "I suggest you move on."

"Ms. Fielding, have you ever been to Carrie Lamb's apartment?"

"Yes."

"Do you remember anything unusual about her home?"

"No." Amanda instantly visualized Carrie's one-bedroom apartment in Capitol Hill with beige carpets and white walls enlivened by brightly colored posters. There were lots of books, knickknacks and candles. And guns. Carrie owned three handguns.

"Nothing unusual?" Metcalf persisted.

Amanda didn't want to mention the guns. "Why are you asking all these questions about Carrie?"

"After she was taken hostage this morning, we—"

"Excuse me." A sudden chill raced across her skin, raising goose bumps. An ill wind blew across the empty horizons of her mind. "Did you say Carrie was taken hostage?"

Metcalf and his partner exchanged a glance. "Yes, ma'am."

"She wasn't hurt, was she? What happened?"

It was Agent Hess who responded, "One of the robbers used her as a shield when he came out of the bank. They took off on a motorcycle. She was riding behind him, so the snipers couldn't get a clear shot. This was after the SWAT team stormed the bank."

"They stormed the bank?" She was stunned. "Why? How could that happen?"

"Negotiations broke down," Agent Hess said. "The local police were doing the talking. If the FBI had been called in sooner, we never would have risked the lives of hostages."

Metcalf, the senior agent, corrected him. "The locals did the best they could. There were only three hostages left."

"Carrie Lamb, Tracy Meyer and me." Icy dread flowed in her veins as she turned toward David. "I remember."

He took her hand. His warm gaze encouraged her. "Tell me, Amanda. Tell me what you remember."

Her eyelids squeezed shut. Cold. She was so cold. "Near the teller counter. There were three robbers. All in black, wearing ski masks. And three of us. Me, Carrie and Tracy."

As if from a distance, she saw herself and the other two

women, clinging together. They were helpless, utterly helpless, and she couldn't make things right. The situation was out of control. Amanda's worst nightmare.

"Oh, David. I couldn't stop them. It was my fault."

A blizzard of confusion blanketed her mind, and she clutched his hand convulsively. His warmth was her lifeline. Trembling, she opened her eyes.

"It's all right," he said. "There wasn't anything you could do."

She wanted to believe him, but his words went against everything she'd taught herself. Never give up. There was always something she could do. Always.

She clung to his steady gaze. David was the only anchor against the gale-force winds that buffeted her mind, tearing away her defenses.

"Ms. Fielding." She heard the voice of Agent Metcalf. "What else do you remember?"

"Nothing." The word echoed inside her head.

"Back off." David spoke forcefully to the two federal agents sitting across the table. His focus remained steady on Amanda. "You're going to be okay. Do you hear me, Amanda?"

"Yes."

Struggling to regain control of herself, she tried to make sense of an incomprehensible disaster. Carrie had been taken hostage. What about Tracy Meyer?

Fearful of what she might hear, Amanda asked, "The other hostage…Ms. Meyer? Is she safe?"

"Yes," Metcalf said.

Tracy had a child, a seven-year-old daughter who had a sizable trust fund at the bank. "I was supposed to have a meeting with Tracy Meyer on July 1."

"Today is the first," Agent Metcalf noted.

"Of course," Amanda said.

But she didn't recall whether their meeting had taken place or not. Today's events had fallen into an impenetrable blankness. All she really wanted was to sleep, to allow herself the luxury of forgetting, leaving the answers to someone else.

Get over it. She was the president of Empire Bank. This was her responsibility.

Tearing her gaze away from David, she faced the FBI. Stiffly, she said, "Is Carrie Lamb all right?"

"She's still a hostage. And we have reason to believe she's a willing hostage."

"Absurd," Amanda said. "Carrie is an excellent employee."

"The local police were on the verge of apprehending the robber, and Carrie Lamb fired on them."

"Impossible!" Had Carrie been involved in the robbery attempt? Had she betrayed bank routine to the robbers? "I can't believe she'd have any part in this."

"But you can't remember?"

Amanda gritted her teeth. "That is correct. I can't remember."

Metcalf clicked off his tape recorder and rose slowly to his feet. "That's all for now, Ms. Fielding. I'll be in touch."

Still holding David's hand, she walked the agents toward the door. "If I recall anything that might be useful, how shall I get in touch with you, Agent Metcalf?"

From his wallet, he produced a business card as he gestured toward the painting on Amanda's living-room wall. "That's a very good copy of a Monet."

"How do you know it's a copy?"

"I know that your mother gave it to you as a housewarming gift when you moved in here. And she had to borrow money to buy it."

Taken aback, Amanda could only stare at him.

Quiet as the hissing of a snake, he added, ''I also know your net worth and that of your family. I know that you and your brother are paying the mortgage on your parents' refinanced home in Chicago. I have information on your credit history, your phone calls and the number of speeding tickets you've had in your lifetime.''

Suddenly, she realized why he had questioned her, why he had focused on her relationship with Carrie, who was presumed to be a bank robber. ''You're investigating me.''

''Background, Ms. Fielding. The motive for a bank robbery is usually money, and this attempt was well financed. It's standard procedure to check the background of all the principals. We're investigating everyone.''

He handed her the white business card. ''If Carrie Lamb contacts you, call me immediately.''

''Of course I will. And it goes without saying that I'll do anything to help find her.''

She closed the door behind Special Agents Metcalf and Hess.

David was close beside her. When he gently wrapped his arm around her shoulder, she didn't object.

''Are you all right, Amanda?''

''They think I was involved in the robbery.''

''It's their job to investigate everyone.''

But so many facts pointed to her. Amanda had the necessary codes to turn off the video cameras and to abort the silent-alarm system. Carrie was her friend, and Carrie was behaving extremely suspiciously. Who better to pull off a robbery than the bank president and her accomplice, a bank teller?

Certainly, there were rational explanations for this circumstantial evidence. The problem was, she couldn't remember much of anything associated with the bank. The operational systems were clear in her mind, but the day-to-day events were hazy at best.

Her eyes sought David. "Is it possible, with this short-term memory loss, that I could have blanked out something really big and important?"

"It's possible," he said.

Though he caressed her cheek and smiled reassuringly, she couldn't accept his comforting touch. Somewhere in the forgotten depths of her mind, she had the key to this robbery attempt. Amanda sensed that the answer was there, just beyond her reach.

"David, could I have forgotten that I was involved in the planning of this bank robbery?"

He didn't respond. He didn't need to. She could see the unspoken answer in his gaze. Anything was possible.

Chapter Four

After David returned to emergency at Denver General, he was too busy to think about Amanda's crisis. In any case, her notion that she'd been involved in the attempted bank robbery was too crazy for him to take seriously. Though her stubborn attitude was enough to drive a cardcarrying AA member to drink, David was damned sure she wasn't a bank robber.

While he dealt with the usual E.R. workload—a combination of accidental injuries and sudden illnesses, blood and vomit—he considered what might have happened at the bank. David checked on the condition of Mr. Nyland, the injured bank customer. He'd survived surgery but remained in ICU, regarded as extremely critical. The bank robber who had been shot, a man named Temple, was also in the hospital with a uniformed policeman posted outside the door to his private room.

At the end of his shift, still dressed in his scrubs and lab coat, David decided to pay a visit to the injured bank guard, Harry Hoffman, who had been moved from ICU to a private room. Possibly, Hoffman had information that David could use to jog Amanda's memory.

With his hospital bed in a sitting position, Harry Hoffman stared fiercely at the television across the room. His square jaw was darkened with afternoon stubble. His head had been wrapped in bandages. Above the white gauze, his hair was graying. His age, David guessed, was midfifties. Physical condition, except for his injuries, appeared to be excellent. The short-sleeved hospital gown revealed Popeye-sized forearms. On his left wrist, he wore an Ace bandage for the sprain. Just below the right elbow was a tattoo of a lion's head.

"Mr. Hoffman," David said.

Without taking his eyes off the television, he muttered, "Another doctor? I haven't seen you before."

"I've been taking care of Amanda Fielding. She's home now and wanted to send her regards."

The expression in Hoffman's dark eyes was unreadable. "Did she send you to fire me?"

David shook his head. "No, sir."

"I blew it," he growled. "You tell Amanda I'm sorry for what happened. She's a fair boss, stood up for me when everybody else said I was too old."

"How'd you get into this line of work? Are you a former cop?"

"I had military training in the Marines, did two tours in Vietnam. I tried lots of other stuff before I got into security work." His thin lips stretched in a grin. "Guess I always preferred the kind of job where I carry a firearm."

David hoped he was joking. "Do you mind telling me what happened this morning during the robbery attempt? I could pass that information to Amanda."

"I don't think so." He dropped the remote control for the television and picked up a cell phone. "If she wants information, I'll call her myself."

"Don't bother. Her phone's off the hook."

"Reporters, huh?" His lantern jaw stuck out. "Damned vultures. I hate to think of them flapping around Amanda."

"She's really worried about the robbery." David wasn't sure how much to reveal. "It might put her mind at ease to hear what you have to say."

"Sorry, Doc. It don't seem right to tell you. I'll talk to Amanda, though. Give her my phone number."

As David scribbled down the number, he said, "When the FBI talked to Amanda, they seemed real interested in the silent alarms and security cameras."

"It's okay. You can tell Amanda that I kept her little secret."

"Her secret?" That didn't sound good.

"It's between her and me." Gruffly, he added, "Tell her I'm glad she's okay."

"Have you experienced memory loss from your head injury?"

"Not a bit." He stared at the television, where a weatherman made sweeping gestures at a map of Colorado. "I'm too tough for anybody to knock any sense into or out of me."

AFTER A QUICK SHOWER in the hospital locker room, David changed into his Levi's and a white polo shirt. *Amanda's secret?* Apparently, she'd conspired with Hoffman. About what? David couldn't believe she'd been involved in committing a major crime. Yet she hadn't been forthcoming about her baby's parentage, and David couldn't help but suspect he was Laurel's biological father. If she hadn't told him, it was a hell of a deception.

Outside, the summer skies blushed at the beginning of a hot, red sunset. He crossed the parking lot and went to his Porsche. Might be a good idea to pick up a hamburger before returning to Amanda's condo. She was likely to call pasta and a salad dinner, and he was hungrier than that.

Firing up the car engine and turning the air-conditioning

to full arctic blast, he cruised south on Broadway and parked outside a fast-food joint. Next door was a liquor store.

David read the neon sign. The back of his throat remembered the velvet taste of fine Scotch whiskey and the satisfying afterburn. He hadn't taken a drink in over four years, not since he returned to the study of medicine as an intern. Four years and three months. In all that time, not a day passed without the desire.

A perverse logic told him he could handle one drink, maybe two, maybe just a beer. Being around Amanda made him damned thirsty.

When he got out of the car, he paced off the distance to the liquor store and entered. It was a familiar haven, cool and quiet. A dim overhead light reflected dully on a battalion of rounded wine bottles. Beyond the dry whites and rich reds, he found the glistening amber of rum and whiskey in cut-glass decanters.

The guy behind the counter watched without comment, and David realized that he'd been in here before. He walked between the rows, greeting the bottles like old friends. As if the all-night parties, the overindulging and subsequent retching had been fun. Driven by urges he never understood, he'd come as close as he could to total meltdown. His brain was fried. Nerves were shot. It was hell. And still, he craved that first drink.

His fingers curled around the neck of a whiskey bottle, shaking hands with the devil. What if he was Laurel's father? A vision of her pink cheeks and laughing blue eyes flashed in the back of his head. He could hear the baby's laughter.

With a sharp pivot, he left the liquor store, went to the fast-food place and placed his order.

"Would you like fries with that?"

"What I'd like is a double martini," David said to the teenager behind the counter. "But I'll settle for a milk shake, chocolate."

After quickly downing the burgers and shake, he drove to the high-rise, parked and pressed the front buzzer. He'd arranged with Vonnie to say his whole name before she opened the door for him. "It's me, David Underwood Haines."

The buzzer sounded and David entered. He rode the elevator to fourteen and went to Amanda's apartment. When Vonnie opened the door for him, her eyes sparkled with excitement. "You were just on the news," she said. "Elaine Montero is broadcasting from right across the street."

"Swell." David hadn't even noticed the television truck and the intrusive reporter. "How's Amanda?"

"Really, really quiet," Vonnie said. "Especially for her."

"What do you mean?"

"Amanda's so intense. She always does ten things at once. Writing a letter while she's painting her toenails and taking care of Laurel. But after her nap, when I woke her to check her eyes, like you said, she just asked me to bring Laurel into her bedroom. She hasn't moved." Vonnie shuddered. "It's kind of scary."

"How so?" David asked.

"It's like she's plotting something."

More likely, David suspected, she was trying to remember. Knowing Amanda as he did, she probably considered her inability to remember a personal failure instead of a physical symptom of her concussion.

"I talked to my mom," the red-haired nanny blurted out.

"And?"

"She told me I should quit and move away from here before something bad happens to me."

"Hang in, Vonnie." He patted her freckled arm. "It's important for you to stay. Amanda needs you."

He knocked before entering Amanda's bedroom.

"Come in."

He had always been fascinated by her large bedroom. The rest of her condo looked as if it might have been put together by a decorator, but this room held a clutter of pretty, delicate things. Slender green vines patterned the wallpaper in a dainty, controlled jungle. There were also photographs in fancy frames. Her parents, Jack and Shirley Fielding. Lots of Laurel photos. There was even one of Stefan in his rock-climbing gear, looking too damned healthy for his own good.

The predominant color was white—white eyelet on the duvet bedcover and a flounce on the windows, white velvet on the chaise longue. Dozens of mysterious bottles, mementos and jewelry boxes covered the surfaces of the dresser and bureau. The scent of the room was subtle and feminine.

Amanda looked frail and small on the queen-size bed with lace-covered pillows propped behind her back. She slipped off her reading glasses and set aside the paperback novel she'd been reading. Beside her on the white duvet, Laurel was on her back, playing with a brightly colored set of oversize plastic keys.

David's gaze was drawn to the bandage on Amanda's forehead. The left side of her face was slightly discolored and swollen. Otherwise, she was beautiful in a peach-colored nightgown with a square neck. The skin above her breasts was lightly tanned, and she wasn't wearing a bra.

His hands remembered her silky flesh, and the sweet tremors that went through her body when they made love.

He forced himself to look only at her face. Her almond-shaped blue eyes beneath precisely sculpted brows held a silent appeal that sorely tested his self-control. "How are you feeling?"

"As long as I stay quiet, I'm fine." Her tense smile reflected determined bravado. "My head barely hurts."

"And your memory?"

"Not much better. I keep getting flashes that don't make any sense."

He sat on the edge of her bed. The baby was between them. When Laurel saw David, she offered a bright-eyed, gurgling welcome. "Hey, cutie," he said. "What do you have there?"

She shook the keys and stared at them with cheerful concentration. When David pulled at a key, she yanked them back. Then she flipped to her stomach and aimed for the edge of the bed.

David scooped her up. "Is it okay if I put her on the carpet?"

"Sure. The whole condo is baby proof. Though that won't last for long. She's almost able to reach the top of the dresser."

Laurel took off crawling like a baby dragster. She even seemed to be making a *vroom-vroom* sound.

David glanced at Amanda. "Tell me about these memory flashes."

"I remembered three names—Dallas, Temple and Sarge. And I think those are the robbers. During the robbery, I must have heard someone say the names."

When she averted her gaze, he guessed she was hiding something. "You don't have to keep secrets from me, Amanda."

She frowned. "What do you mean?"

"Your memories could be distorted. If you tell me about

them, I can help you sort them out. I promise I won't tell anybody what you say.''

"I can't trust promises," she said bitterly. "I used to be a lawyer, remember? I made a living from people breaking their promises.''

"Then trust me, damn it.''

"How can I trust you?" She eyed him coldly. The ice princess again. "When we were engaged, you betrayed me in every possible way.''

He shoved off the bed and went to the window facing west. He had an urge to push open the glass and let the hot, fresh air inside to disrupt the sterile air-conditioning. When was she going to forget the past and give him a break?

After she'd broken their engagement, he'd known she was right. His life had been a mess. If he hadn't stopped pouring liquor down his throat and making stupid decisions, he wouldn't have made his thirty-fifth birthday.

But he had changed. At first, when he'd started to pull himself together, he did it from anger, to show Amanda that he could be serious and responsible. He'd swallowed his pride and gone back to medicine to prove he could handle the work. Only later did he realize that his career was something he wanted for himself.

"I didn't mean to bring up the past," she said.

But their history kept cropping up like a virulent weed that couldn't be killed.

"It was Carrie's voice," she said.

He turned back toward her. "What do you mean?''

"I remembered Carrie saying the name Dallas as if she knew the man. And I saw her with a gun in her hand.''

"A gun?''

"It was a revolver with a stainless-steel barrel and a

wood handle. Carrie took out five bullets. I could hear them dropping one by one.''

''That sounds a little like a dream,'' he said.

''Maybe that's it. Maybe it didn't really happen.'' She seized on the possibility. ''The bullets made a plopping noise, as if they'd fallen in water, and there's certainly not a stream that runs through Empire Bank. I must have been dreaming.''

''Tell me about Carrie.''

''I knew her a long time ago, while I was growing up in Chicago. We were friends, but we weren't close. We went to different high schools. Two years ago, she showed up here in Denver, and she looked me up. When she asked if I could get her a job at the bank, I knew something was wrong.''

''Why?''

''Carrie was from a very wealthy family. Not like my parents, who like to give the appearance of having money when they're really broke. Carrie's father was rich. It seemed strange that she'd want to be a bank teller.''

''But you decided to help her, anyway.''

She bit her lower lip. ''David, if I tell you these things, you can't repeat them to anyone. Especially not to the police or the FBI.''

''No problem. Haven't you ever heard of doctor-patient privilege?''

She rolled her eyes. ''I believe that has to do with information about a patient's physical condition.''

''I take a broad interpretation,'' he said. ''I won't tell anyone.''

Laurel's cross-carpet crawl led her to a full-length mirror. She sat back on her bottom and babbled to her reflection.

Amanda took up her story again. ''Carrie told me she'd

had a bad marriage. She hardly knew the guy when she'd eloped with him. Within a few months, she found out how abusive he was. She divorced him, but that wasn't enough. He kept coming after her.''

"Couldn't she turn to her wealthy father for help?"

"They were estranged," Amanda said. "Carrie disappeared. She bought fake identification and came out here. To work at the bank, she needed to be bonded. And she bought that, too. I hired her, knowing that her identification was completely phony."

Helping out a friend in trouble didn't seem outrageous to David, but he knew how difficult it must have been for Amanda to bend the rules, much less break them. "You're acting like this is the first time in your life you've ever told a lie."

When she shook her head, her hair fell forward and covered her face. "It's not the worst lie I've ever told."

Was she talking about the "secret" she shared with Hoffman? Or was this more personal? David returned his focus to her. He sat on the bed, close and intimate. "Tell me."

When she looked at him, there was something stark and tragic about the set of her lips. In spite of her cool facade, she was vulnerable. "I can't."

"What are you afraid of?"

"Everything. Nothing. I can't remember." The tendons on her throat stood out in sharp relief as she inhaled a deep breath. In the grip of fierce tension, she spoke in a slow, measured cadence. "I'm terrified that Carrie was involved in the bank robbery, and I helped her."

"Why?"

"The money. Empire Bank always gets a Wells Fargo delivery on the first of the month. There must have been a million dollars in that vault."

"I don't get it." He looked around the condo. It wasn't exactly skid row. "You're not broke, are you?"

"No. But a million dollars is a huge temptation. I can't help thinking about all that money. Sometimes, when I'm at the bank, I have to stop and stare. All that cash. Do you know what it feels like, David, to hold crisp stacks of hundred-dollar bills in your hand?" She leaned back on the pillows. "It's almost sexy."

She was sexy. "Tell me more."

Slowly, she shook her head. "I don't know what's going on, David. I can't help wondering if the real reason I feel so guilty is because I *am* guilty."

"Be rational," he said. "There's no actual evidence."

"I know every operational system in the bank. The alarms. The surveillance cameras. The delivery schedules."

"There must be other people who have the same information. Just because you know how the bank works doesn't prove you planned a heist."

"What about Carrie? Apparently, she's on the run with one of the bank robbers. And Carrie is one of my best friends."

"Friendship doesn't count as evidence."

"There's something else," she said. "I was watching the television news with Vonnie, and there was a secondary story about an escaped federal prisoner."

David had heard this news. "Jax Schaffer."

"I recognized him," Amanda said.

"That's no surprise," he countered. "His photograph has been in every newspaper. The guy's a major crime boss."

"I'm telling you that I know him, David. From back home in Chicago. I think he belonged to some of the same clubs as my father. He might have even been a guest in our home."

"So what?"

"His escape occurred at almost the same time as the robbery attempt at Empire Bank. Don't you think the timing is too coincidental? The two crimes have to be related."

Her logic made sense. If the SWAT teams were busy at Empire Bank, there wouldn't be as many officers available to respond to a call for help in stopping Jax Schaffer's escape.

"And I knew him," she said. "When he escaped this morning, two federal marshals and two policemen were killed."

"And you think it's your fault?"

"I don't know. That's the worst part. I'm building a case against myself, and I don't know if there's any foundation in truth."

Laurel gave a happy shriek as she flung her plastic keys at the baby in the mirror. She flipped athletically and began crawling, butt high in the air, toward the bed.

David watched her, mesmerized, as he considered truth as it applied to Amanda's suspicions of herself. She made a fairly decent case against herself, piling up associations and bits of circumstantial knowledge. What if she had been involved in the bank robbery? What if she was the inside contact for crime boss Jax Schaffer?

Laurel reached the bed. Energetically, she pulled herself upright using the comforter, and David gave her a boost onto the top of the mattress. She wriggled over to Amanda and snuggled close. They made a beautiful picture, with Amanda's darker blond hair mingling with her daughter's pale platinum. When they both turned to him, their matching blue eyes were breathtaking.

She sure as hell didn't look like a bank robber. But she was a woman with secrets. Of that, he was certain.

"At the hospital," he went on, "I stopped in to visit Harry Hoffman."

"How is he?" she asked.

"In spite of a sprained wrist, he looked like he was capable of bench-pressing the hospital bed."

"Seriously, David."

"His condition is listed as fair. He'll be going home tomorrow." Not wanting to tell her the less positive news about the bank customer who was shot, he added, "Harry has no memory loss, and I think he might have some important information. But he wouldn't give me a message for you. Said you had to call him yourself, and he gave me the phone number."

"He's a crusty old guy," she said. "I'm surprised the robbers got past him."

Following that logic, David said, "Maybe they didn't. It's possible that Harry was the inside contact."

"No way. He's completely loyal."

"He wanted me to tell you that your secret was safe with him. He didn't tell the cops or the FBI."

"My secret?" Her eyebrows pulled together in concentration, then she sighed. "I have no idea what he's talking about. Harry tends to be a little melodramatic."

Was she lying? It was difficult for him to concentrate on crime while he watched mother and child at play. "You and Laurel are beautiful together."

"She's wonderful." Amanda rubbed noses with her tiny daughter. "Aren't you? You're wonderful. You and me against the world, kiddo."

"What about her father?"

Her sudden stricken expression told David that he'd chosen exactly the wrong thing to say. Her maternal serenity vanished. "David, this isn't something I want to talk about. Not right now."

The identity of the father was painful for Amanda. If she'd been making love with David at the same time as with Laurel's father, their one-night stand might have destroyed her other relationship. Or, the inescapable alternative, he might be the father of her child.

He should ask her, point-blank. He didn't think she could look him in the eye and lie. But he wasn't sure, and he didn't want to take the chance.

At one time, he'd loved her. They were going to be married. Even when he'd embarked on his journey to self-destruction, she'd been the bright spot in his life. Their passion had been the only thing that had silenced his demons and given him peace. She'd been the pure, clean center of his filthy life.

Then she'd left him cold.

Being with her again wakened a lot of old feelings. This afternoon, he'd almost purchased a bottle. He wasn't ready for the truth. Not yet.

David pushed himself off the bed. "Try to rest. Forget about the robbery. Forget guilt. Forget truth. Your only concern at present is to get better. Let your body heal."

"Are you speaking as my doctor?"

"Your doctor...and your friend."

She straightened in the bed, jostling Laurel, who protested with a little squeak. "Is there something I can take to help me sleep?"

"Nonnarcotic painkillers. With a concussion, the idea is to avoid deep sleep that might become coma."

"Maybe a drink? There's vodka and rum in the liquor cabinet."

"No booze." David gritted his teeth. Was this a test? Why had he agreed to stay the night here? His instinct for self-preservation urged him to run like hell. "I'll take Laurel and give her to Vonnie. You try to sleep."

Unfortunately, there wasn't any way to take the baby without touching Amanda. As he leaned close, he caught a whiff of her light floral perfume. Mingled with the scent of baby, the smell was tantalizing.

His hand brushed Amanda's breast, and he groaned inwardly.

"Thank you," she said crisply.

Her cool demeanor had slipped back into place. And David matched her detachment. Inside, his frustration seethed. But his voice stayed calm. "I'll be checking on you throughout the night. Don't be alarmed when I come into your room."

"Fine." Her lips were tight.

David passed the rest of the evening with Vonnie in front of the television. When she made dinner for Amanda and carried it into her room on a tray, he didn't join them.

The longest hours came after eight o'clock when Laurel was in bed.

On the ten-o'clock news, he watched Elaine Montero as she reported no new developments on the bank robbery or the escape of Jax Schaffer. She outlined the progress in the case with shots of Empire Bank, the hospital and the front entrance to Amanda's high-rise condo. When she showed an ID photo of Carrie Lamb, David studied the face of Amanda's good friend. She didn't look like a bank robber, but she also didn't look like a woman who carried fake identification and was on the run from an abusive ex-husband.

After Vonnie went to her room, he was left alone on the sofa with a comforter, staring up at the very good copy of Monet's water lilies. He'd set an alarm clock to wake him in three hours so he could monitor Amanda, but he doubted he would need the alarm. David couldn't sleep.

His tension held slumber at bay. A couple of drinks

would've knocked him out, and he yearned for the unthinking, blissful state of unconsciousness. Something, anything, to take the edge off his awareness of Amanda and what she'd meant to him. A year and a half ago, they'd made love on the sunporch beneath the stars, and he'd made the mistake of thinking they'd get back together again. Dead wrong.

At one in the morning, he was still awake to hear the click of a key being fitted into a lock. He saw the shifting of shadows when the front door to Amanda's condo slowly opened.

Chapter Five

In her bedroom, Amanda rested uneasily upon her queen-size bed. It was a little after one o'clock in the morning. The loneliest hour of the night. After midnight, there should be new hopes for a new day, but she dreaded the suspicions that loomed beyond the dawn.

Rubbing at the base of her throat, she tried to massage her tension away. She felt suffocated by the weight of all the questions, the coincidences, the doubts. Even here in her bedroom, a sanctuary, the delicate ivy pattern on her wallpaper seemed to constrict around her. Her gaze darted from wall to wall. God, there was so much furniture in this room! Too much clutter. A dresser and bureau and chaise in addition to the bed. Amanda needed more room to breathe.

She concentrated on the vertical blinds. With bright moonlight streaking the edges, the cream-colored blinds looked like prison bars beneath an eyelet flounce.

Her veiled memories hinted that she was a criminal, an accomplice in the attempted bank robbery. Though she'd never thought of herself as that sort of person, Amanda could trace a pattern of failed expectations regarding her personal growth. More clutter. No wonder she felt claustrophobic.

Seeking release, she rose from the bed, went to the window and cranked it open. In her high-rise, above the city, she inhaled the sultry air of a summer night.

Relationships were her downfall. She had several acquaintances but few friends. Even fewer lovers. David had been the only man to whom she'd ever made a serious commitment. Being with him again unlocked a treasure trove of memories, good and bad. It was ironic. In the midst of this odd amnesia, she recalled her time with David so clearly. Sunlit days and starry nights under a lovers' moon. Spontaneous laughter. When times were good with him, she'd never felt so carefree.

She had to savor the memories, because she would never have the reality again. Sooner or later, she'd have to tell him about Laurel. And he'd hate her for the deception. She'd deprived him of nine precious months in his daughter's life. How could he ever forgive her?

Earlier tonight, when they'd spoken of truth, she should have told him. But she was afraid. She didn't want him to leave. *Get over it.* He deserved to know.

Leaning against the casement beside the window, she heard him coming down the hall to check on her. *Tell him now. Right this minute.* Talking to him at night would be easier. In the darkness, she wouldn't see the loathing in his eyes.

The door to her bedroom swung wide, and he stumbled through. Poor David, he must be exhausted.

In the faint glow of moonlight, she saw the outline of his head and shoulders. But he didn't look right. His posture was odd. As he groped for the light switch beside the door, she sensed that something was terribly wrong.

The overhead light flashed on. Instead of David, she saw a man dressed all in black. He wore a black ski mask. In his right hand, he held a gun.

His arm extended straight from his side. He aimed at the rumpled comforter on her bed.

Standing at the window, she tried to shrink, to become invisible. But he'd seen her. An executioner, he slowly rotated his arm. The gun pointed at her breast.

Then David dived through the door.

Amanda ducked.

The gun fired. The muffled explosion echoed inside her head, jolting other memories of recent terror.

Huddled on the floor, she watched in horror as David wrestled with the masked intruder. Bare chested, David pressed the assault. The muscles in his arms flexed as he caught hold of the other man's gun hand.

Locked in combat, they staggered against the foot of her bed and crashed to the floor. The gun dropped to the carpet.

Instinctively, Amanda snatched up the automatic pistol. It was cold and black and deadly. Her fingers trembled, and she used both hands to steady the barrel.

"I'll shoot," she yelled. But with the two of them struggling, there was no way she could get a clear shot at the intruder.

David landed a solid blow to the intruder's chin, and the man fell back, slamming against her dresser. Perfume bottles and a small lamp went flying.

He kicked at the chaise, and the edge caught David's knee. But he wouldn't be stopped. David bobbed and weaved like a prizefighter. His eyes glinted like steel. He cocked his arm and drove his fist hard into the other man's stomach. When the intruder doubled over in pain, David hammered the back of the man's head.

The would-be assassin sprawled across her bedroom carpet.

Reaching down, David yanked off the black woolen ski mask. "Do you know him?"

His face was very young. Midtwenties. "I've never seen him before."

"Get something to tie him up."

Adrenaline surged through her body, but she felt paralyzed. Though David had exerted all the effort, she was the one panting.

"Amanda," he said, "hurry."

"I don't have any rope. I have ribbon for wrapping packages."

"How about duct tape?"

"Why would I have duct tape?" she demanded. "I live in a condo. Other people do my repairs."

Vonnie appeared in the doorway. Her eyes were wide, and her hair stuck out in wild ringlets, a brilliant red contrast to her pink terry-cloth bathrobe. When she saw the man on the floor and the gun in Amanda's hand, she unleashed a piercing wail.

"Stop it," Amanda ordered.

"You killed him!"

"Hush, Vonnie. You'll wake Laurel."

David went toward the nanny. "It's okay. We have everything under control. I want you to go into the front room and call the police. Can you do that?"

Dumbly, she nodded.

"Go in the other room," he repeated. "But first, let me use the sash on your robe."

She quickly unfastened the sash, handed it to him and fled.

As he approached the still unconscious intruder, David flexed the fingers on his right hand and winced.

"David, are you all right?"

"I'd feel a whole lot better if you put down the gun."

Still grasping the weapon with both hands, she aimed it toward the floor. "What happened? Who is this person?"

"I don't know." David felt for a pulse before he flipped the man onto his stomach and tied his hands securely behind his back. "I heard him come in. He had a key."

"My purse," she said. "I never got my purse back. Somebody must have stolen my keys."

He finished with his knots and came toward her. "You're okay, aren't you?"

He held her arms and looked into her eyes, much the same as when he'd checked for symptoms of concussion. His hazel eyes held a depth of concern. "You're cold," he said.

"Warm me."

His strong arms embraced her, and she crushed tightly against his bare chest. He had saved her life, this wonderful man she'd once rejected.

From the nursery, she heard Laurel's cry. Only a few yards away, her baby had been sleeping while a masked intruder had broken into her bedroom and tried to murder her. Horrified, Amanda broke away from David and stared at the pistol in her hand. What might have happened if the intruder had entered the wrong room?

Gently, David took the weapon from her. "You can't stay here. Not even for tonight."

She surveyed the damage to her bedroom. The broken bottles. The overturned chaise. "But this is my home. I don't want to leave."

"Your building has been on the evening news, Amanda. This guy had a key, and there may be duplicates." He tossed the gun on the bed. "After we talk to the police, I'm taking you and Laurel and Vonnie home with me. To my house."

Never in her life had she felt less like a decisive, hard-driving career woman. The assault had devastated her confidence. All she wanted was to lean against David's bare chest and have him take care of her and her daughter. *Their daughter.*

"Come on, Amanda. Pull yourself together."

She nodded, trying to draw on the internal poise and strength that had never failed her. But fear made her helpless. She had no control over these terrible things that kept happening.

He directed her toward the bedroom door. "Take care of Laurel and wait for the police. I'll stay here and watch this guy."

In the door of her bedroom, she paused and looked back at this incredibly virile man with a gun in his hand. His Levi's slung low on his hips. His tanned torso was lean, sprinkled with crisp black hair. His shoulders were broad, strong enough to protect her and Laurel.

The truth might drive him away, and she didn't want that to happen. In this time of confusion, she desperately needed him, more than ever before. But he deserved to know about Laurel.

RELOCATING HER HOUSEHOLD in the middle of the night was easier than Amanda would have expected. In deference to her injury, David and Vonnie had taken charge. They'd hurried the police through the arrest of the assailant, answered questions from Agents Metcalf and Hess, packed the suitcases and retrieved Amanda's minivan from the bank parking lot.

It was four in the morning when Vonnie, driving the minivan, followed David's Porsche down University Boulevard toward the south suburbs.

Amanda checked on Laurel, who was sound asleep in her car seat, then turned toward the red-haired nanny, who was concentrating hard on David's taillights, though there was virtually no other traffic on the road. "I'm sorry about all of this, Vonnie."

"It's kind of cool," she said. "I'm going to have something to tell when I go back to college in the fall. I mean, getting attacked and everything makes a much better story about what I did on my summer vacation."

Amanda envied her youthful resilience. "Really?"

"I've never even gotten a parking ticket before, and now I'm on a first-name basis with an FBI agent."

"With Agent Metcalf?"

"With his partner, Hess. *Greg* Hess. The tall guy with the incredible blue eyes." Vonnie all but twinkled. "He told me he's partial to redheads, like Dee Gallant."

"Who?"

"She's on my favorite soap opera."

Amanda seriously doubted that Agent Greg Hess watched the soaps, but the fantasy seemed to make Vonnie happy as she followed David's taillights into the exclusive Bow Mar area in Littleton.

"Nice part of town," Vonnie said enthusiastically. "David lives out here?"

"Yes."

"He's really a catch, Amanda. I think you should go out with him."

"We were engaged. It didn't work."

"But he still has feelings for you. I can tell."

Unfortunately, this wasn't one of Vonnie's soap operas where people dated and mated with little regard for what had happened in their pasts.

The peppy little redhead continued, "I mean, you like Stefan, and he's a nice guy. But David is…incredible."

Vaguely amused by Vonnie's matchmaking, Amanda said, "Last week, you thought Stefan was a major hunk."

"Well, he is, and I know you've got lots of important reasons to stay with him."

"Such as?"

"The family stuff. Over the phone, your mom and I have talked about Stefan, you know."

"And mother approves of him," Amanda said.

"You bet she does. I mean, she's already got the wedding planned and everything."

"But you think I should go with David."

"It's like this," Vonnie said. "In *Gone with the Wind,* Scarlett was in love with that blond guy, but as soon as you saw Rhett Butler, you knew she ought to be with him."

"And David is my Rhett Butler?"

"You got it." Vonnie followed David's Porsche into a circular driveway and parked behind him. "Oh, my God! This is a great house!"

Amanda remembered the Tudor home from when she and David were engaged. When he was only twenty-seven, he'd inherited this property from a favorite aunt who'd passed away. Though everyone had expected him to sell the house, David settled in, discovering an unforeseen talent for gardening.

From what Amanda could discern by the glow from security lights, he'd kept up the yard work. "Do you like the landscaping, Vonnie?"

She squinted through the windshield. "From what I can see, it's really nice."

"David does it all himself."

"Wow! Rhett Butler and gardening, too." She glared at Amanda. "You have got to dump Stefan and go with David."

While the modern-day Rhett and Vonnie unloaded the back of the van, Amanda lifted her sleeping baby from the car seat and supported the little bundle in her arms. After a bit of wriggling, Laurel eased back into peaceful slumber.

Unfortunately, Amanda was nowhere near so complacent. Returning to David's house brought back a painful flood of regrets. When they were engaged, Amanda had planned to live in this charming home with peaked roof and shake shingles. Though the three-bedroom house was small in comparison to some of the mansions in this area, it was more than adequate for two people, and she'd explored the possibility of adding another bedroom above the garage, possibly redesigning the kitchen to be more efficient. This would have been her home.

She followed David and Vonnie inside, watching as he punched a code into the keypad near the front door.

"Alarm system," he said. "Unless it's disarmed within three minutes of opening the door, a siren goes off and the security company is alerted. The same thing happens if any of the windows are broken."

"This is new," she commented.

"I needed it. Working at the hospital, I'm gone a lot and I needed to protect against break-ins."

Other than the security system, he hadn't made many changes. Down a step from the entryway was a large front room with a leather sectional sofa. The dining area was beyond that. On the right was David's office. On the left, the kitchen.

Still holding Laurel, Amanda wandered into the kitchen with its adjoining breakfast area. The oak cabinets were exactly the same as she remembered. On the countertop were a couple of empty pizza boxes. David might be a terrific gardener, but he'd never been fond of cooking.

"Amanda," he called out. "Bring the baby up here."

She climbed the stairs to the second story and entered the large master bedroom where David had already unloaded the playpen from the car. It would act as a makeshift crib for Laurel.

"I figured you and Laurel would sleep in here," he said.

After she'd ended their relationship, she'd never thought she'd see the inside of this room again. Being here with him disconcerted her. Quickly, she settled Laurel in the playpen and tiptoed toward the door, not wanting to waken her.

Downstairs, Amanda offered to help with the other suitcases.

"Not necessary," David said. "If you want to make yourself useful, brew some coffee."

"Why? We all need sleep."

"Can't do it. I'm scheduled at the hospital for an early shift. I'll be even more tired if I go back to sleep."

"Can't you take the day off?"

"I could, but that would mess up my schedule for the rest of the week, and I want to be off on Friday and Saturday so I miss the Fourth of July madness in the emergency room." He gestured toward the coffeemaker near the sink. "Do you remember where I keep the beans?"

She crossed the white tile floor and pointed to a vacuum-sealed canister that held exactly a pound of beans. "Sumatra blend, brewed with distilled water," she said. "You were always fussy about your coffee."

"And I still am." He headed back to the car, calling over his shoulder, "Some things never change."

People never change, she reminded herself as she went through the remembered ritual of preparing David's coffee. No matter how wonderful he seemed, this was the same David she'd broken up with five years ago.

Leaving the dark, rich, aromatic liquid dripping steadily through the Braun coffeemaker, she climbed the stairway to the master bedroom. Her feet trod heavily on the carpeted steps. So many times she'd raced David up the stairs to the bedroom. They'd torn off their clothes on the way to bed, feverish and anxious to make love.

Now they kept a careful distance when they met in the hall outside the bedroom. Avoiding eye contact, they carefully stepped around each other so they wouldn't accidentally touch.

"I brought in three suitcases for you and Laurel," he said.

"That's all of them." Their exchange felt stilted, overly formal. "Thank you."

"No problem. I do this kind of thing for all my patients."

"You've got a great bedside manner, Doctor."

"So I've been told."

Her gaze lit upon a grouping of family photos that decorated the hallway above a cedar chest. She indicated one of the pictures. "How's your big brother and his family?"

"Fine. Josh is still bigger than I am. I told him it was because Nancy fed him too well."

"Do they still live in Evergreen?"

"Right. Josh is handling all the mountain construction work for the family business." David stared at the picture as if he'd never seen it before. "Their three boys are growing like weeds."

"I remember how Nancy always wanted a girl."

"She always liked the girlish things. Sewing and crafts. Now that the boys are in school, she's started selling some of her custom clothing designs, and she's thinking about opening a boutique in Evergreen."

"I'm sure she'll do well. Everything your family touches seems to turn to gold."

"We've been lucky," he agreed.

As far as Amanda knew, David was the only person in

his large extended family who wasn't involved in Haines Homes, New Construction and Renovation. After he'd graduated from medical school and wasn't accepted at his first choice of hospitals for an internship, he'd tried to make a niche for himself in the family business. Unfortunately, David was terrible with numbers and such a perfectionist when it came to the construction work that it took him four times too long to complete a job.

His father created a position for David in negotiation and advertising. It was roughly similar to the duties of a prince in a royal family. David's obligation was to show up at social events and be charming.

"Your parents?" she asked.

"They're good. Sometimes they ask about you."

"Really?" She'd always been fond of David's parents.

"Mom tells me I was an idiot to lose you. Nobody ever blamed you for breaking up with me, Amanda. It was pretty much the consensus that I was a spectacular disaster."

She hadn't wanted to get into this. "David, I—"

"Forget it." Staring straight ahead, he continued, "I put Vonnie in the guest room, and I gave her instructions to check on you at nine in the morning. You're not to do anything strenuous tomorrow."

"But I feel all right," she protested. "I'm tired and my head still hurts a bit, but I'm really fine."

"Fine? Do me a favor, Amanda. Don't tell me you're *fine*. You keep saying that you're *fine*. And it's not true. You had a brain injury, okay? A concussion is serious. You need to rest and heal. Promise me you won't take on the world for at least another day."

"Okay," she said meekly.

As they mumbled their goodnights, she hoped he might stroke her cheek or kiss her lightly on the tip of her nose. But he made no such gesture.

Though it was unreasonable to feel desolate, that was her state as she closed the bedroom door behind her. If things had worked out differently between them, this might have been her bedroom, *their* bedroom.

She checked on Laurel, who continued to sleep soundly on her back. One tiny hand curled against her rosy cheek in the blissful repose of the innocent. She was such a beautiful baby, *their* baby.

BY THE TIME DAVID HAD showered and shaved, it was four-thirty in the morning. There was no point in going to bed. He needed to leave for work in an hour and a half.

He threw on a pair of khaki trousers and a shirt before staggering out to the kitchen for a dose of caffeine.

The refrigerator light was on. When David turned on the overhead, Vonnie's head popped around the edge of the refrigerator door. "There's nothing to eat in here."

He poured himself a cup of coffee. "I'm not much of a cook."

"Well, I've got to go shopping tomorrow."

He pulled out his wallet and took out four twenties, which he placed on the countertop. "This should get you started at the grocery store. Be sure you get everything Laurel needs."

"You bet."

She stuffed the cash into the pocket of her beltless bathrobe, closed the refrigerator door and grinned at him. She was a cute little thing. The tangled red hair and freckles made her look like a kid. "How old are you, Vonnie?"

"Almost twenty."

He had observed her skills in child care enough to know she was competent to care for Laurel. "What made you decide to be a nanny?"

"I have six younger brothers and sisters. But this isn't,

like, a career choice. Being a nanny is just a summer job. I'm in college.'' She planted her fists on her skinny hips. ''David, we need to talk about Amanda.''

He sipped his coffee, hoping the caffeine would do its work. ''Aren't you tired, Vonnie?''

''After all the awesome stuff that's happened today? I mean, the bank robbery and the guy who broke in and that really cute FBI agent. It's totally a Mel Gibson movie.''

Her excitement was like a whirlwind. Oh, to be nineteen again. David could barely remember that wide-eyed age when every day was a fresh start, and life was a grand adventure.

''About Amanda,'' Vonnie said. ''She told me you guys were engaged a long time ago, and I think she still likes you. You should, you know, take her out to dinner or something.''

Unfortunately, life wasn't that simple anymore. They weren't talking about a date to the senior prom. ''Thanks for the advice, Vonnie, but—''

''Just because she had a kid with another man doesn't mean you two can't get back together.''

Another man? David came suddenly awake. Did Vonnie know the identity of the father?

Though he couldn't imagine Amanda sharing heart-to-heart confidences with this bouncy red-haired pixie, they were two women living together. They were likely to talk about the baby. And the father?

''I consider Laurel to be an asset,'' he said.

''You like kids,'' she said with a knowing grin. ''I could tell. Oh, my God, you and Amanda have to get back together.''

''What about Stefan?''

''He's like, really cute. And I've talked to Amanda's mom about him. A lot. She wants Amanda and Stefan to get married. But I don't think so. I mean, he's..." Her voice trailed off. "Well, you know."

"I don't know," David said. "Shed a little light for me on her relationship with Stefan."

"Well, he should have gotten married to Amanda as soon as he knew she was pregnant with his baby. That would have been the right thing to do."

David's mug fell from his hand and crashed to the floor. Numbly, he watched the dark liquid splash across the kitchen tiles. Laurel was Stefan's daughter. Not his.

Chapter Six

The coming of dawn splashed pink across the cloudless skies outside David's kitchen window. He poured himself another cup of coffee. He'd been sitting here for an hour, coming to grips with the knowledge that Laurel wasn't his child.

Until yesterday morning, when Amanda had told him about her nine-month-old baby, he hadn't considered the prospect of fatherhood. And then, for a few hours, he'd imagined the possibility. And he'd liked the feeling. Now the dream was gone.

It was better this way. At least he knew the truth.

When he heard the sound of footsteps on the staircase, he was momentarily startled. It had been a long time since anybody else had shared his home, and he was accustomed to silence.

Amanda appeared in the doorway, dressed in cutoff jeans and a pastel blue T-shirt with her hair freshly washed. "I couldn't sleep," she said.

He stared down into the circle of his mug, unable to look at her. "Help yourself to coffee."

He listened to the sounds of Amanda bustling about in his kitchen, finding sugar and milk for her coffee. When he looked up, he noticed that she'd selected the same mug she'd always used when she stayed with him—white with yellow daisies. They had a history but no future.

She sat at the small kitchen table across from him. "There has to be a reason that man tried to kill me."

"Nice wake-up topic, Amanda."

"What else would we discuss? The weather?" She sipped her coffee. "What do you think? Why did he come after me?"

"Sex or money. Those are the usual motives for murder," he said. "In E.R., most of our victims come from accidents. However, when the violence is premeditated, the reason is almost always sex or money."

"But those motives don't apply to me. The man who came into my apartment wasn't intent upon robbery. And I never saw him before in my life, so it couldn't be sex."

When it came to Amanda, he would never rule out sex. Despite the hour and their mutual lack of sleep, she looked great. Her freshly washed blond hair fell neatly to her shoulders, and she'd discarded the bandage on her forehead.

If he hadn't known better, he never would have suspected that she'd been in the hospital emergency room less than twenty-four hours ago. A hell of a lot had happened since then, but only one fact stood out: Stefan Phillips was Laurel's father.

Consciously, David put his disappointment behind him. He wasn't angry at Amanda. It was more the opposite. He was relieved that she hadn't purposely kept Laurel's birth a secret from him. She simply hadn't told him because it wasn't any of his business. He wasn't the father.

And Vonnie's perception of him was true. David wouldn't reject Amanda because she'd had another man's child. Laurel was still an asset as far as he was concerned. And Amanda? She was now—and always would be—one of the best things that had ever happened to him. "How are you feeling?"

"I'm all right," she said. "I took some aspirin."

"Let me check that head wound."

"Stop being a doctor, David. I want to talk about the person who attacked me."

"The motive was money. It's obvious. Somebody must have paid him to come after you."

"Who?"

"I'll take a wild guess and say it was the person who planned the bank robbery."

"Why?"

Again, David thought the conclusion was transparently obvious. "They want you out of the way. You must know something that could implicate the criminals."

"I can't think of anything."

"Do you have your memory back?"

"It's getting better." Her eyes took on a soft, dreamy look as she concentrated. "I remember getting up, getting dressed for work and feeding Laurel her oatmeal and bananas. I even have a few flashes of the robbery, like being with Carrie and Tracy and hearing the robber's names. Then I woke up in the hospital and saw you."

When her blue eyes stared directly into his, he felt a dangerous tension, the prelude to arousal. There was no medical explanation for his reaction to her. Nor was there a prescribed drug he could take to stop the palpable symptoms of desire. But he could tell that he was coming down with a bad case of Amanda. He wanted to make love to her.

His body was on superalert. His senses peaked. He could smell her clean fragrance from six feet away. He marveled at the way her dimples appeared when her jaw tightened. Though Amanda had an expressive face, she generally kept herself impassive and cool. She did the ice-princess facade very well, but he knew different. He'd seen Amanda when she was hot, sweaty and passionate.

He couldn't resist much longer. Pushing his chair back from the table, he stood. "I've got to hit the road. I suggest you go back to bed."

"I can't sleep. I have to figure this out."

"As your doctor—"

"You're not my doctor. My regular physician is gray haired, never makes jokes and is a woman." She gave one quick nod as if her statement was some kind of conclusion. "Now, what do you think about this Jax Schaffer theory?"

"You mean the idea that the bank robbery was only meant as a diversion to get the SWAT team out of the way so this super-bad guy could escape?"

"Is that possible?"

"Sounds too complicated." As a doctor treating the victims of violent crime, he knew that the solution was usually simple. "On the other hand, this Schaffer guy is supposed to be a crime boss. If he wanted you dead, he'd hire a killer."

Her eyebrows raised. "Do you think that man who came into my condo was a hit man?"

"Maybe." The idea of a professional hit man was intimidating, and David was glad he hadn't been aware of that possibility when he jumped the guy. Not that it would have stopped him. He would have fought a dozen bad guys to protect Amanda and Laurel.

"I'm going to figure this out, David."

Her expression hardened, and he knew exactly what she was thinking. Amanda viewed the world as a morass of incompetence, where no one was as capable as she. She was about to confront the problem head-on. "So, you're going to become a supersleuth? Columbo in a skirt?"

"A designer skirt," she corrected. "Only because it's a little hot for a trench coat."

"I know better than to argue with you," he said. "So here's the bottom line. You're still not totally well. You could still have major headaches and vertigo. You need to take it easy. Don't leave the house today."

"But I—"

"No," he said firmly. "Do your investigating on the phone. And don't tell anybody where you are. Promise you'll stay here."

"I'll try."

Not much of a promise, but he figured that was the best he was going to get. "I have to leave, Amanda. But I should probably take a look at your stitches before I go. Did you use antiseptic after your shower?"

"Only a moisturizer."

"Don't move."

David went to the downstairs bathroom and opened the medicine cabinet, where he found a bottle of antiseptic and a tin of bandages.

When he returned to the kitchen, she was perched on the edge of a chair, facing him.

Before touching her, David braced himself. Yesterday, when he'd treated her at the hospital, it was clinical. Here in his kitchen, sharing a cup of coffee, a natural intimacy overwhelmed him.

Carefully, he pushed her bangs aside to reveal her temple. Though the area was swollen and discolored, she was healing nicely. He'd done a neat job of patching her up using clear surgical thread. "I don't think you'll have much permanent scarring."

"I hadn't even thought of that. Will I need plastic surgery?"

"It's up to you. A slight imperfection might make you more beautiful."

"You think I'm beautiful?"

"You know what I think."

From the first moment he had seen her, David had thought she was the perfect blonde. Not a buxom bimbo but a cool, sophisticated blonde, sculpted from porcelain.

As he tilted her head toward the light above the kitchen table, his thumb caressed her jaw, feeling the hard bone beneath her velvet skin. His gaze followed the line of her throat to the beginning hint of cleavage at the scoop neckline of her T-shirt. Her breasts, he knew, were full and perfect.

As a doctor, his examination was over. As a man, he'd just begun to look.

"Am I all right?" she asked.

Very much so. "Yes."

"I don't need to wear that stupid bandage, do I?"

"No." Her silky hair slipped through his fingers as he raked it back behind her ear. The scent of her shampoo teased his nostrils. "You smell like flowers."

"It's my shampoo. I told Vonnie to pack everything in my bathroom, and she was thorough. Probably a good thing. I wouldn't want to use that harsh soap of yours."

He agreed. Her delicate skin deserved the finest ointments. She was so dainty, so utterly feminine.

Since he didn't have cotton balls handy, David saturated a paper napkin with antiseptic and lightly daubed at the area where her skin had been broken and he'd sewn her back together.

"That stings," she said with a shudder.

Her slight movement aroused him. He remembered how she would tremble when they made love. Her body was amazingly sensitive.

"I'm almost done," he said, screwing the top back on the bottle. "After this dries, I'll put on a Band-Aid."

He leaned closer, still holding her hair away from the stitches, and lightly blew on her skin.

Amanda wriggled on the chair. "Is that necessary?"

"Absolutely. Recommended treatment in the first-aid manual."

He was too close. He couldn't stop himself. Breathing lightly, he circled her ear.

She gasped. Her shoulders stiffened. "Are you sure you do this with all your patients?"

His tongue outlined the helix edge of her ear. Again, he blew softly.

"David, stop!"

She pulled away. But when their eyes met, he saw the reflection of his own desire in her gaze. "You don't want me to stop."

"No." She stood. "I mean, yes."

"You want me, Amanda." She couldn't deny the sizzling electricity that flowed between them. "You want me as much as I want you."

He pulled her into a tight embrace and ravaged her mouth, tasting deeply of her honeyed passion. Her body molded to his. Her lips parted, and her tongue darted into his mouth.

His need for her almost overwhelmed him. His male instincts told him to sweep the coffee mugs off the table and take her right here. But he wouldn't allow himself to lose control, not again.

When he loosened his grasp, she rubbed herself against him, torturing his hard erection.

Inhaling a ragged breath, he held her away from him. "I can't let this happen."

He stepped back, and she sank bonelessly into the chair. "Why not?"

"Things are different now. You have a child. I have responsibilities."

He had to leave. Now. "I'll be at work. I left my beeper number by the phone. Stay here and rest. I'll see you tonight."

Without looking back, David fled from his own desire.

WHEN AMANDA OPENED the door to her air-conditioned minivan, the afternoon heat smacked her in the face. For an instant, her dizziness returned and she hesitated, with one sandaled foot in her car and the other sinking into the steaming asphalt of the Denver General parking lot. Her sleeveless, bronze-colored shift felt unbearably heavy, even though the knit material was lightweight and the above-the-knee dress was the skimpiest outfit she could wear without feeling unreasonably casual. She yanked off the long leopard-patterned silk scarf she'd worn at her throat for accent. It was simply too hot for fashion.

Coming here might be a huge mistake. David had advised rest. Agent Metcalf certainly wouldn't approve. But she'd slept as much as she could and couldn't bear the inactivity of sitting around the house, watching soap operas with Vonnie. Most especially, she couldn't be comfortable in David's house where every corner brought back memories of a time when they'd been together, and every window reflected the guilty feeling that she hadn't tried hard enough to make their relationship work.

This morning, he'd encapsulated the barrier between them in just a few words: things were different now because she had a child. She was a mother.

It wouldn't be right for them to get together for a fling and then separate again. Their relationship needed to be all or nothing. She needed to tell him the truth. Even if things never worked out between them, Laurel deserved more than an occasional father.

She entered Denver General, signed in at the guard's desk and picked up a get-well bouquet at the hospital florist. From an earlier phone call to Harry Hoffman, she'd ascertained that he was in a private room on the fifth floor. But she hadn't discussed anything else over the phone. Amanda wanted to talk to Harry in person, to question him about their "secret."

Taking the elevator to the fifth floor, she inquired at the nurse's station. "I'm looking for Harry Hoffman."

"He's a popular fellow. Fourth door on the left. You can't miss it. There's a police guard."

"Thank you."

"Tell Harry you're the last one until somebody else leaves. He's only allowed to have four visitors at a time."

Though she'd hoped to have a private talk with the injured bank guard, Amanda would take what she could get. After identifying herself to the uniformed policeman in the hall, she pushed open the door to Harry's private room, where an air of festivity brightened the bland hospital decor. There were several bouquets and a bunch of balloons. Harry's wife, Muriel, sat closest to his bed. Frank Weathers paced back and forth, blabbing. The head teller, Jane Borelli, seemed to hang on Frank's every word.

Frank halted midsentence when he saw her. "Amanda," he said. "Well, well. You must be feeling better."

"Better than yesterday," she said coolly.

"I'm sure the board will be delighted to hear of your progress. There's a meeting tomorrow." His eyebrows raised. "But you've surely been informed."

She hadn't heard. Though she'd checked the messages on her home answering machine, there was no mention of a board meeting for Empire Bank. The omission worried her. Her career would suffer if she was out of the loop, but that was something she'd deal with later.

Disregarding Frank, she approached the bed where Harry sat. His expression was stern, but he was almost comical in the outrageous magenta brocade smoking jacket that he wore over his hospital gown. There was gauze wrapped around his head like a turban, holding bandages in place. "What about you, Harry? How are you feeling?"

"I'm good." He straightened his posture. "I'm ready to get out of this joint."

Muriel patted his hand. "Settle down, dear. You're not leaving until tomorrow."

Amanda turned to the small round woman. "I'm so sorry about everything, Muriel. This must be difficult for you."

"I knew the risks when my Harry took a job as a security guard. When your husband goes out the door every day with a gun strapped to his hip, you've got to be prepared for danger." She took the bouquet and found a place for it amid the others. "Thank you for the flowers, dear. Aren't they nice, Harry?"

Though he made a grumbling noise in the back of his throat, his fondness for his pleasant little wife was apparent, and Amanda guessed that he rather enjoyed being fussed over.

"No need for you to be sorry," he said to Amanda. "The hostile takeover can't be blamed on you."

"Nor you," she assured him. "You're the best security guard we've ever had."

"Then why did this happen?" The question came from Jane, the head teller, who always reminded Amanda of a neat brown wren, an impression that was enhanced by Jane's frequent choice of brown-and-beige clothing that matched her dishwater-blond hair. Her dark eyes darted as she continued, "I don't mean to put the blame on anybody, certainly not on either of you. But how could this terrible thing have happened to us?"

"Maybe we can figure it out," Amanda said. She didn't think it would improve employee confidence to mention her memory loss. "Jane, why don't you describe the robbery attempt for us from your perspective?"

"Fishing?" Frank Weathers asked her.

"I beg your pardon."

"You don't have any idea what happened. Yesterday, you couldn't remember a thing."

So much for keeping her memory loss a secret. "As soon as my concussion heals, I'll recall every detail."

"I wish I could forget," Jane said quietly. Her sallow cheeks quivered with the effort of smiling. "But the victim-assistance woman said it was important to talk about the hostage situation. She said I shouldn't repress my feelings."

"You need to talk about it," Muriel said. Leaving the floral display, she moved toward the other woman and gently took both of Jane's hands in her own. "I've been in therapy for seven years, and I know about these things."

Swell, Amanda thought. Just what they needed. An amateur psychologist with good intentions.

Muriel continued, "Tell us about it, Jane. How did you feel?"

"Helpless," she said. "And scared."

"Of course you were. Those men had guns, didn't they?"

Biting back sobs, Jane nodded. Her eyes washed with tears.

Imperiously, Amanda watched. Her chin lifted. Her shoulders pulled back. She'd never been a touchy-feely person. Too much emotion embarrassed her. She didn't enjoy hugging, especially not with an employee. It wasn't appropriate, wasn't right. An individual's demeanor was a clear indication of breeding and background.

Yet, she understood Jane's trauma. Though Amanda couldn't recall much about the attempted robbery, she had a residual sense of panic, anger and fear—intense emotions that threatened her identity as a bank president. It was as if she knew the melody but couldn't remember the title of the song.

"I was too scared to breathe," Jane said. "They could have killed us all. We were trapped. There was nowhere to hide."

"Just awful," Muriel said. "What else?"

"It was…intense. I can't explain. I was…"

"You don't have to explain." Amanda understood her confusion, her terror and unreasoning fear. "I know what you were going through."

"You do?"

"You're going to be all right, Jane." Though she'd never been good at sympathetic reassurance, Amanda spoke from the heart. "We're all going to make it through this."

"You were so brave, Amanda. You stood up to them."

"Brave? I was scared as a rabbit."

As she looked at Jane, she felt a kinship. As hostages, they had shared a profound helplessness that couldn't be explained. Emotion built within Amanda like a tidal wave, eroding her regal control, crashing against her defenses.

Slowly, Jane approached her, and Amanda stumbled forward. It seemed that no one else was in the room, no one else could understand. They hugged tightly, sharing their pain.

Never before had Amanda been so demonstrative. Now she was crying. Oh, God, she was ruining her mascara. Her reputation as an executive would be decimated. Frank

Weathers would make sure Bill Chessman and the rest of the Empire Bank board of directors heard about her breakdown.

But she didn't give a damn. This time, she wouldn't just get over it. She couldn't deny the way she felt. She wouldn't fight it, not anymore.

Jane stepped away first. "I'm sorry. I didn't mean to grab you like that."

"I'm glad you did." Amanda was sorry, too. Sorry for all the years she'd worked with this woman and had never really seen her. Things were different now. "We've been through hell, Jane. But we'll stick together and hope the worst is over."

"I hope so."

"Can you tell me what happened to you at the bank?"

"Ladies," Frank Weathers called out, "we're here to cheer up Harry. Remember?"

Dismissively, Amanda said, "Shut up, Frank."

"Excuse me?"

"No, I don't think I will. It's quite possible that I'm not following proper bank protocol. And I don't care." She squeezed Jane's hand. "Every single person who was held hostage in the bank needs to talk about it, to work through it."

"Fortunately," he said stiffly, "we have excellent insurance benefits at the bank. I believe several visits to the shrink of your choice will be covered."

"Get out," Harry Hoffman thundered.

"I'm looking out for *your* interests," Frank protested. "You don't need to be surrounded by weeping women."

"You've got five seconds." Harry glowered under his bandages. "Or else I get out of this bed and kick your skinny butt out the door."

"Fine, I'm gone. Have a nice little crying game."

When the door closed behind him, Harry patted the edge of his bed. "Amanda and Jane, come over here."

Amanda perched at the foot of his bed and looked toward Harry expectantly, like a little girl waiting for her storytime. Two days ago, she never would have shared her fear. She would have been on Frank's side as they both sprinted toward career advancement. But now it felt right to talk with the bank guard and the head teller. They were the victims; they were the survivors.

"You start, Harry."

"I was in the video-surveillance room, keeping an eye on the cameras. A guy came into the room. He was wearing a black knit cap, which I thought was pretty weird for July. Then he pulled the ski mask over his face. He was holding a gun on me."

"To get to the surveillance room, he must have walked through the bank," she said. "And he didn't have his mask pulled down. That means we must have a video picture of him."

"Doesn't matter," Harry pointed out. "The cops have one guy under arrest. Another one is here at the hospital. The third guy is the one who made the escape, and there are lots of pictures of him. He's still at large."

"With Carrie. She's still a hostage," Amanda said. She and Jane exchanged a look and shuddered at the thought of what Carrie might be going through.

"Anyway," Harry said, "the guy in the mask told me to back up. He went to the computer and keyed in the code to turn off the video surveillance. Then he ordered me to walk to the door. Halfway across the room, I went for my gun. That's when he knocked me out."

"Back up a minute," Amanda said. "He knew the correct computer information? How is that possible?"

"I kind of wondered about that. As far as I know, only you and the people at Summit Security have the codes."

She didn't need to be reminded. "Maybe it was some kind of computer-hacker thing. Is that possible, Harry?"

Relieved, Harry nodded. "You don't suspect me, do you?"

"Of course not," she said firmly. "You're the best security guard we've ever had."

"You see?" his wife said. "I told you so. You aren't going to lose your job."

"Not if I have anything to say about it," Amanda reassured him. Then she turned to Jane, "When did you first realize there was a robbery in progress?"

"Well, it wasn't hard to figure out," she said. "There were three of them. All with black masks. All with machine guns. They ordered us to lie down on the floor. Facedown."

As she relived the moment, Amanda saw the panic return to Jane's eyes. "It's okay. Go on."

"I was too far away from the counter to press my silent-alarm button. I curled up on the floor and stayed there, praying that nobody would be hurt."

Amanda hugged her again. "I'm so sorry you had to go through this."

"It's not your fault."

But it was. The robbers had chosen this particular branch of Empire Bank for a reason. They seemed too professional to simply wander into a bank at random. They had selected *her* bank. Which was why an assailant had come to her condo last night and tried to kill her. "Then what happened?"

"I froze. I really couldn't move. One of them wanted me to use my key with you to open the vault, but I couldn't do it. Carrie took the key from me and helped you open the vault."

"Carrie took the key?" That sounded suspicious.

"She had to. One of the robbers was going to hurt me." Her dark eyes pleaded with Amanda. "I know what they're saying about Carrie, that she's involved with the robbers. But I don't believe it for a minute. She was trying to help me."

"I'm with you, Jane. I don't think Carrie is a criminal."

Jane exhaled and looked down. "They were unloading the money when the police and the SWAT team showed up. And that customer got shot. I didn't see what happened, but I heard the gun blast. It was the loudest noise. Then the robbers let all the hostages go, except for you and Carrie and that woman you had the meeting with that morning."

"Tracy Meyer," Amanda said. Poor Tracy! Amanda needed to call her.

"It was awful." Jane's lips were tight. "I feel like such a coward."

"You're not," Harry said. "I should have been there to protect you."

They could second-guess each other forever, but that wouldn't explain why the robbers had chosen Amanda's bank. She needed to figure it out, to clear her reputation, to end the threats. Harry Hoffman might have the answer.

Amanda asked Muriel and Jane to wait in the hall for a moment. After they'd left the room, she occupied the chair at bedside. "Tell me about our secret, Harry."

"I've kept it quiet. I haven't told the cops or anybody about the secret camera."

"A camera." Remembrance teased at the edge of her consciousness. "Where? Why?"

"You caught some of that amnesia, didn't you?"

"But it's going away," she said. She remembered a private conversation with Harry. It had taken place a few days ago. "I suspected someone at the bank of going through my desk, but I wanted to avoid a confrontation. I asked you to set up a secret camera in my office."

"And I got the equipment from Summit to do the job. The camera only activated when your desk drawers were opened."

This secret camera could provide important evidence. If someone had gone through her desk, he might have taken the security codes that were used in the robbery. "I need to get over to the bank," she said. "Thank you, Harry."

"Don't mention it." His gaze drifted past her shoulder, and she turned.

David stood in the door to Harry's room.

His eyes were angry. "You're supposed to be home in bed, Amanda."

"There's too much else to do."

"I told you to rest," he declared. "Why are you here?"

"I could ask you the same thing," she said. "Aren't you supposed to be in the emergency room?"

"There's been another kind of emergency. The entire hospital is on alert."

He opened the door wider. Jane Borelli and Muriel squeezed back into the room. Two uniformed police officers were right behind them.

"What's going on?" Harry Hoffman demanded.

"There's been a murder," David explained. "One of the bank robbers—his name was Temple—was shot and killed."

Chapter Seven

A chill crept into Harry Hoffman's hospital room. The danger that started with the robbery attempt at Empire Bank reached out again toward Amanda. She shivered, imagining the grip of ice-cold, skeletal fingers on her shoulder. She wasn't safe. Death was in the air. One of the robbers had been murdered.

Immediately, her defenses went up. She stood, straightened her posture and directed her question to the two officers who stood behind David. "May I ask how such a thing could happen? I assume this person was under police protection."

The cops exchanged a glance before the older one said, "We're not at liberty to discuss—"

"Might as well tell her," David interrupted. "Trust me on this. She'll poke around until she finds out. Besides, I'm real sure this story is going to break on the five-o'clock news."

The cop shifted his weight and adjusted the holster on his belt. His tone was matter-of-fact as he explained, "The officer guarding Temple abandoned his post for a few minutes. The killer entered Temple's room and shot him once in the face. When the officer resumed his duties, he failed to check on his prisoner. When the shift changed, ten minutes ago, the new officer in charge discovered the murder.''

The utter incompetence appalled her. "You don't even know the precise time the murder was committed?''

"That's not my department, ma'am.''

Another faceless killer. Another brazen assault, similar to the one unleashed on her by the assailant who had come into her condo in the dark of night. She was struck by the lack of subtlety in these attacks. A killer simply marched forth, aimed a weapon and fired. "Didn't anyone hear the gunshot?''

Harry piped up from his hospital bed. "Must have been using a silencer. Some of those babies are doggone effective. The only noise you hear is a thud, like dropping a book on the floor.''

Amanda never dreamed it would be so easy to commit murder and walk away, especially not in a hospital under police guard. No one was safe. Her mind flashed back to the image of a man in a black ski mask aiming a gun directly at her heart. She could have died. If David hadn't been there to protect her...

Authoritatively, Harry asked, "Have you found the murder weapon?''

"Far as I know,'' the cop said, "we don't have it.''

"What about witnesses?'' Harry demanded.

"It's a full-scale investigation.''

At one time, Amanda would have taken solace in the assurance that the police were investigating. But now? The sense of security she'd lived with all her life faded, chased away by brutal reality.

Acting on intuition, Amanda moved toward Jane. Before the hostage situation, Amanda had thought of Jane Borelli as a bright, efficient head teller, capable of supervising others. They shared a pleasant working relationship. Now, they were close as sisters. Amanda felt Jane's fear. Her dark eyes glistened with stark terror. Poor Jane trembled at the brink of total collapse.

She grasped Amanda's hand and held on tightly, as if their physical contact were the rope that kept her from plummeting into dark, endless despair.

"We survived before," Amanda whispered. "We'll survive again."

"It's so senseless. Things like this aren't supposed to happen."

"Life is fragile." She wouldn't succumb to this devastating vulnerability. She wouldn't live in fear. "But it's precious, too. We have to grab every moment."

"Excuse me, ma'am," the senior cop said. "I have to ask all visitors to leave this room."

"I don't think much of your protection," Harry said as he swung his legs off the bed. "I'm getting the hell out of here."

"Whoa, there." David stepped forward. "I'll notify Dr. Spangler."

"You don't get it, Doc. I'm leaving. I don't want to stay here anymore."

David appeared to be near the end of his patience. His expression was haggard. Dark circles ringed his eyes. A smear of blood stained the front of his pale blue scrubs. "Lie down, Harry. You can't leave until your doctor releases you."

"The hell I can't." He turned to his wife. "Muriel, where are my pants?"

"I've had it," David growled. "Don't give me crap, Hoffman. There's been a murder in the hospital, and I'm not in the mood to play games."

"You can't keep me against my will."

"Lie down before these officers put you under arrest."

"On what charge?"

"Suspicion of murder," David said. "Have you left this room in the past hour?"

"I went for a walk. To test my balance, get my sea legs." Harry drew back his chin like a turtle going into his shell. "Are you accusing me of killing that guy?"

"You could have done it," David said.

"Oh, really," Amanda protested. "Harry didn't—"

"I'm making a point," David said. "This situation is serious. It's life-and-death. All of you people need to co-operate without fussing and without questions. Do you read me, Harry?"

Resentfully, he climbed back onto his bed. "Loud and clear, Doc."

"Good." David transferred his steely gaze to her. "Amanda, you're coming with me."

Though she didn't like being ordered about, now probably wasn't the best time to raise objections with David. He appeared ready and willing to throw her over his shoulder and physically remove her from the room.

Amanda gave Jane's hand a final encouraging squeeze and preceded David into the hallway. "Was that really necessary?" she asked. "Did you have to be so mean to Harry?"

"Don't tick me off, Amanda."

He paused at the nurses' station and told the RN in charge to contact Dr. Loretta Spangler and have her check on Harry Hoffman before he tied his bedsheets together and escaped from his room. Then he herded Amanda into the elevator.

"Where are we going?" she asked.

"Don't talk," he said. "Don't even think about giving me a hard time."

Her annoyance built as she followed him through the

first-floor lobby and out the exit, where they walked through a newly erected metal detector. In the parking lot, he led the way past four police cruisers. Spotting her minivan, he escorted her to it. Finally, he turned to her. "Go home."

But she wasn't prepared to leave. "Doesn't Temple's murder sound a lot like the attack on me? Of course, it can't be the same guy, because he's in custody. But I need to figure out the connection. Possibly, Agent Metcalf could—"

"You need to go home." His voice rasped like a knife blade grating against stone. Anger tensed the muscles and tendons in his arms. "Go back to my house, lock the door and stay inside."

"I won't," she retorted. "And I don't appreciate you ordering me around."

A vein in his forehead began to pulse. Though it was hot outside, his red complexion had nothing to do with sunburn. "You're in danger."

"It's *my danger. My choice.*" If she gave in to her fear, she'd be cowering in a corner, weeping and helpless. That wasn't her way. "If I choose to handle these threats by investigating them, that's my option."

"Use some common sense. Yesterday, you were a hostage. Last night, you were almost killed by an assassin. How much can you conveniently arrange to forget?"

"I didn't ask for memory loss," she said. Her own temper rose to match his. "You're not being fair."

"Damn it, Amanda. Ignoring your own personal safety is bad enough, but you need to think about Laurel."

How dare he drag her daughter into this! Furious, she went up on her toes and got right in his face. "Are you saying I'm not a good mother?"

"I'm saying that if you get yourself killed playing detective, your daughter will suffer. You're all she's got."

"She has a father," Amanda said.

"Where is he?" He gestured wide, encompassing the parking lot, the hospital, the entire state of Colorado. "Where is the supposed mystery dad? Is he invisible?"

"Unfortunately, he's not."

She caught her lower lip between her teeth, forcing herself to remain silent. This certainly wasn't the way she wanted to break the news that David was a daddy.

Turning away from him, she stared at the far end of the parking lot, where the police had set up a barricade in front of a long line of cars trying to exit. She pointed. "Look."

"A stop-and-search," he said.

"I guess I can't leave," she said smugly. "It appears the crackerjack Denver police department is in the process of closing the barn door after the cows have run away."

"Oh, this is great! Just dandy."

He paced two steps away from her, raised his arms as if imploring the heavens, then allowed them to drop to his sides. For a moment, he stood very still. Then his shoulders began to shake. When he confronted her again, he was laughing.

"David?" Had he snapped? "Are you all right?"

He exhaled a final chuckle. "I guess this is what they call payback time."

"Whatever do you mean?"

"As you know, I spent some time being an irresponsible son of a bitch. Everybody else had to look out for me and cover my butt. Now, I'm trying to do the sensible thing, and everybody else is nuts."

"I'm not."

"Whatever you say, Nancy Drew." He started back toward the entrance. "Come on, let's go back to the hospital and wait for things to settle down. You stick with me."

"Isn't it against hospital policy for me to follow you around?"

"I've already broken most of the rules," he said. "Might as well give the disciplinary committee a few more infractions to consider."

"Disciplinary committee?"

"According to some people, I'm too arrogant to be a good little resident. Dr. Loretta Spangler filed a complaint about my behavior yesterday. According to her, I shouldn't have released a certain patient who refused a CT scan."

"I'm so sorry," she said. It was her fault. If she'd disrupted his career, she would never forgive herself. "Is there anything I can do?"

"No."

"But if I can help"

"No, Amanda." Stuffing his hands in his pockets, he sauntered under the covered walkway leading to the main building. "Being a bank president doesn't give you any influence at the hospital. And, by the way, you're not a detective, either. Don't mess with things you don't understand."

"What's the alternative?" she asked.

"How about this—leave the doctoring to the doctors and the detective work to the cops."

"I can't stand around and wait until the next time I'm taken hostage. The next time an assassin comes into my bedroom with a gun, I might not be so lucky."

"You've never been a passive woman." A smile quirked the corner of his mouth. "I like that. Especially in the bedroom."

Amanda definitely wasn't going there. "I'm going to figure this out, David. With or without your help. Now, let's consider Temple's murder. What was the motive?''

"Sex or money," David said. "What do you think about sex, Amanda?"

Ignoring his innuendo, she said. "I think Temple was killed so he wouldn't give information to the police."

"Sounds reasonable."

"What information did Temple have? Who could he hurt?"

"The other two bank robbers?" David guessed.

"But one of them, Sarge, is already in custody. The other, Dallas, is the subject of a manhunt. How could he hurt them?"

"By testifying against them. Or he could give away the hideout location of the guy who grabbed your friend Carrie."

"True."

She mulled over a wider range of possibilities. There was a question in her mind about the computer codes to turn off video surveillance at the bank. Not to mention the escape of a federal prisoner, which took place at the same time as the robbery. There was Carrie's possible involvement to consider.

"How could Temple be murdered in the hospital?" she questioned. Though security at Denver General wasn't top-notch, the murder of a guarded prisoner seemed impossible. "Do you think his police guard was bribed to look the other way? What if the police are involved?"

"It would explain a few things," he said. "Like the sloppy hostage negotiations. And the pathetic inability to nab this Dallas character."

"This might be a conspiracy, David."

"And who's behind it?"

"Jax Schaffer," she said.

WHEN DAVID DRAGGED Amanda back to the emergency area, Stella didn't seem surprised at all. The appointment nurse gazed at Amanda through her huge eyeglasses and said, "You look a lot better today."

"Thank you. I don't suppose you happened to find my shoes or my purse?"

"The Guccis? No luck." She shook her head. "You might check with the cops. But I wouldn't advise doing it right now. They're a little paranoid."

David counted three uniforms in the immediate vicinity. Their presence seemed excessive and useless; he agreed with Amanda's assessment that it was too late to lock the barn door. Whoever killed Temple was long gone.

"Doc Haines," Stella said. "There's a guy in the waiting area who insists on talking to you. Not a patient. His name is Stefan Phillips."

David was tired, frustrated and worried about Amanda's safety. Her cheery assumption that they might be involved in a giant crime conspiracy didn't brighten his mood. A confrontation with Stefan—the father of Amanda's child, who should have done the right thing and married her—would not be the high point of his day.

He turned to her. "Come on, Amanda. I'm sure the only reason Stefan wants to see me is because he's looking for you."

In the emergency-care waiting room, Stefan lounged casually in a far corner. In his madras plaid shirt, preppy shorts and loafers without socks, he looked like an L.L. Bean catalog model. The moment he saw Amanda, he came at her with his arms outstretched. Ignoring David, he enveloped her in a muscular embrace.

"Where have you been?" Stefan asked her. "I went to your condo this morning, and the concierge told me you'd spent the night somewhere else."

"Didn't Vonnie call you? I gave her a list of people to contact."

"There was a message on my machine, telling me that you were fine and would be in touch."

She stepped away from him, and David had the impression that Amanda didn't particularly like for Stefan to hold her. She seemed unresponsive and cold. "As you can see," she said, "the message was correct. I'm just fine."

"Come on, Amanda. I deserve more than a message from the nanny."

David had to agree. Stefan was Laurel's father. Even if Amanda had refused to marry him, she should keep him informed as to the whereabouts of his daughter.

David was actually feeling a little bit sorry for Stefan. He looked genuinely upset as he nodded a greeting to David and said, "I'd like to talk with Amanda alone."

"The nurse said you needed to see me. Is there anything else I can do for you?"

"No, Doctor," Stefan said. "I was looking for Amanda and Laurel, and I thought you might know where they were."

"Then I'll leave you alone." He started back toward the emergency-care unit.

"David, wait!" Amanda caught hold of his sleeve. "I'll just be a minute. There really isn't anything else for Stefan and I to talk about."

"But there is," Stefan insisted. "Damn it, Amanda, I'm talking to your mother more often than to you. What's the matter? At least tell me where you're staying."

"I'm recuperating at a friend's house," she said. "My condo was broken into last night, and I don't feel safe there."

"Broken into? Why didn't you call me?"

"Because I didn't need to." She forced a smile. "I'm

sorry if you were worried, but I really can take care of myself. You don't need to feel any obligation to look out for me and Laurel."

"But I want to," he said. "You could stay with me. Better yet, we could go out of town for a few days. Take a trip. You could forget all about this mess at the bank."

"Forget about it?" She raised an eyebrow. "What an odd suggestion! I've been desperately trying to remember."

David averted his gaze. Their conversation made him distinctly uncomfortable. There should have been an intimacy between these two people. They shared a child; they should be close. Instead, they acted like casual acquaintances.

Amanda concluded with, "I'll call you later, Stefan."

He caught hold of her arm and spun her around to face him. "Don't brush me off. Tell me where you're staying."

"Let go of my arm."

"I know what's best for you, Amanda."

But when she yanked away from him, he let her go. He wasn't willing to stand up to her, nor to fight for her. His blue eyes were sullen beneath his floppy blond hair.

"Goodbye," Amanda said as she headed back toward E.R.

David fell into step beside her. He didn't understand how her relationship with Stefan worked, but he sure as hell wasn't going to let her roll over him like a bulldozer.

David directed her back to the emergency-care unit, where two armed security guards flanked the metal detector. "Don't ever do that to me again, Amanda."

"What?"

"Keep me standing around while you have a personal conversation."

"I'm sorry," she said. "That was rude. But I really didn't expect Stefan to be so...concerned."

David didn't get it. Stefan was the father of her child. Of course he'd be worried when he couldn't reach them. No matter how big a jerk he was, the guy had some rights.

"What's wrong?" she asked.

"When you freeze somebody out, you don't do it halfway." But he knew that. When she'd ended their engagement, she'd never looked back. After their one-night stand, she closed the door tight. "It must get lonely," he said, "being an ice princess."

She winced slightly. "You have no idea."

"Then give it up. Do a meltdown," he advised. "You'd be surprised at how much fun you can have with the rest of us warm-blooded creatures."

Instead of backing off, he saw a warmth in her eyes. "You know what, David? That's exactly what I'm going to do. A meltdown."

Back at Stella's desk, he picked up his next assignments. The patients were stacking up, and he needed to get back to the job of doctoring. "Stella, I need for Amanda to stay here with you for a while. I'll be done shortly."

"Sure thing." Stella patted a plastic chair at her left. "Sit down. Make yourself comfy."

"Thank you."

As soon as David disappeared into an examination room, Amanda was aware of the other woman's scrutiny. Those huge eyeglasses focused on her like a microscope on an amoeba.

"So," Stella said, "what's the deal with you and Doc Haines? You used to date, didn't you?"

"We were engaged."

Stella clicked her tongue against the roof of her mouth. "You're getting back together. I can tell."

Just like Vonnie. Rather than argue with Stella, who

seemed to be in control of this area, Amanda offered a congenial smile. "Nothing is impossible."

"It would be good for him," she said. "Doc Haines acts like a goofball half the time, but he's a family man waiting to happen."

"David?"

"You should see him with kids. He's super."

From watching David with Laurel, she knew he had a touch with children. Still, that was a long way from being a good father. Or a husband.

"So?" Stella encompassed her in a questioning gaze. "Are you going to start dating?"

Amanda was uncomfortable with this topic. She'd never been one to confide the details of her love life. An ice princess didn't do that sort of thing. "Would you excuse me? I need to use the ladies' room."

"Down the hall." Stella pointed. "Take the first left, then left again."

"I'll be back."

Her headache had started up again. The dull throbbing behind her eyes reminded her of how tired she was. Tonight, there would be no waking every four hours. She could really sleep, and she was looking forward to uninterrupted slumber.

In the bland hospital bathroom, she stood at the sink, washed her hands and checked her appearance in the mirror. The bruises from her head wound were mostly hidden behind her bangs. She didn't look much different now than she had before the robbery, but something inside her was different.

People don't change. And yet, she felt a transformation growing within her. She was melting. It was more and more difficult to assume the guise of an ice princess. This morning, when David had kissed her, sensuality had flooded her body and she'd felt truly alive. This afternoon, she'd embraced the head teller at the bank, and they'd wept in each other's arms. Maybe she was becoming a warm-blooded human being, after all.

She heard the door to the bathroom open and turned on the faucet. Water splashed in the sink as Amanda laved her hands as carefully as a surgeon preparing for a life-or-death operation. There was so much to consider. Not only the bank robbery, but a life-changing transformation.

"Amanda," said a familiar voice.

Startled, she looked up. A brunette woman in a white lab coat stood beside her, reflected in the bathroom mirror.

"Carrie?"

THE AFTERNOON SUNLIGHT beat down hard on the pavement, but the Iceman ignored the July heat. He never sweat, never let nerves get to him.

Today had been a test. And he'd succeeded. He'd stayed cool.

Earlier today, when he'd been inside the hospital dressed in scrubs and a cap like a surgeon, he hadn't flinched. He'd timed it exactly right.

Everybody had known Temple would have to be killed if he was taken into custody. The guy was too weird to be trusted—always blabbing about reincarnation.

Temple's murder shouldn't have been the Iceman's responsibility. He wasn't a professional killer, not like the assassin he'd hired to kill Amanda in her condo.

After that failed attempt, Iceman figured he'd kill Temple.

It went down according to plan—smooth as a touchdown pass on third and ten. Every detail clicked into place.

He'd found the gun right where it was supposed to be.

At the exact right moment, the paid-off cop guarding

Temple had stepped away from his post.

That had been the plan. The Iceman had done his part.

He'd found Temple, sedated and asleep in his room. His right leg in a cast, and the left cuffed to the bed.

The Iceman had taken out his gun and screwed on the silencer. The last whisper from his conscience had told him that killing Temple was wrong. But he'd barely heard it. Murder was the culmination of years of petty crimes. After he committed murder, people would take him seriously, he'd thought. He'd get noticed.

He'd stuck a pillow over Temple's face and fired through it.

He'd left the room and taken his time cleaning off the blood and getting rid of the gun. Everything had gone according to plan. He'd committed murder, and he was getting away with it.

His next job was to get rid of Amanda. It ought to be a snap.

Chapter Eight

Amanda reached out toward the wall mirror in the hospital bathroom, fearing that she'd lost her mind and that the face reflected beside hers was an illusion. Carrie couldn't possibly be here! She was a fugitive. Her photograph was being broadcast on every news station and published in the newspaper. The entire police force was combing the city, searching for her.

An elfin smile lit up Carrie's features. "You're all right. I'm glad."

"Are you really here?"

"Yup."

Amanda spun around, half expecting that the slender woman in a white lab coat with an official-looking hospital-ID badge would disappear like smoke when directly confronted. But she didn't vanish, not even when Amanda looked directly into her friendly gray eyes. Nor did Carrie dissolve when Amanda pulled her into a ferocious hug.

She hugged back. "Amanda?"

"What?" An amazing sense of relief washed through her. She'd been so worried. "What is it?"

"What's happened to you?" Carrie whispered. "I don't think you've ever hugged me before."

"Of course I have." Gasping for breath, Amanda drew

back and dabbed at her eyes, wiping away the beginnings of happy tears. "Well, perhaps I've never physically embraced you, but I've thought about it. In my mind, I've hugged. What does it matter? You're here. You're safe."

"It matters a lot," Carrie said. "You've changed."

"People don't change." She studied her friend carefully, noting the odd, brownish hairdo that really didn't become her at all. "What did you do to your hair?"

"It's a wig."

A disguise. The only reason for a disguise was to avoid recognition. Apparently, Carrie was not being held against her will. She was in hiding. "You're not really a hostage."

"Not in the usual sense," she admitted. "But don't draw any conclusions from that. Do you remember when I first came to you, before you gave me the job at the bank?"

"You were on the run. Escaping from your abusive ex-husband." Amanda had known Carrie's identification was false and that her bonding certificate was forged. "I trusted you then."

"Trust me again," Carrie said.

"Did you have anything to do with the robbery?"

"No way," she said.

Could Amanda believe her? Carrie was hiding from the police. She was at the hospital just after Temple had been murdered. She had guns in her apartment and knew how to use them.

Amanda's heart wanted to believe that her old friend was innocent, but the evidence weighed heavily toward her guilt.

"Listen, Amanda, I don't have much time. I wanted you to know that the robbery was an inside job. Somebody in the bank gave information to the robbers so they could override the security system."

"Who?"

"I don't know. But these are violent, terrible people. You've got to be very careful."

Bits and pieces of memories swirled like debris in a tornado. There was one thing that concerned her more than anything else. She could live with the danger and the threats, but she couldn't stand any more self-doubt. "Was I part of the robbery? Tell me."

"Can't you remember?"

"I have short-term memory loss from the concussion." A dark fear crept over her. "I was involved, wasn't I? You and I planned some sort of—"

"You and I? How could you even think that?" Carrie stared hard into her face. "I've known you since grade school, and you're the most law-abiding person in the world. You'd never even steal a stick of gum, much less commit a major felony."

"But I had access to all the computer codes to override security. And I can't remember. I just can't remember."

"Use your brain, Amanda. You've got everything going for you. A career that you love. A beautiful daughter. You don't need to rob a bank." She checked her wristwatch. "I've got to go now."

"Don't leave. If you turn yourself in to the police, they'll protect you."

"I have to do this my way. Can you trust me?"

A brave smile touched the corners of Carrie's mouth, and Amanda found herself smiling back. She wanted to believe in Carrie's innocence. And in her own. She wanted desperately to believe they were both victims of a larger plot, a vicious scheme that had killed and wounded other innocent people.

As Carrie went toward the door, she pulled a pair of black-framed glasses from her pocket and slipped them on. It was disconcerting to realize how easily she could blend into the hospital population. Of course, there were always a lot of people coming and going, especially at a city hospital, but Amanda had always thought there would be better security. "Carrie!"

"What is it?"

"I'm going to figure this out. In the meantime, watch out for yourself. I don't want anything bad to happen to my best friend."

"I've never seen you like this." She held out her hand, and Amanda gripped it tightly. "It's a change for the good."

She pulled her hand away, waved and slipped out the door.

AFTER FINISHING his shift at four o'clock, David changed from his scrubs into street clothes and headed toward Stella's emergency-room counter. He wasn't surprised that, during their time together, Amanda and Stella had become bosom buddies. Despite their difference in income and status, they were both highly organized women who reigned supreme in their separate domains.

With their combined powers of persuasion, they'd managed to summon Agent Metcalf and Agent Hess to Stella's desk.

As he approached, David nodded to Hess. The young, skinny FBI agent had been friendly to David when they discussed the midnight assailant who'd tried to kill Amanda. Though David suspected Hess's confidential attitude might be part of a good-cop–bad-cop scenario, he was willing to take that chance in exchange for a contact with someone who was on the inside of the investigation.

Hess winked back at David, then turned his attention toward Amanda, who was addressing Agent Metcalf.

"There's one more thing," she said. "My purse and my shoes."

Stella passed out copies of a typed, one-sheet description of the missing items under the heading, Wanted! Reward!

Amanda said, "I've distributed this information throughout the hospital," she said. "But, if you ask me, I think the shoes and purse are still at the bank, and that's where we should search."

"The bank is a crime scene," Metcalf informed her.

"Of course," Amanda said smoothly. "And I'd like your permission to enter and search the premises."

"All this for a pair of shoes?"

"May I remind you that I am the president of Empire Bank. And I'm not above pulling strings to get what I want."

David noted Metcalf's tension. Beneath his tidy white shirt and Windsor-knotted necktie, Metcalf's chest heaved. His breathing was labored. It was as if he were being slowly strangled.

"Ms. Fielding," he said, "the scope of our inquiries has spread through several law-enforcement agencies and security forces. We have included the escape of federal prisoner Jax Schaffer in our investigation. The body count, including dead and injured, is approaching double digits. My question, ma'am, is, why should anybody give a good goddamn about your Gucci shoes?"

"It's a clue." Amanda showed no sign of intimidation. "The assailant who entered my apartment used a key. Since I am not in the habit of dispersing keys to my home, I assume he found the keys in my purse."

"She's got a point," said Agent Hess.

Metcalf's head whipped around to glare at his partner. "We don't have time to—"

"There might be fingerprints," Amanda interrupted.

"Also, if my purse and shoes were in police custody when my keys were stolen, you might consider police corruption in your investigations. Will you allow me access to the bank?"

His resistance slowly deconstructed. The frustration on his face looked like a building imploding on itself. "I'll meet you there, Ms. Fielding. Tomorrow. Two o'clock in the afternoon."

"One more detail." Amanda smiled with deceptive sweetness. "If Agent Hess isn't already married, I should inform him that my nanny, Vonnie, finds him very attractive."

"The little redhead?" Hess grinned in spite of himself. "I like her, too."

"This is not the dating game," Metcalf snapped.

"Lighten up," Hess said. "We've got this under control. Once we take the fugitives into custody, we—"

"Good day, ladies," Metcalf interrupted his partner. Briskly, he retreated before Amanda could think of even one more little thing.

David took his place at Stella's counter. "Shame on you, ladies. Having a little fun at the expense of the uptight FBI."

"I wouldn't call this fun," Amanda said. "What do you suppose Hess meant when he referred to the fugitives?"

Stella supplied the answer, "The third bank robber and Carrie Lamb. They're the main suspects."

"But they didn't do it."

She sounded completely convinced, which was enough to make David suspicious. What had she been up to? "Don't be so quick, Amanda. I think it's safe to assume that the armed robber who held you hostage was involved in the robbery."

"Of course he's involved. But he's not the *real* criminal mastermind."

"Just a pawn," Stella agreed. She patted Amanda's shoulder and looked up at David. "I like her, Doc Haines."

"I'll bet you do. Amanda is going to teach you even more tricks about how to run this area."

"As if I need any help," Stella scoffed. "If I wasn't sitting behind this desk, the city of Denver would bleed to death before you doctors got yourselves organized. Which reminds me, Doc, the head of administration wants to talk to you."

Couldn't be good news. "Sorry, I'm off. And I won't be back until Monday."

"Gotcha. Have a happy Fourth of July."

As he escorted Amanda through the hospital, David congratulated himself on avoiding the impending confrontation about his supposedly unprofessional behavior. So far, nobody'd had a chance to reprimand him. Dr. Loretta Spangler and her complaints would have to wait until after his three-day weekend.

Not that he expected to relax over the Fourth of July. Not with Amanda staying at his home. She'd keep him on his toes, dancing like a dervish.

As they crossed the parking lot, he observed, "You're quiet."

"Thinking," she said. "I tried to contact Tracy Meyer on the phone and got her answering machine. Could we stop by her house?"

"Sure."

As she approached the minivan, a stillness came over her, as if she were holding her breath. The sunlight glinted off her shining blond hair, and the light tan on her bare arms blended delicately with the darker brown of her simple dress. She was beautiful, but that wasn't what he noticed.

David studied the diffident set of her shoulders and the stubborn tilt to her head. Though he didn't consider himself the most perceptive man in the world, he could read her moods as easily as he could diagnose strep throat, and he knew she was withholding information. "What haven't you told me?"

"The bank robbery was an inside job." She unlocked the driver's door on her minivan.

"Why are you so sure?"

"Some things are better left unsaid."

He caught hold of her right hand and deftly took the car keys from her. "No more games. Tell me."

Aghast, she looked up at him. Her blue-eyed gaze flicked across his face like a slap. "I can't believe you grabbed my keys."

"I'm too damned tired to play guessing games."

"I see. So, you're playing keep away with my car keys instead."

She made an undignified snatch for the car keys, and he held them over his head. "Tell."

"No."

"Damn it, woman. Exactly how many assassins does it take to convince you?" He opened the door to her minivan wide, allowing the sweltering air trapped inside to escape. "You're in danger."

"Fine. I'll hire a bodyguard."

Midsummer heat flowed over them like lava, and David's temper was firing on all eight cylinders. "There's not a man on earth who can protect you better than I can."

"Oh, really? Do you have a gun?"

"Don't need one."

"Do you know karate?"

"I know you," he said.

She planted her fists on her hips and scowled up at him. "What difference does that make?"

"I know what to expect from you. I know when you're tired, when you're angry, when you're pleased. I remember once at a party, you stuck your nose in the air and acted condescending, but it was because you were hurt."

"Oh, really?" She retaliated with a vengeance. "During your partying days, I would have thought you were too blitzed to notice anything."

"I always noticed you. I saw you pretend to be efficient when you felt out of control. Sometimes you say no when you mean yes. And vice versa."

He slipped his hand behind her neck. Beneath her hair, the skin was moist. "For example," he said, "if I asked you right now to kiss me, you'd say no. But you want to. You remember what it feels like to have my mouth on yours."

The chemistry between them was unmistakable. Her eyes glistened like cool, soothing ice on this blazing July afternoon, and he longed to hold her against him. Signs of her own arousal were subtle. A quickening of her breath. A slight movement toward him.

"I can take care of you," he said, "because I know you, Amanda. I know how to protect you from yourself."

He removed his hand from her neck and took a step back. "Be as stubborn as you want, but you're stuck with me. You can't stop me from caring about you. And about Laurel."

"I don't want you to stop caring."

"What do you want, Amanda?"

Her blue eyes were a sultry invitation, painting an unmistakable desire. He gazed at the fullness of her lips.

"I want you to be my friend." Her chin lifted. "And I

want you to help me figure out what happened at the bank.''

He didn't have much choice. If he wanted to be sure she was safe, he had to stay with her. And she was determined to investigate. ''I'll do it. On one condition.''

Her eyebrows lifted. ''What's that?''

He dangled the keys over her head as a reminder. ''No secrets. No holding back. You tell me everything.''

''Everything?'' Her eyes clouded with doubt, and he could see that she still didn't completely trust him. She obviously still remembered the broken promises when they were engaged.

It killed him to realize how deeply he'd hurt her. The wound might never heal, but continue to fester until the only possible treatment was amputation—cutting her out of his life. As if he hadn't tried. A hundred times, he'd told himself to forget Amanda Fielding. He'd dated with a vengeance, hoping he'd find someone else who would take her place. Nothing worked. He might as well cut out his own lungs and try to keep on breathing.

''Tell me, Amanda. Why are you so sure that the bank robbery was an inside job?''

''Someone told me.''

''Metcalf?''

''Why would I believe him? Every time I talk to the man, it's obvious that he's itching to slap a pair of handcuffs on my wrists.''

''Then who?''

''It was Carrie. I saw her here in the hospital. She was disguised in a wig and a lab coat, like one of the doctors.''

''Carrie Lamb was here? At Denver General?'' That took some kind of nerve. ''How'd she pull that off in the middle of the biggest manhunt in Denver's history?''

''For one thing, the security at Denver General sucks.

For another, Carrie is amazing with disguises. Keep in mind that she's been on the run from her ex-husband for two years. She even had one of those little ID badges on her lab coat.''

"I'm impressed."

"But that's not the important thing, David. Carrie told me that the robbers had inside information about the security system at the bank. She asked me to trust her, and I do."

He didn't like the way this sounded. If Carrie was disguised, she had to be a willing hostage, which meant she was on the run with the bank robber named Dallas. Why did Amanda have to pick a woman who was on the lam, hiding from the cops, as her best friend? "Did it occur to you that Carrie herself might be the inside contact at the bank?"

"Then why would she tell me to be careful? Besides, she didn't know all the codes. Carrie was only a teller." Amanda pushed the hair off her forehead. "It's hot. Can we go now?"

He nodded once. "Get in the car. I'll drive."

"What about your Porsche?"

"Not a problem." With Amanda belted into the passenger's seat, he pulled even with the parking attendant's booth at the exit and called to the young man inside, "Tom, would you do me a favor?"

Eagerly, the uniformed attendant came to the window. "The Porsche? Can I drive the Porsche?"

David handed over the keys. "You know where I live. Get it back tonight."

"You bet!"

Amanda shook her head disapprovingly. "Honestly, David. You know he's going to take the car for a joy ride."

"The Porsche might as well have some thrills," David

said as he turned the minivan's air-conditioning to full blast and rolled up the window. "God knows, I don't."

As he exited the parking lot and headed east on Eighth Avenue, David belatedly considered the implications of volunteering to help Amanda investigate. This sure as hell didn't seem like the act of a sane man.

A year and a half ago, after she'd dumped him for the second time, he'd vowed never to get involved with this woman again. Yet, he'd signed on for another bout, another chance for her to tap-dance on his heart. He had to be crazy.

But something about being with her felt so damned good.

"Don't forget," she said. "We're going to Tracy Meyer's house."

"Why?"

Amanda recited an address in the Washington Park area. "Don't worry. This visit doesn't have anything to do with dangerous investigating."

"Then why?"

"I remembered something that happened right before the attempted robbery. I had a meeting with Tracy and Carrie, and I should have handled it differently."

The air-conditioning had made the temperature inside the van bearable. "How so?"

"She wanted access to a trust fund, and I was advising against it. Instead, I should have figured out a way to help her. Maybe a loan, even though she's mortgaged to the max."

David glanced in the rearview mirror. He was slow in pulling away from the stop sign, but the pearl-gray Cadillac sedan behind him was waiting patiently. Maybe a little too patiently. "Could you do that? Make a loan with no collateral?"

"An unsecured signature loan. Of course I can do that. I'm a bank president." With a sigh, she added, "Although, at present, I don't much feel like an executive business-woman.''

"How do you feel?''

"I'm not sure. At the hospital, I found myself embracing Jane Borelli, the head teller who was terrified during the robbery. We were practically sobbing in each other's arms. And you know how much I disapprove of casual hugging and kissing.''

"I know.''

He made an unexpected left turn, doubling back toward the hospital. The Caddy followed. He couldn't see the driver or passengers through the tinted windows.

"It might be for the best,'' she said. "In the past, I've been a little too reserved. Cold. Like you said.''

"An ice princess.''

"I don't mind thinking of myself as a wintry person, shielded by glistening snow and ice. It feels…clean.''

"Clean,'' he repeated. Though he was listening to her, his attention was riveted on the Caddy, which followed as he took another sudden left.

"Maybe I'm on schedule for a meltdown.''

"That's good, Amanda.''

"No big deal. It's just a different side to me, and that's not really a change. I'm the same person I always was.''

"There's nothing wrong with change.''

"It doesn't happen! I've made many decisions based on the solid premise that people don't change.''

"If you're wrong?''

"Then I've made a lot of terrible mistakes,'' she said. The biggest of which was ending her relationship with David. "Too many mistakes.''

She sank back against the seat, absorbed in her own thoughts. Amanda wanted her world to be painted in clean, crisp black and white without smudging. Instead, confusion blurred the lines and created ominous shadows of gray. She was afraid, torn with a fear that went deeper than threats to her life. Could people change? Had David changed?

She'd based her decision to end their engagement upon the firm belief that he was too wild and irresponsible to be a satisfactory mate. When she'd discovered she was pregnant, she'd called upon that core belief, knowing that to tell him would only bring heartache for both of them. But if he'd changed…

In turmoil, she studied his profile. The firm jaw and strong nose contrasted full lips that always seemed to be grinning. There were no secrets in his face. He had always been unfailingly honest, willing to admit when he erred. During their engagement, he'd piled one broken promise on top of another, but he'd never made excuses when he'd missed appointments or shown up late in a partying mood.

"Take a look through the back window," he said. "Do you recognize the car?"

She twisted in her bucket seat to see through the rear of the minivan. "Gray sedan with tinted windows? It's not familiar."

"He's tailing us," David said. "And he's not being subtle about it."

Another assailant? She cinched her seat belt more tightly, almost relieved to abandon her agonizing emotional doubts in the face of a tangible threat. "Are you sure they're following us?"

"Pretty sure."

"Can you speed up and lose him?"

"If I was driving the Porsche, you bet. But this happens to be a minivan. It's not the vehicle of choice for a high-speed chase."

When he stopped at a traffic light, she peered at the Caddy behind him. Were they really being pursued? It seemed so unlikely in this stop-and-go traffic that led south to the suburbs. On either side of University Boulevard were towering, leafy elms and neat brick houses. Sprinklers watered the well-tended lawns.

At the cusp of rush hour, commuters were headed home from work. Parents transported their children to Little League games or picked them up from day care or drove to the supermarket. Real danger seemed inconceivable.

Yet, she felt her heart beating faster. In the air-conditioned van, she'd begun to sweat. Was it only last night that a masked assailant had pointed a gun to her breast? "I wish we were armed."

"No guns," he said. "In the E.R., I've treated too many accidental-gunshot wounds."

Much as she would have liked to debate NRA policy with him, now was not the time. "This is different."

"Maybe." When the light turned green, David eased forward. "I'm going to lead him to the police station at I-25."

"Then what?"

"I'll pull up close to the door of the station house. You jump out and run inside as fast as you can."

"What are you going to do?"

"The same." His gaze flicked to the rearview mirror. "See if you can read the license plate."

She angled between the seats, trying to catch a glimpse, as David changed lanes. "I can't see the plates. There's another car between us."

"That's good. The police station is right ahead. I'll speed up to give us more time to get inside. Take off your seat belt and get ready to run."

Chapter Nine

Amanda braced herself as David floored the accelerator. After two screeching blocks, he careened into a hard right turn at the police station. The minivan fishtailed into the lot. He parked at the entrance and yelled, "Go, Amanda."

She flung the door open and leaped out. Her sandals weren't made for sprinting, nor was the narrow hem of her dress. Still, she raced up the sidewalk, expecting to hear the sound of gunfire, to feel the slam of a bullet in her back.

"Ms. Fielding, wait!"

At the door to the police station, Amanda halted. *Ms. Fielding?* That didn't sound like a thug. The voice was female.

Amanda turned and stared. The Caddy had come to a stop nose to nose with the minivan. Elaine Montero stood at the passenger's side, microphone in hand.

"Ms. Fielding," she shouted again. "May I ask you a few questions? I'm not going to hurt you."

Amanda's momentary relief was overwhelmed by righteous indignation. How dare this newsperson stalk them! Quite obviously, Elaine Montero had the scruples of a cockroach who didn't have the sense to hide when the lights came on.

She smiled and waved. "May I call you Amanda? Just a few questions, please."

David advanced on her. "I'd call this harassment, Ms. Montero."

"It's my job, Doctor. I want to be the first to get an interview with Ms. Fielding, and she hasn't made herself available to the media."

She flashed a professional smile as Amanda came nearer. "I'm pleased to finally meet you, Amanda."

Apparently, Elaine chose to disregard their earlier encounter, when Amanda had been a mohair-clad bag lady in a wheelchair. "I have no comment."

"You've been really elusive. Nobody even knows where you're staying."

Amanda grasped the passenger's door handle on the minivan. "I intend to keep it that way."

"Last night, you were attacked in your home by an armed assailant," Elaine said.

"How do you know that?"

"You reported it to the police, and I have a scanner. I've been following this story. Especially from your angle."

"No comment."

"Think again, Amanda." Her voice turned harsh. "You need to make a statement. I'm giving you a chance to defend yourself."

"Against what?"

"Allegations have been made."

Elaine's companion had emerged from the driver's side. He opened the rear door and took out his portable camera, which he hefted onto his shoulder. In minutes, Amanda's likeness would be captured on video for the ten-o'clock news.

If she hopped into the van and drove away, there would be a story about how she was avoiding the ace newswoman's questions. The implication, of course, would be that Amanda had something to hide.

Annoyed, Amanda strode toward Elaine and her cameraman. As she walked, she adjusted the hem of her sleeveless bronze shift, wishing that she'd worn something more professional. Would it help if she added the leopard-print neck scarf? She decided against it. Better to be understated.

She assumed the poised, professional facial expression that had helped gain a promotion to bank president before her thirty-fifth birthday. "Ms. Montero, I will make a statement."

David stepped up beside her. "You don't have to talk to her."

"If people are accusing me, I have to face them." She spoke softly so the camera's microphone wouldn't pick it up. "If I don't answer, it looks like I have something to hide."

"Be careful. This Montero woman is slick."

She smiled coldly. "So am I."

When the cameraman was set, Elaine offered her introduction, "We're talking with Amanda Fielding, the president of Empire Bank who was held hostage yesterday during the attempted robbery."

Unsmiling, Amanda stared into the eye of the camera. "I would like to take this opportunity to express my sympathy for those who were injured during the robbery attempt, most especially Mr. Harry Hoffman and Mr. Horst Nyland. Our prayers are with them. Throughout the hostage situation, I was proud of the Empire Bank employees. They behaved with courage and common sense."

Elaine Montero said, "According to my sources, the security system at the bank was bypassed."

How did she know? "It's not appropriate for me to discuss the ongoing investigation."

"But you're the bank president. Don't you know how the security works?"

"Of course." She looked directly into the eye of the camera and launched into a dull explanation that couldn't possibly be chopped up to provide an embarrassing sound bite. "Every person who has been inside a banking institution has noticed video-surveillance cameras. They're placed above eye level and maintained by a security company."

Amanda listed frames per second, looping of videotape, transmission and playback capability. In an equally detailed manner, reminiscent of her college math professor who could talk for hours on the Pythagorean theorem, she described the silent-alarm buttons and standard banking procedures. When Elaine Montero's eyes had glazed over, Amanda asked, "Shall I continue?"

"God, no," Elaine said. "What do you know about the robber who's still at large?"

"I'm sure the police and federal agents are doing everything in their power to apprehend—"

"Would you comment, please, on Carrie Lamb, the teller who's with the fugitive."

Amanda turned her gaze from the camera to the reporter. "Ms. Lamb is a model employee. I pray for her safety."

"When you hired her, were you aware that her identification was false?"

Suppressing an urge to snarl at the overaggressive reporter, Amanda responded, "This is the second day Carrie Lamb has been held hostage by an armed, dangerous man. It's hard to imagine the terror she must be feeling and the helplessness."

"But Carrie Lamb is suspected of—"

"Until I was held hostage and beaten unconscious," Amanda said as she turned toward the camera again, "I felt safe. Like any other citizen, I thought, I can walk down the street without looking over my shoulder. I'm not afraid. No one can touch me. But that's not true. Fear is now my ever present companion. I realize just how vulnerable we all are. I'm sorry, Ms. Montero, there is nothing else I can say."

Amanda pivoted quickly and slipped inside the minivan. She closed the door with a click and glanced at David. 'Let's get out of here before she tries to follow us again."

David flipped the minivan in reverse and circled the parking lot to the exit. "You handled that well."

"My years as a lawyer ought to count for something," she replied. "Even though I never got to present a defense in a courtroom, I was always good at closing statements."

"Maybe you missed your true calling."

"I love my career at the bank." And she was disturbed by the sly accusations from Elaine Montero, the implications that she and Carrie were somehow involved in the robbery attempt. "Do you really think people are saying I was involved in the robbery?"

"I've never paid much attention to gossip."

That was a gross understatement if she'd ever heard one. David had almost complete disregard for the opinions of others. "If I remember correctly, you used to start rumors about yourself to see how quickly they would spread."

"It's that practical-joke habit. I've never broken it."

She leaned back against the seat and sighed heavily. "I think we should just go home."

"But you wanted to see Tracy."

"Not today."

Today had been an emotional roller coaster, with more hugging than she'd done since her college graduation. She didn't wish to face even one more tense emotional confrontation.

That wish, however, was not to be granted.

As soon as she walked in the door to David's house, Vonnie called to her. "Thank goodness you're here, Amanda, your mother's on the phone."

Amanda glanced at her wristwatch and mentally calculated the time difference. It was almost six o'clock in Denver, which meant it was just about seven in Chicago—well past the beginning of cocktail hour. Long ago, she'd learned not to contact her parents in the evening when her father was sure to be incoherent. But this couldn't be helped. Her mother had probably been watching the news and was worried.

Amanda accepted the portable telephone that Vonnie thrust toward her and went to sit at David's kitchen table. "Hello, Mother."

"Finally, we've reached you! We've been so upset."

"Vonnie called you yesterday, didn't she?" Amanda had given the nanny a list of several routine calls.

"Oh, yes. She rang me up," her mother said dismissively. When she was nervous, Shirley Fielding's voice assumed a fake, upper-crust British accent, even though she was born and raised in the American Midwest. "And she telephoned again today with the changed phone number. But I wanted to talk to you in person, darling."

"And here I am," Amanda said.

"The news said you were in the hospital."

"I had a bump on the head. A slight concussion. It's nothing serious."

"Shall I come out and help you?" her mother offered.

"No," Amanda said quickly. The last thing she needed was to be burdened with the additional responsibility of caring for her parents. "I'm fine. Don't pay any attention to the news reports. I'm sure they're exaggerated."

"And what should I tell the others?"

"The others?"

"A dozen people must have called me to inquire about you. Really, Amanda, I had no idea you were so popular."

Her mother had been a sought-after debutante. Popularity was important to her, and Shirley Fielding had always been disappointed that her only daughter excelled in academics rather than cheerleading. Only grudgingly did she offer approval for Amanda's career achievements, even though Amanda's financial success allowed Shirley and Jack Fielding to maintain the life-style to which they'd become accustomed.

According to Shirley, Amanda should have married well and gotten her husband to contribute to the Fielding family coffers. As if marriage could be counted as an achievement. As if Amanda would feel justified in dumping all her family baggage onto a husband. It took all her willpower not to point out to her mother that her own dysfunctional marriage was not exactly a portrait of heaven on earth.

Brusquely, Amanda said, "Tell the others whatever you want, Mother."

"There's no need to be snippy, young lady. I'm merely expressing a natural concern."

"Naturally."

She couldn't help but notice that Shirley hadn't yet inquired about Laurel. When Amanda had opted to be a single mother, it was the last betrayal of her supposed position in society. Shirley had been devastated...which was fine with Amanda. She hadn't been having a baby to please her parents, anyway.

"I say, Amanda..." She sounded like the Queen Mother. "This phone number is familiar. You're staying with David Haines, aren't you? Is your engagement back on?"

"David is a friend."

"Then I suppose it's off with that handsome Stefan Phillips."

"It was never really *on*," she said.

"Don't be sly, darling. I know you and Stefan are much, much closer than you've ever admitted."

Whatever she wanted to believe was fine. Amanda didn't have the will to argue. And there was the slight possibility that she could turn this conversation into something useful. "Mother, do you remember a man named Jax Schaffer?"

"Yes, I do. Such an unusual first name. He had an operation for cancer of the larynx and always talked in a whispery voice. Rather an attractive man, if I remember correctly."

Her mother was possibly the only person in the country who hadn't heard of Jax Schaffer's arrest and the trial at the federal courthouse in Denver where the Oklahoma City bomber trial had taken place. "Was he ever a guest at our house?"

"I don't believe so. He was more your father's friend."

That figured. "Is Daddy home?"

"Yes, but he's indisposed."

"I'd like to talk to him, Mother."

"Hold on."

Holding the portable phone, Amanda left the kitchen and went into the spacious front room. Vonnie was nowhere in sight, and David had taken over with Laurel, playing peek-a-boo. He stretched out full length on his stomach on the carpeted floor. On a pink blanket with satin edging, tiny Laurel lay facing him.

David covered his eyes with his hands, then popped out at her. The game was much to Laurel's delight. She giggled hysterically at the funny faces he made.

The fading light of dusk gave a softness to the warm picture of a father and daughter at play. David's attention was completely consumed with their game. He seemed content, even happy.

Amanda was certain that when she finally got up the courage to tell him that he was the mystery dad, David would be a devoted father, the kind of father that Laurel deserved. Unfortunately, she feared he would never be able to forgive her for deceiving him. This time, she was sure, David would dump her instead of the other way around.

Sadly, she could have avoided this tragedy if she'd been smart enough to believe him when he told her he'd changed. If only she'd trusted him.

"Hello, princess."

Her father's voice came through the telephone, and Amanda returned to the kitchen. "Hi, Daddy. I wanted to tell you not to worry."

"I knew my little girl could handle a couple of bank robbers. No problem."

Ironically, her irresponsible father had always believed in her. He'd dreamed big dreams for her future.

"You're right, Daddy. I can handle this."

"Just another game of cops and robbers. Bang, bang and they're dead." He chuckled. "You want me to come out there and give you a hand, kiddo? I can catch those bad guys for you."

Even after all these years, he was quick to make promises that he could never fulfill.

He continued, "I'll come to Colorado and lasso those bastards with a rope. Yee-haw! That's how you do things in the Old West. Am I right?"

"Sure, Daddy."

"How's my little Laurel? I've got that picture you sent me in my car."

Probably, the photograph was taped right above the Breathalyzer lock her brother had installed so their father wouldn't drive while under the influence. "She's beautiful, Daddy."

"So were you when you were a baby. It was the happiest time in my life." For a moment, he almost sounded sober. "There's something very special about a father and daughter."

"I know."

Amanda choked back a sudden poignant pang. She couldn't deprive Laurel of that relationship with David. It was too important.

"Your mother said you wanted to talk about Jax."

"What can you tell me about him?"

"He's a crook, Amanda. But I'm sure you know that. I saw on the cable news that he just escaped from federal custody in Denver."

"That's right," she said.

"I hope you're not involved with the likes of Jax Schaffer."

"No, Daddy. I saw his picture on the news, too. When I recognized him, I wondered if he was ever close to our family."

"Not to us," her father said. "Jax had a hell of a lot more money than I've ever seen. The bastard used to think he was better than me because he owned the prettiest little yacht you ever saw. He was one of those outdoorsy types, always had something to prove. The bastard."

She knew this conversation was about to head down a familiar path, complaining about the unfairness of life and her father's business misfortunes.

"Gotta go," she said. "I love you, Daddy."

"That's my princess. Love you, too."

She returned to the front room, where David and Laurel had progressed to a game where he held her fingers and she practiced walking on her tiptoes.

As Amanda sank into a chair, he glanced at her.

"There's nothing like a baby to make you feel that all's right with the world."

Laurel shouted, demanding his full attention.

"That's right," he said to her. "You're my favorite kind of person."

"I had no idea you were so fond of infants."

"Neither did I. It was sometime during my first years of internship that I decided to specialize in pediatrics. I got to spend a lot of time with these little critters."

He directed Laurel's staggering walk across the carpet to her mother, and Amanda lifted the baby onto her lap, giving her a tight squeeze.

David stood over them. "Hungry?"

"Starved."

Right on cue, Vonnie came back into the room. "About dinner," she said. "I did some shopping today. We can have a salad. Or pasta."

"Not to worry," David said. "Tonight, we're having my specialty."

"What's that?"

"Pizza."

While he went to the kitchen to call pizza delivery, Vonnie sat on the sofa opposite Amanda. The red-haired nanny projected a very businesslike attitude as she opened a spiral notebook in her lap. "I made all the phone calls you wanted," she said. "And I have a lot of messages for you."

"Did you manage to contact Bill Chessman, the chairman of the board for Empire Bank?"

"What a nice man! He said you should take care of yourself and feel better. There's an emergency board meeting tomorrow morning at ten, but he doesn't expect you to be there."

Still, it might be wise to attend. With all the rampant

accusations and suspicion, Amanda should show herself and clear the air. "What else?"

"I left a message on Tracy Meyer's phone machine. I said you were concerned about her. And that you were feeling much better." Vonnie consulted her written list. "I left pretty much the same message for everybody else you asked me to call. I returned calls to a couple of people who wanted to know if you were coming to the Fourth of July party at the country club. And Frank Weathers. God, he's called ten times. I wrote it all down for you to look at."

"Thank you, Vonnie. I don't know what I'd do without you."

When Amanda reached over and patted her hand, Vonnie looked surprised. She tossed her red curls. "I kind of enjoyed it. Being a nanny is just my summer job, you know. I was thinking that when I went back to school in the fall, I might change my major to business."

"Excellent choice. I'm sure you'll do very well, and the world needs more female executives."

"Thanks, Amanda." She beamed, then looked back at her notes. "And I've talked to Agent Hess three times. I think he likes me."

"Did he have any information?"

"He asked that David call when he got in."

Interesting, she thought. David had cultivated a contact with the FBI. That might be extremely useful in their investigating. "Be sure to tell him."

It was much later when David finally made contact with Agent Hess.

At ten o'clock, Laurel had settled down for the night, and a weariness surrounded Amanda. She stared at the moving images on the television screen, not seeing what she was watching, not hearing the laugh track. She longed for a good, long, deep sleep.

The news came on with Elaine Montero reporting. In spite of her obnoxious attitude, she presented herself well on the television. Her black hair shone with highlights. Her navy blazer looked serious and efficient. On the screen behind her was a picture of Empire Bank.

"Look," Vonnie said. "She's talking about your robbery."

"It's not *my* robbery."

A particularly unflattering photo of Amanda took the place of the bank, and Elaine Montero said, "Earlier today, I spoke with bank president Amanda Fielding. When asked about the alleged possibility that the bank robbery was an inside job, Ms. Fielding had this to say."

Amanda winced as she saw herself on tape. And she heard her own voice say, "I'm not afraid. No one can touch me."

"What?" She bounded out of her chair. How could Elaine Montero do that? With clever editing, she'd made it look as if Amanda were boasting that she could get away with the robbing a bank.

"Did you really say that?" Vonnie asked.

"It's out of context. I was talking about fear and the hostage situation."

David returned to the room. "What's going on?"

"That Montero woman made me look like a criminal," she ranted. "You were right, David. I never should have spoken to her."

When she turned to him, she noticed a solemnity in his expression. What else could possibly go wrong? "Did you talk to Agent Hess?"

"That was him on the telephone."

"Did he say anything about me?" Vonnie asked.

"No." David focused on Amanda. "The bank robber in

custody, the one named Sarge, has offered to testify in exchange for immunity.''

''Good,'' she said. ''Now, maybe the FBI will get to the bottom of this.''

''I'm not so sure,'' David said. ''In his confession, Sarge implicated you.''

Chapter Ten

When Amanda wakened the next morning at seven, the first thing she noticed was an absence of pain. No more headache. The air-cooled temperature in the bedroom felt pleasant. Bright morning light around the window blinds promised another sunny day. Refreshed by the night's sleep, her sense of optimism lasted for nearly thirty seconds before she remembered that her life was like the *Titanic* and she'd just hit an iceberg.

She buried her face in the pillows and groaned. Thanks to Elaine Montero, everyone in the city of Denver suspected Amanda was bragging about how she could get away with robbery. Sarge the bank robber had done his best to convince the FBI.

It was definitely time for damage control, because she couldn't abandon ship. Amanda had never been one to give up without a fight.

Given the circumstances, the ten-o'clock meeting of the Empire Bank board of directors took on far greater importance. She needed to attend and convince the directors that she wasn't a crook and could manage the Cherry Creek branch of the bank with renewed efficiency and skill. She had to save her job.

After the meeting, she would meet Agent Metcalf at the

bank. Though her supposed reason was to search for her purse and shoes, Amanda really wanted to find the secret camera that she and Harry Hoffman had rigged to see if anyone was getting into her desk. More than likely, the FBI had already found the camera. If so, she wanted the information. She had to solve the crime.

That should do it. Save her job and solve the crime.

Throwing off the sheets, Amanda went to the playpen and checked on her sleeping baby before rushing through her shower and hair wash, being careful near the stitches where her scalp was still tender.

Though her headache had not returned, she packed a vial of aspirin into the white purse that matched her open-toed shoes. The accessories complemented the subtle white-and-peach pattern of her silk shirtwaist dress. She added a gold choker and matching earrings. For the first time since the robbery, she applied full makeup.

Then she tiptoed downstairs to sneak in a cup of coffee before Laurel awakened.

David was already in the kitchen, hovering over his coffeemaker waiting for the final brew. Though his hazel eyes were sleepy and his dark stubble was almost a beard, he looked sexy in pajama bottoms and a lightweight robe that hung open, revealing his muscular chest and flat torso.

From the many mornings they'd shared, she knew what to expect from him. David was slow to waken but not at all irritable. Before his first cup of coffee, he moved like a three-toed sloth.

"You look great," he murmured as he turned toward her.

His bathrobe flapped open, and her gaze rested on his dark, flat nipples. The pattern of black, springy hair arrowed down past his belly button. "You look pretty great yourself."

"Where are you going?" he asked.

"Board meeting downtown."

The coffee was done. David sloshed the dark liquid into his mug and took a sip. "Good," he grunted.

Amanda took down the daisy mug from the cabinet and prepared her coffee with milk and sugar. She'd always enjoyed mornings with David, when his black hair fell artlessly across his forehead and his manner was unguarded. They had never argued in the morning.

"Know what I miss?" he asked, staring into his mug. "Amaretto in my coffee."

"For breakfast?"

"Anytime of day. And Irish coffee." A lazy half smile lifted the corner of his mouth. "It's better to be liquor free, but sometimes, I miss it. A lot."

When she heard Laurel's morning chirp, she and David turned simultaneously toward the baby sound. Already he'd taken on the role of caregiver.

"Should I get the baby?" he asked. "You're all dressed up. Probably don't want to get messy."

"I can take care of Laurel without mussing myself." Automatically, she set down her coffee mug and prepared a bottle. Laurel was always hungry when she woke up. "This is usually the way I'm dressed before work."

"It must be hard to leave her every morning."

"Sometimes." A familiar knot tightened in her stomach. "On the other hand, I really appreciate my time with Laurel because I can't always be with her."

"What made you decide to be a single mother?"

"When I found out I was pregnant, I was glad. More than glad—I was ecstatic. From that moment on, the world was a brighter, more wonderful place. I could always hear birds singing." She screwed the nipple onto the bottle. "I wanted a baby. In my thirties and unmarried, being pregnant was a precious gift."

"Did Laurel's father feel the same way?"

She'd never given him the opportunity to say how he felt. Selfishly, Amanda had been so wrapped up in herself, her own happiness, that she never even told him.

She'd been so horribly wrong. She had to tell him. "About Laurel's father…"

"I already know," he said. "Vonnie told me."

Her eyelids squeezed shut. Tension spread through her, radiating from the gnarl in her gut, setting her nerves on edge. But how could Vonnie have told him? Vonnie didn't know the identity of Laurel's father.

"I was disappointed," he said.

So deeply, she regretted not telling him the truth. She should have believed in him, believed that he could change. If she could turn back the clock, she would do everything differently. But it was too late. "David, I don't know how to tell you how sorry I am."

"It's not your fault. You can't blame biology."

"I guess not."

He came up behind her and lightly placed his hands on her shoulders. The gentleness of his touch was a painful rebuke. "It all turned out for the best. Laurel is a wonderful kid." Quietly, he said, "I wish she was my daughter instead of Stefan's."

Stefan's? He thought Laurel was Stefan's child. She had to explain to him. *Say it! Get it over with!* Even if it meant losing him forever, she had to tell the truth.

She turned in the circle of his arms and looked up into his eyes. Therein, she saw forgiveness. He didn't hate her. There was even a hint of caring. In his smile, she saw the possibility of a future for them.

"Do you believe in second chances?" she asked.

"Sure. Even third chances," he said.

She'd made a mistake in not telling him, but it wasn't a

fatal error. There was still hope for a relationship between them. She just had to be sure to explain it all correctly....

From upstairs, Laurel gave a demanding shout at the precise moment that the phone rang. The moment was broken, and Amanda knew she needed more time to figure out how to explain it all to David. She stepped away from him as both Laurel and the phone shrieked again. "You get the phone—I'll grab Laurel."

"The machine will pick it up. I'm going to get dressed."

"I thought you had the day off."

David stretched his arms over his head and issued a huge, gaping yawn. "I'm coming with you."

"But David—"

"Dangerous stuff is going on. You need a bodyguard, and I'm your man. Whether you like it or not."

She liked it.

DAVID TOOK THE PORSCHE, which had been returned without dents or nicks by the parking-lot attendant. In case of another high-speed chase, he wanted to be prepared.

But the drive to her board of directors' meeting in downtown Denver was uneventful. The streets were a little less crowded than usual, since this was the Friday before a holiday weekend. Because there were fewer cars, he easily found a parking space near their destination.

David straightened the knot on his Jerry Garcia necktie. It was the first time this summer he'd worn anything but casual clothes or hospital scrubs. The navy sports jacket felt like too much clothing for July.

As he and Amanda crossed the street from the parking lot to the twenty-two-story Heiser Building, he realized that he hadn't been downtown, except for Rockies baseball games, for most of the summer. The trendy LoDo area had once been his favorite stomping ground, and he hadn't even missed the constant parties.

"I'm getting old," he said as they entered the skyscraper.

"Are you referring to those few little gray hairs at your temples?"

"My hair?" He hadn't even thought about his hair turning, though his brother, Josh, who was only four years older, was almost completely gray. "At least, I'm not going bald."

"I like the gray," she said. "You look distinguished."

"That's just another word for *old*." He turned toward her. "You're not aging. If anything, you're prettier now than ever before."

"Thank you."

Her smile was pure delight. Her lipstick matched the peachy color of her dress, and she looked cool and sweet as a butterscotch sundae. But he didn't make the mistake of assuming she was a fluffy bit of confection. Amanda was wearing her game face—the cool, poised mask of a highly trained executive.

Outside the boardroom, they ran into the chairman, Bill Chessman. He was an average-sized man with a high forehead and a thick black mustache. David was acquainted with him from the country club, where Chessman had the reputation of being one of the most consistent golfers in town. They shook hands.

"What are you doing here, David?"

"Keeping an eye on Amanda."

She said, "David was the doctor who treated me at Denver General."

"A doctor?" He gave him a thumbs-up sign. "Good for you, David."

Chessman focused his attention on Amanda. "I'm glad

you could make it. Are you sure you've recovered enough from your injuries to be here?''

"Mostly," she said. "If you want a professional opinion, ask David."

Chessman turned to him expectantly. His eyebrows, as thick as his mustache, rose. "Well?"

"Amanda sustained a concussion from a blow to the left temple. When the ambulance brought her in, she was also suffering from shock. As you can see, she's recovering nicely."

"That's a relief," he said. "I'd heard you had amnesia and could barely remember your name."

"Who told you that?" she asked.

"Must have been Frank Weathers. He's been real helpful, keeping us updated. It's lucky that at least one of the branch executives wasn't inside the bank during the robbery."

"How lucky," Amanda said coldly.

"But you're all right? You don't have any of this amnesia?"

Again, she turned to David. "I'll let the doctor explain."

"It's called short-term memory loss," he said, "and it's typical of a concussion. A few recent events are unclear. She might never have total recall of the incidents surrounding the traumatic injury."

"The robbery attempt itself?" Chessman asked.

"Correct."

"Doesn't matter," he said. "We have reports from several other employees, and I want to commend you, Amanda, on the way you handled yourself."

"Thank you, sir."

"I have only one question," he continued, "before we go into the meeting."

"Yes?"

"I talked to the president at Summit Security. He told me the silent alarms were disabled and the surveillance cameras shut down according to all the proper computer codes. A genius computer hacker could have done almost all of it."

"Except for the one last code," she said. "I spoke to Harry Hoffman, and he told me that before he was knocked unconscious, the robber plugged in the final code to shut down the system."

"Who had access?" Chessman asked.

"As far as I know," she said, "only you and me. I keep all my computer information in a locked drawer in my desk."

"Someone could have broken into your office. Or into mine."

"Yes, sir."

Chessman encompassed David in his rueful glance. "It's a hell of a thing. We have all this expensive high-tech security equipment, and the police were alerted to the robbery by an anonymous 911 call. A hell of a thing."

He ushered Amanda into the meeting, and David took a seat outside to wait for her.

The last person bustling up to the door was Frank Weathers. He glanced at David, then did a double take. His perfect grooming was off-kilter this morning. The silk handkerchief in his lapel pocket was askew.

"Dr. Haines," he said. "Why are you here? Of course, it's lovely to see you, but—"

"I brought Amanda."

"Oh. Is she well enough to attend?"

David recalled his first encounter with this ferret-faced man and said, "She's marvelous."

The doors to the conference room closed behind Frank, and David settled back to wait. He was glad to be outside instead of sitting around the table. He'd gone through a couple of years of being bored by meetings associated with the family construction business. Bored by the board.

He straightened his necktie. Big business definitely wasn't his thing. Even at the hospital, he was always in trouble with the committees. The restrictions of group decisions made him want to be outrageous.

After flipping through a magazine and pacing around the carpeted area outside the conference room, David was beginning to feel stifled. How could Amanda function in this atmosphere? She must always be holding back, impersonating an ice princess.

At noon, the boardroom doors opened. Frank Weathers was the first one out. His ferrety little face flushed bright red, a symptom of stress and possible high blood pressure. This time, he didn't bother with being friendly to David.

"Give Amanda a message for me," he said. "Tell her she has enemies on this board."

"Are you one of them?"

"I could be." He tugged on his shirt collar as if to let out steam. "God, I hate being on the hot seat."

As soon as Amanda emerged with her features paralyzed in her typical ice-princess smile, David whisked her away from the others, claiming they had another appointment.

"Thanks," she whispered in the elevator going down. "The key to a good meeting is a fast exit."

David suggested lunch at a restaurant around the corner from the bank on the Sixteenth Street Mall. They were soon seated at a booth inside, and the air-conditioning was pleasantly cool. Still, Amanda looked wilted.

"Tell me about it," he said.

"Elaine Montero must die," she said. "Everybody saw the sound bite on the news. No matter how I explained it, I look like an idiot for talking to her."

"But that's just public relations. Did they talk about anything important?"

"I don't know where these people get their information," she said, "but they knew about Sarge's testimony. He said I was the inside contact at the bank, and I made it possible for their computer expert, disguised as a technician from Summit Security, to get inside our systems." She gave him an ironic smile. "This guy must be really good. I think he was the robber called Dallas. He not only fooled me, but he got past the people at Summit Security, the bank guards and even Frank Weathers, who signed him in one time when I was out of the office."

"Frank, huh? He's a little weasel."

"He had all kinds of information on Carrie. The only way he could have gotten this stuff was by sneaking it out of my office."

Their waitress came, and David was pleased when Amanda ordered more than a salad. Now wasn't the time to be eating like a waif. She needed protein for energy.

"Is there any way you can prove that Frank got into your office?"

"That's what I hope to find out when we meet Agent Metcalf at the bank. Harry Hoffman and I put a secret camera in my office. It activated when anybody turned the key in my locked desk drawers."

"You did that before the robbery," he said. "Why?"

"Once, when I came back from lunch, my desk drawers were unlocked. It's possible I forgot to lock up. Nothing was missing, but it worried me."

"When was this?"

She hesitated, thinking. "It was two weeks ago today. I remember because I went out to lunch with Stefan, and he was talking about his rock-climbing trip, which was scheduled for the next day, Saturday."

Stefan. David hated the sound of his name, but he wasn't going to dwell on it. This morning, they'd cleared the air, and he meant to make a fresh start with Amanda.

The waitress returned with their beverages, nonalcoholic, and David took a sip. The aroma of food was enticing, and he was getting hungrier by the minute.

"The good news," she said, "is that I looked at some photos of the interior of the bank, and I remembered details about my meeting with Tracy and Carrie. Everything is coming back to me, David."

"Tell me about it."

"There was a gun. Tracy had a gun that belonged to her deceased husband in the safe-deposit box, and Carrie removed the cartridges and dropped them on the table."

"You talked about this before," he said. "You remembered the bullets making a plopping sound, like drops in a bucket."

"I know," she said.

"Do you remember anything else about Tracy?"

She thought for a moment, then her hand flew to her mouth. "Oh, my God!"

"What is it?"

"I just had a flash. I was lying on the marble floor near the teller's counter, and Tracy was holding me, taking care of me. Even after I'd been so coldhearted in our meeting, she was an angel."

"It's good that you're remembering," he said. The recollections were returning to her conscious mind more quickly. Within a few days, he expected her to have almost total recall.

"I really need to tell Tracy I'm sorry. All she wanted was to use the money from her stepdaughter's trust fund so she can stay home with the child." Amanda's gaze turned inward. "I advised against touching the principal because of legal problems. But I was wrong."

He raised his eyebrows. "What did you say?"

"I was wrong?"

"That might be the first time I've ever heard you admit that you'd made a mistake."

"Oh, please. I'm not that rigid."

"Yeah, you are." He regarded her curiously. "And you even want to apologize to Tracy?"

"I want to make things right for her."

"Amanda, honey, I hate to say this, but maybe you got clunked on the head for some big, fat cosmic reason. You've changed."

"So have you," she said. "You've gone back to medicine. You're fulfilling your dream to be a doctor."

"We're both different," he said, thinking of the fresh start. "But we're still the same."

"What do you mean?"

He came around the table and sat next to her on the booth. Holding her face in his hands, he forced her to look into his eyes. "You and I, we feel the same way now as we did five years ago when we were engaged. Do you remember the good times?"

"Yes," she whispered.

"Do you remember what we were like in bed?"

"David, we're in a public place. We shouldn't be—"

"Let me remind you."

He gently tasted her lips. As his tongue penetrated the satin interior of her mouth, he felt her responding to him. Lightly, he caressed her. His hand rested on the edge of her firm breast. His thumb flicked toward her nipple.

When he was certain that she was aroused, he returned to the opposite side of the booth. "I'm right."

"You're insufferably arrogant."

The dreamy look in her blue eyes told him she liked it. Tonight, he decided, they would share his bed.

AT TWO O'CLOCK, they parked in the lot outside Empire Bank. The destruction to the premises made Amanda's stomach turn. A lot of the windows had been broken and were covered with ugly sheets of plywood. As they approached, she cringed to see the trampled landscaping. The double doors at the entryway were draped with yellow crime-scene tape. The glass on one door was shattered, and shards of glass sparkled underfoot.

"Looks like a war zone," she commented. "How could I have forgotten what happened here?"

"Maybe it's better that you don't remember," David said.

An armed guard from Summit Security Services stood beside the doors. Unlike Harry Hoffman, he was youthful and muscular as a commando. He asked, "Can I help you?"

"We're waiting for Metcalf and Hess," David said. "Federal agents."

"Yeah, I know. Metcalf is inside."

Amanda peered through the one glass door that was still intact. "It's dark in there. Is the electricity turned off?"

"That's right."

"And how many guards from Summit are on the premises?"

"Me and one other guy."

This morning at the board meeting, when they'd discussed beefing up security until the building could be repaired, Amanda had voted to increase the number of guards, especially at night. Though the Wells Fargo trucks had removed the cash from the vault on the first floor, there were many other bank assets, including the safe-deposit boxes on the lower level, that needed protecting from looters.

The guard unfastened the yellow plastic tape and pushed open the door. He called out, "Hey, Metcalf. Somebody's here to see you."

The increasingly tense FBI man appeared at the door. He'd taken off his suit jacket and rolled up the sleeves of his white shirt. He was sweating profusely. "Hot enough for you?"

"Are you all right?"

"There's no air-conditioning inside," he explained. "It's like an oven."

"I'm here to look for my purse and shoes," she said.

He held open the door and gestured with a large flashlight. "Don't touch anything unless I give the okay. We've completed our search, but this is still a crime scene."

Amanda eyed him suspiciously. He was being awfully cooperative. Every other time she'd met with Metcalf, it was a confrontation. Why the change in attitude? Logically, he should be even more hostile since Sarge had named her as a coconspirator. Amanda had the feeling she might be walking into a trap, and she stepped cautiously into the bank.

The familiar lobby had been transformed from a clean, well-lit space to a dark ruin with only enough diffused light from the few unbroken windows to make it possible for them to avoid bumping into things. And it was hot, unbearably hot.

David pulled off his sports jacket and necktie. "So this is where you work. Empire Bank and Sauna."

"It's awful in here." She looked toward Metcalf. "When will we be allowed to repair this mess?"

"Soon," he said. The beam of his flashlight darted up

and focused on a security camera that hung like a bat near the ceiling.

At the board meeting, Frank Weathers had offered to supervise the first phase of cleanup involving the insurance adjusters, and she was grateful for his offer. It would be too painful to tally up these losses.

She peered through the sweltering air. Dingy shadows streaked the teller counter. On the floor, directly in front of her, was a rust-colored smear.

Amanda blinked. Behind her eyelids, she saw fresh, crimson blood oozing across the pristine marble floor. That man had been shot. He'd been dying.

Just as quickly as it had come on, the memory vanished. But the sense of shock and nausea remained. A metallic stench stung her nostrils. Her knees felt weak, and she grasped David's arm for support.

Stepping around the dried blood on the floor, she crossed the lobby into the area where five personal bankers, including Frank Weathers, worked. Their desks had been trashed. One of the computer monitors was shattered. Papers and files littered the floor. It was going to be hell sorting everything out.

She pointed toward the corner. ''My office is back there.''

A brass plaque on the door read, Amanda Fielding, President.

She waited for Metcalf to open the door. Compared to the outer area where the SWAT team must have broken through, her office was in good shape. Natural light blazed through the corner window that faced west. The north window was covered in plywood. One of the chairs rested upside down opposite her desk. A blank computer screen stared darkly. Her bookshelves and credenza appeared to be untouched, but paper from her In box spilled across the desk.

She bent down and picked up an unbroken bud vase from the floor. Beside it lay a single rose, dead and withered.

"I like flowers on my desk," she said quietly.

"It'll be okay," David assured her. "After they clean up."

"It'll never be okay again," she declared. The destruction. The violation. The indelible blotch on her career. "My God, did they have to destroy everything?"

"The SWAT team isn't real tidy," Metcalf said without apology.

With one window boarded over, her office felt small and claustrophobic. She wanted to escape from here as quickly as possible. "I usually keep my purse in the corner closet. Is it all right if I look in there?"

"Don't bother." He reached behind the desk and held up her purse. "Is this it?"

"Yes."

He dropped it in the middle of the desk. "Open it and see if anything's missing."

She unfastened the snap. By the morning of the robbery, she'd been carrying this large purse for a couple of days and had accumulated the usual junk: a lipstick, a nail file, a receipt from the drugstore, a napkin from a coffee shop. In the front pocket was her cell phone and pager.

"My wallet," she said. A quick check showed her credit cards and cash had not been stolen. Her checkbook was also tucked inside.

She fished around on the bottom. "Here they are. My keys."

"Interesting," Metcalf said. "Then we can assume that whoever used a key to break into your house didn't steal it from your purse."

"I guess not."

"Who else has keys?"

"Only me and the nanny." Amanda tried to concentrate, but she couldn't think. She'd been so certain about the keys being stolen. "I keep an extra set at the condo, but they aren't missing."

"Are you sure?"

"I'm positive." She shook her head. "I just don't understand. How else could the intruder get a key to my condo?"

"It's not hard to make a key," David said. "Anybody who had access to your purse could make an impression then take it to a locksmith."

"But that would have to be someone I knew. Or someone who worked at the bank." The realization took solid form in her mind. Someone she knew had made a key to her apartment, and had given it to the intruder. "Agent Metcalf, do you know the identity of the man who broke into my condo?"

"It's not your concern, Ms. Fielding."

"Of course it is. The man tried to kill me. You can share this information with me now, or I can go down to the police station and go through arrest records. I used to be an attorney, I know how to—"

"He's a professional criminal with a record," Metcalf said. "The lawyer who showed up to defend him doesn't come cheap."

"A hit man," David said. "Do you mind if we get out of here? I'm boiling."

Metcalf suggested that she look around before she left. "Is there anything else you have in this office that might be useful to our investigation."

"There was a camera," she admitted. "I had thought

someone was tampering with my desk, and Harry Hoffman set it up for me.''

"We found it," Metcalf said tersely.

"Did you play back the tape? Was there anything on it?"

"Ms. Fielding, let me explain something to you. This is an FBI investigation. It's our job to collect the evidence and make the arrests. Your job is to cooperate."

"I understand," she said.

"I allowed you to come here for a reason," he said. "Take a look around you. I assume this used to be a nice bank, now it's broken glass. Smashed computers. Chaos. There's a man in the hospital who's fighting for his life. This isn't fun and games."

"I never thought it was," she said.

"You hid information about Carrie Lamb, alias Carrie Leigh. You didn't mention the secret camera in your office." He mopped his forehead with a handkerchief. "I'm willing to believe you have short-term memory loss, but I want you to tell me every detail as you remember it."

"I'll try."

"You'll do better than that," Metcalf said. "You've been implicated in this robbery. If I find one more incident of noncooperation, I will arrest you. Do you understand?"

"Yes, sir."

She knew he was right. Somewhere in the back of her mind was a detail she hadn't yet recalled—a detail so important that a hit man had come after her to make sure she wouldn't talk.

But she would remember. Until she did, she would remain a suspect—a suspect in danger.

Chapter Eleven

In the parking lot outside Empire Bank, Amanda blinked owlishly in the brilliant sunlight. Though the July day was seasonably warm, the temperature was nothing compared to the pressure cooker inside Empire Bank. Another dead end.

Did the secret camera in her office show the face of the criminal mastermind who'd planned the bank robbery? Or was the tape blank? She would never know.

Agent Metcalf would never share that privileged information with her. Amanda supposed she should be glad that the FBI agent had, at least, allowed her to take her purse.

Standing beside the Porsche, she transferred her cell phone and beeper to her other bag. And her keys. Never again would she allow her keys to be out of her sight. She tossed the empty purse inside the car. "Let's take a walk, David. I need to figure a few things out."

He glanced down at her open-toed white pumps. "Those don't look like walking shoes."

"Actually, they're quite comfortable. That's one of the benefits of expensive footwear."

Beautiful, costly shoes were a luxury she might be forced to forego in the future. If she lost her job, she wouldn't be able to afford to shop at designer boutiques.

"Where to?" he asked.

"The creek."

They crossed the south lanes of Speer Boulevard and descended a stone stairway to a wide sidewalk and bike path that ran in the middle of the boulevard, following the course of Cherry Creek. The foliage on either side was full and green. At midsummer, the waters were low but still enticing, sparkling like liquid fire in the afternoon sunlight.

Amanda often jogged along this urban trail after work. Less than a mile away was her condo, and she thought fondly of the view from the fourteenth floor, the furnishings she'd selected so carefully, the nursery she'd decorated for her baby daughter.

With all her heart, she wished she could truly go home again, lock the door and be free from this ever-tightening web of uncertainty and suspicion. Seeing the devastation at the bank had affected her. Though the attempted robbery wasn't her fault, the result was her responsibility.

She and David stepped to the right of the sidewalk, allowing joggers and a bicyclist to pass.

"A plan," she said, "I need a plan."

"How about this—do what Metcalf said. Settle down and wait until the feds and the cops solve the case."

"What if they don't figure it out?"

"Call me crazy, but it seems like a whole police force and the FBI will do better at investigating than Amanda Fielding, girl sleuth."

Of course he was right. The law-enforcement officers had manpower and the authority. Unfortunately, they seemed to be as stumped as Amanda herself—and the FBI couldn't claim amnesia.

"I don't have much faith in their ability," she said. "They still haven't managed to apprehend Jax Schaffer. Or even Carrie and the other robber fugitive. They failed to protect Temple in the hospital. As far as we know, they haven't got a single clue or witness."

"Except for you," he said. "The attack at your condo proves you know something."

"A clue that I can't remember." She paused beneath the shade of a lilac bush that had lost its fragrant blooms. "I can't stand this helplessness, this out-of-control feeling. David, what if I lose my job?"

"You'll find another."

She shook her head. "I'll never find another position as good as this one. How will I support Laurel? How can I send money home to my parents? It feels like my future is going up in flames. It isn't fair."

"Life doesn't come with guarantees."

"Not unless you have money," she said. "I grew up in a world where everybody had more cash than I did. We weren't starving, and we still had the advantages of a good family name, but we were broke. When my friends went looking for jobs, they were interested in the prestige or the fun value of a particular career. I was looking at the net take-home pay. I can't afford to lose my job."

"It's not the end of the world," he said.

"But it is. It's the end of *my* world."

When David spoke, his baritone was low and measured. "Two weeks ago in the emergency room, I worked on a team trying to save the life of a young girl. She was seventeen, a good girl, a straight-A student who was well loved by her family and friends. Her only mistake was being in the wrong lane when a drunk driver crossed the line and hit her car head-on. Her body was shattered. After three days of operations, we lost her."

His lips tightened in a thin line, and a muscle in his jaw twitched. He seemed to be fighting tears, but he had never seemed so manly and strong to Amanda. And wise. How

did he get to be so smart? She was astonished to realize
that David Haines, practical joker and man-about-town, had
an unseen depth of real wisdom.

"If you lose your job," he said, "that's a setback. But
it's not a tragedy."

Had she ever really known him? Reaching up, she
stroked his jaw. With her thumb, she felt the hard bone and
muscle beneath his flesh. "I've misjudged you."

His hand rested upon hers. He turned his head and kissed
the soft pad beneath her fingers. The touch of his lips
caused an electric shock to chase up her arm and spread,
tingling, through her entire body.

Slowly, he lowered her hand, gliding her fingers along
the outline of her own torso and hips. Though they were
outdoors in a public place, the daylight narrowed around
them, microscoping to a taut sexual awareness as if they
were enclosed in a glass bell jar.

Joggers bobbed past them. On either side of the boulevard, the hectic rush-hour traffic surged, but she felt as if
they were alone in a separate reality. His gaze held her
captive, and she had no desire to escape from the tender,
fierce energy that flowed between them.

Abruptly, he stepped away from her, breaking the spell.
"We'll figure this out, Amanda."

"Yes," she breathed.

His smile brightened her world—a place that had, only
moments ago, seemed bleak and angry.

"I'm always on your side," he said. "The important
thing is to let your memory work."

Lightly holding her hand, he faced forward on the path,
and they started walking again. For a distance, they said
nothing. The frustration inside her began to settle, and she
felt strangely refreshed, cognizant of the sunlight and the
gentle afternoon breeze. She felt alive.

"The way I see it," David said, "there are three pieces of evidence working against you. First, you hired Carrie when you knew she had fake ID, and she's looking very suspicious. Second, you had access to inside information. Third, you must know something important, because the bad guys tried to kill you."

"Let's start with number three, the man who broke into my condo," she said. "From what Metcalf told us, he's obviously a slick, professional hit man, and—"

"Not that slick," David interrupted. "He got beat by a resident pediatrician."

"Super doc." She grinned. "With fists of iron."

"And buns of steel."

"I like your buns."

"Not as much as I like yours," he said.

When he reached over and patted her bottom, she didn't object. "Are you trying to distract me from this investigation?"

"Is that possible?"

Most definitely! Her sexual attraction to him was becoming a major preoccupation. With an effort, she dragged her thoughts back to the hit man. "Do we have any way of knowing who hired him?"

"Not unless he confesses," David said.

"Then we need to look at the problem of the keys. I was disappointed to find them inside my purse. It seemed so obvious to me that the crooks took advantage of the confusion at the bank and stole my keys."

"Not likely," he said. "Somebody made a copy of your keys long before the bank robbery. Who had access to your purse?"

"Anybody who was in my apartment. Or an employee at the bank."

He guided her toward the edge of the sidewalk to allow

another bike to pass. "You said it yourself, Amanda. The robbery was an inside job."

She hated to think that one of her trusted bank employees had slipped into her office, stolen the keys to her home and made copies. "Why would they want my keys?"

"If they were planning to rob the bank, they needed the security phone numbers and codes."

"But I don't carry such vital information around with me. I keep that data locked in a desk drawer at the bank."

"And where's the key to the drawer?"

"In my purse," she said. "Oh, David. You're right."

When she reasoned through the details with David's help, it all seemed clear. "Since the robbers had inside information, the robbery had to be an inside job, perpetrated with the help of someone who worked at the bank. They stole my keys. They broke into my desk. Now we just need to figure out who it was."

"My money's on Frank Weathers," David said. "That little ferret wants your job, and he wants it bad."

But it was difficult to think of Frank as a daring coconspirator in a bank robbery. He was too conservative. His greatest flaw as a personal banker was a fear of risk taking. In all the times he'd come to her for authorization on a loan or credit line, she never remembered an instance when he'd argued in favor of the client.

He was an office gossip, petty, sniping at other people behind their backs. "He's a creep but not a bank robber. Frank with a gun? I think not. He'd be trembling too hard to aim."

"He wasn't the triggerman. It was his job to find out the security codes and phone numbers."

"Information I had access to."

"Right," David said. "The fact that you had the vital

info logically made you a suspect instead of him. Framing you for the crime is a bonus for Frankie boy.''

''He'd be delighted to see me in trouble,'' she agreed.

''Let's make Frank Weathers our number-one suspect.''

''Okay.''

Now it felt as though they were getting somewhere.

As they strolled in silence, her mind raced through a list of other personal bankers and tellers who had been on duty. Their faces appeared like photos in a yearbook. Beyond their personnel file, she knew little about them. These were people she saw five days a week. They spoke to each other. She would recognize them on the street. But they were strangers.

Few people were true friends. Yesterday in Harry's hospital room, she'd been closer to Jane Borelli than ever before in the years they'd worked side by side.

''What about Harry Hoffman?'' David said.

''Harry?'' She liked and respected the bank guard. She didn't want to suspect him. ''But that doesn't make any sense. If Harry was working with the robbers, why would they knock him out?''

''So he wouldn't be suspected.''

She frowned and walked a little faster, as if by speeding up she could kick her brain into high gear. Logically, Harry Hoffman made an excellent suspect. Not only was he familiar with the security system, but he also had access to her office, the keys, the codes.

''Harry has to be suspect number two,'' David said. ''When the bank robber was killed at the hospital, Harry was there. He could have roamed the halls, and nobody would have paid attention to him. He could have even slipped into a disguise.''

''Frank Weathers was also there. For that matter, Stefan

was in the waiting room outside emergency. And Carrie," she concluded miserably. "Carrie was there, too."

"I hate to say it, Amanda. But it sounds like your friend is on the lam with a bank robber."

"She couldn't have killed Temple in the hospital. I'm sure she's not a murderer."

"What about the guy she's with? The third robber?"

"I don't know."

As they walked in the shadows of overhanging tree limbs, a dark apprehension rose within her. Though Amanda clung to an unshakable loyalty to her friend, she couldn't escape the cold, hard facts. Carrie was willingly in contact with one of the bank robbers. If not an accomplice, she was his associate.

Unwittingly, she might give him information that would be useful for him. "Oh, my God," she whispered. "Carrie knows about you."

"What do you mean?"

"About us, David. She knows we were engaged. What if she mentions something to the robbers? They might come to your house, looking for me."

The thought chilled her to the bone. Alone at David's house, Laurel and Vonnie were virtually defenseless.

"Call the house," he said. "My security is state-of-the-art, but these guys managed to disarm the silent alarm at a bank. My system would be child's play. Call now!"

Amanda plunged her hand into her purse and grabbed the cell phone. She tapped out David's number and waited impatiently through three rings until the answering machine picked up. "Vonnie," Amanda said. "I know you're screening calls, but this is Amanda. Pick up."

Static crackled through the line, and she listened with single-minded attention, trying to hear a voice that wasn't here. Why wasn't the nanny answering? "Vonnie, pick up. It's Amanda."

When David grasped her shoulder, she flinched. Her nerves were strung taut. Desperately, she repeated, "Oh, my God, Vonnie, pick up the damned phone."

"She's not there," David said.

Amanda gripped the phone so tightly that her hand trembled. They could have sent another hit man to David's house. Bank robbers. Violent professional criminals. When they didn't find Amanda...what would they do to Vonnie and Laurel?

"Don't panic," he said. "Maybe Vonnie went to the grocery store or something. Did she tell you your plans this morning?"

"The store." Amanda grasped at that shred of hope. "She had to get disposable diapers."

"Okay," he said. "Let's go back to the car and head out there."

They struck out at a quick pace. But soon, they were running along the path, dodging the other pedestrians and bikers. Though she knew they were covering ground, Amanda had the dream sensation of sprinting as fast as she could and not getting anywhere.

Side by side, they raced up the stone stairway. Her pulse pounded in her eardrums. Her heart felt as if it would explode in her chest.

At the street, David caught her arm before she could hurl herself across three lanes of fast-moving traffic. Her personal safety was forgotten in her frantic need to reach her child.

Nothing else was important. Her job. FBI suspicions. Threats. Nothing mattered except Laurel's safety.

They reached the Porsche, flung open the doors and

dived inside. Instantly, David revved the powerful engine.
"We should call the police," he said.

"No," she responded instinctively. "During the bank
robbery, everything was going smoothly until the SWAT
team showed up."

In a flash, she remembered. The blue-and-red flash of
police cars. The bank robbers were spooked, and the customer—a gray-haired man named Nyland—had been shot.
In her mind, she heard the echo of gunfire. She saw the
blood. A terrible crimson. The color of fear.

She snapped back to the present reality. "How long does
it take to get to your house from here?"

"Twenty-five minutes. Twenty if the lights are with
me."

She stared at her wristwatch—4:18. By 4:38, they would
be there.

"Try calling again," he said.

While he darted expertly from lane to lane, she punched
in the number and talked to the answering machine. Vonnie
still didn't pick up.

"No use," she said.

"Hang on, Amanda. Everything is going to be all right."

If only she could believe him. She stared straight ahead
as if her intense concentration would cause the traffic to
part and speed their progress.

She glanced at her watch. They were ten minutes away
from the house. She pinched her eyelids closed, hoping that
she was overreacting.

"Almost there," he said.

Amanda counted off the seconds as David swerved
around the final street corner and approached the house.
There seemed to be no visible sign of a disturbance. A
minivan was parked in front, but it wasn't Amanda's. She'd
put her vehicle in the garage.

The white van in front of David's house had electronic equipment mounted on top. A television station logo marked the side. Leaning against the front fender was Elaine Montero.

Amanda felt her tension break. No one would attempt an assault on the house while the watchful eye of a television camera was poised to record every detail. Inadvertently, Elaine Montero had acted as a bodyguard.

As soon as David parked, Amanda was out of the Porsche. She charged toward the reporter. "Thank you," she said.

Startled, Elaine backed up a pace. "Why are you thanking me?"

"You'll never ever know."

She and David bolted onto the porch. He unlocked the door and hit the disarm buttons on the security system.

Amanda heard a delighted giggling noise and ran into the front room toward the sound. There she found Vonnie sprawled on the sofa, watching television. Laurel was in front of her, bouncing along in her baby walker.

Scooping the baby into her arms, Amanda showered Laurel with kisses. "I love you, sweetie. You're my life."

Laurel cooed in response.

"What's going on?" Vonnie asked. "You two are acting very weird."

"Why didn't you pick up when I called?" Amanda asked.

"I had to turn off the ringer on the phone and turn down the sound on the answering machine. That Elaine Montero person kept calling and calling. I knew you wouldn't want me to talk to her."

"You did good," David told her.

"So did you," Amanda told him.

David had put everything into the proper perspective.

Solving the crime and saving her career were important goals, but the biggest concern in her life was Laurel. Her relationship with her child was number one.

David stepped up beside her and gave both her and Laurel a hug. It almost felt as if they were a real family.

WHILE AMANDA FED Laurel her smashed bananas and oatmeal in the kitchen, David retired to the den and played back a day's worth of messages on the answering machine.

In the morning, there were the usual sales contacts. Then came another whiny call from Amanda's mother, complaining about being contacted by some Denver television reporter. Amanda's mother had given out David's phone number.

That explained how Elaine had gotten the address. Though David's telephone was unlisted, it wouldn't take a great deal of research to find his address using his name and phone number.

Frank Weathers had called with a snotty bit of information about plans for the cleanup work at the bank. David didn't like that guy, didn't trust him no matter how ineffectual Amanda thought he was.

There were three hang-up calls.

After their panic attack this afternoon, David concluded that it wasn't safe for them to stay here. Too many people knew how to find them.

After a half-dozen calls from Elaine Montero, he came to Amanda's attempts to reach Vonnie on the cell phone. The raw terror in her voice resonated through him.

He turned off the answering machine and looked up as she slipped into the room. Gracefully, she came toward him and sat in a chair opposite his desk. Her blond hair fell in slight disarray, and he longed to smooth the silken curtain away from her lovely face.

"Anything interesting on the answering machine?" she asked.

"Frank Weathers wants you to know that the cleanup at the bank will start tomorrow even though it's the Fourth of July. And your mother called to complain about Elaine Montero."

"She called my mother?" Twin frown lines appeared between her arched brows. "I don't know which of them I should feel sorry for."

"Amanda, we can't stay here anymore. It's not safe."

"I thought of that," she said wearily. "I put in a call to Stefan to ask if his mountain cabin is available. He wasn't home, but I left a message."

"He has my phone number?"

"Is that a problem?"

If Elaine Montero could find his address from a phone number, so could Stefan. And Frank Weathers.

David didn't trust either of them. Stefan might be Laurel's father, but that didn't exclude him from suspicion. He'd visited Amanda's condo. He had access to her purse and her keys. "Suspect number four," he said.

"What?"

"The first three are Frank, Harry and Carrie." He hesitated before naming another. "Stefan is number four."

"But he doesn't work at the bank," she said.

"He has access to you," David said. "You'd be able to tell him all the important stuff. Plus, he could've made off with the extra set of keys in your condo to make copies."

He watched for her reaction. There had to be some residual loyalty to the father of her child. Her lips tightened, but she conceded. "Stefan is suspect number four."

David felt strangely gratified. Her willingness to believe that Stefan was a criminal told him a lot. "If he did this, Amanda, he used you."

"That doesn't surprise me."

"He might have hired a hit man to kill you."

"You once told me that the motivation for crime wa usually sex or money. Well, there's no sex with Stefar And he's extremely fond of money." Her voice was calm dispassionate. "We've known each other for a very lon time, but it wouldn't surprise me to find out he'd traded o our friendship to line his pockets."

Her assessment traded purely on logic. Obviously, an love Amanda might have had for Stefan had died.

Expectantly, she looked at him. "Where are we going stay tonight, David? I can't keep Laurel here if we're danger."

"I have a plan," he said.

"Okay, shoot."

"My brother, Josh, lives in the mountains. It's a bi place with plenty of room."

"I wouldn't feel right about imposing on Josh an Nancy."

"Manners are real important," he drawled, "when you life is in danger."

"And what if the bad guys found out we were there? can't ask your brother to put his family in danger for me."

David hadn't thought that far in advance. "You're right Well, maybe there's some kind of FBI safe house."

"Absolutely not. I'm still concerned about my job. Hov would it look if I went into hiding?"

He shrugged. "Like you were intelligently guarding you own butt, as well as Laurel's."

"I want to give the appearance that everything is busi ness as usual." She leaned forward and rested her hand on the desktop. "I have an idea."

Warily, he listened. Amanda was the most stubborn fe

male he'd ever known. When she made a decision, she stuck to it through hell and high water.

"The real issue here," she said, "is Laurel's safety. Frankly, she's not in danger unless she's with me. We could send Laurel and Vonnie to stay with your brother. I would stay right here. Anybody who's looking for me will come here first."

Though David liked the part of the plan that put him alone with Amanda for the weekend, it bothered him that he couldn't necessarily guarantee her safety. "Last time I checked, this wasn't a fortress. I don't have a secret stockpile of automatic rifles in the basement."

She had already snatched the phone from his desk. "I'll notify Agent Metcalf of our plans. If there is, in fact, someone after me, the FBI might want to do a stakeout on the house."

"You're talking about using yourself as bait."

"*Bait* is such an ugly word," she said. Speaking into the telephone receiver, she left a message for Metcalf, hung up and grinned at David. "I think this will work."

As it turned out, so did Metcalf.

Within a few hours, the setup had been arranged. With FBI involvement, the attention to detail became ridiculous. When David and Amanda kissed Laurel goodbye, they were assured that their transport to Josh's mountain home was complex enough to avoid anyone following. Other FBI agents would spend the night doing surveillance on David's house.

At nine o'clock, David and Amanda were alone in the master bedroom. They'd been here before, but not like this.

Chapter Twelve

In the midsummer night, the Iceman cruised slowly past the doctor's house. The gleam from the streetlight reflected against leaded glass windows, but the curtains were drawn. He couldn't see inside, but he knew Amanda was there, hiding from him.

He turned left at the stop sign. There were no other cars on the street. A quiet neighborhood.

Even if she got her memory back, it was possible that she would never make the connection with him. If he were a betting man, he might have taken that chance. But he valued precision. Sloppiness offended him.

Amanda had to die.

Earlier today, he considered killing her when she was on the bike path next to Cherry Creek, but there were too many witnesses. Tonight, she'd made things complicated by contacting the FBI and attaching herself to David Haines.

He needed to have her alone. Just the two of them. He imagined her eyes, wide with fear, when she saw the .38 Special with silencer attached. She'd beg for her life. She'd weep and fall to her knees.

The dark fantasy filled his mind. Her fingers would lace together in pleading supplication. Her round breasts would heave with sobs. *Who's the cool one now, princess?*

He'd pull the trigger. And he'd walk away free.

A smile twitched at the corners of his mouth. It made sense that murder would be another of his talents. Killing Temple in the hospital was only the beginning. After Amanda, he might choose to develop this ability. He could learn about weapons, practice until he was an expert marksman. He'd be an international assassin, a killer who was known and feared around the world. Heads of state would call upon him. The Iceman.

But first, he had to take care of Amanda. He had to get her alone.

AMANDA SAT on the window seat in the bedroom and stared at the blank space on the carpet where Laurel's crib had been. This would be her first night away from her daughter, and she missed her already.

"Did I do the right thing?" She looked to David, who leaned against the wall beside the door with his arms folded over his chest. "Do you think Laurel will be okay?"

He nodded. "But she probably won't get any sleep tonight. Josh and Nancy can't wait to play with a baby girl after all their boys. Nancy was excited when I told her the plan over the phone. She almost crawled through the wire and hugged me."

"I had that impression, too." Nancy had been kind to her when they'd spoken. She hadn't mentioned the bank robbery or the broken engagement.

"She'll take good care of Laurel."

Reassured, Amanda allowed her maternal nervousness to ebb while a more immediate concern rose up to take its place. Namely, the fact that she and David were alone. She couldn't help noticing that both of them had avoided the largest piece of furniture in the room. The bed.

If history were any sort of guidepost, she wouldn't be

able to resist him. No matter what other problems they'd had, they were sexually compatible. David knew exactly the way she liked to be kissed. He knew where to touch, when to move to the next level.

He sauntered across the room toward her. A faint but unmistakable light flickered in his hazel eyes. He spoke not a word. Instead, he extended his hand.

Mesmerized, her gaze focused on his strong hand and muscular forearm, reaching toward her in invitation. If she joined her hand with his, she knew what came next.

Fully intending to walk away from him, she rose to her feet. She didn't need to complicate matters further by making love to him before she'd told him the truth about Laurel. Her world was complex enough, thank you very much. In fact, as much as she hated to put a damper on things, now seemed the appropriate time to break it to him....

Yet her arm moved of its own volition, as if her physical body had a mind of its own and didn't want to risk almost certain rejection. Her fingers fitted perfectly against his. Contrasting his dark tan, her hand appeared graceful and delicate.

His grasp closed. Effortlessly, he whipped her into his arms.

She pressed hard against him. Her head flung back. The last vestige of resistance vanished, and she welcomed his fierce, passionate kiss. Desire surged through her, hot and demanding.

With hard caresses, he tamed her wayward body in a skillful tango, the dance of love. Every shiver became choreographed. The pounding of their hearts sychronized in a tantalizing beat, and they moved as one toward the perfect, inevitable crescendo.

When his hands cupped her buttocks and he pulled her

firmly against his hard arousal, a tortured groan escaped her lips. She shouldn't be doing this. "David, stop!"

Once before, she'd allowed her passion to win the day, and the result was her daughter. Not again. She couldn't allow this to happen again.

"David!"

His head pulled back. Breathing hard, he looked down at her with smoldering eyes. "You don't want me to stop. Oh, baby, we're too good together."

It absolutely destroyed her when he called her "baby." She was a bank president, for heaven's sake. Nobody called her "honey" or "baby" or "sweetie." Nobody except for David when they were making love. "Yes. I want you. But it's not right."

"We're consenting adults." He held her chin and tasted her mouth, lightly tugging at the fullness of her lower lip with his teeth. When he pulled away and locked gazes with her, she felt herself melting.

"Remember the first time," he said. Not shifting his gaze from her face, he brushed the sides of her swollen breasts. Her nipples tightened against the lace of her Victoria's Secret bra. "Do you remember the first time I touched you here?"

"Yes."

It had been a lifetime ago. They'd attended a charity function together. A formal reception. A formal date between a handsome medical student and an aspiring lawyer. Life had been so simple then.

During the presentation, they'd stepped outside onto a stone balcony. In the moonlight, they'd kissed for the first time, and something amazing had transpired. She'd been instantly transformed from an ice princess to a wanton flame, burning white hot at the core.

"Always," he said. "We've got the magic, baby."

They also had a child. She had to explain things before they went any further. But how could she? He'd hate her for the deception. "I'm...I'm a mother."

"Mommies are allowed to make love."

"That's not what I mean. It's..." *Tell him! Tell him!*

He cocked his head and studied her. "Are you afraid I'll be disappointed by changes in your body? Stretch marks?"

"I have something else to—"

"It's you I'm attracted to. The essence of Amanda Fielding. Your body is great, and it pleases me to look at you. But it doesn't matter what shape you're in. Young or old. Skinny or fat."

What was he saying? "Well, of course it matters."

"Not a bit. I'll still be attracted to you when you're seventy and your butt sags and you have wrinkles."

"Oh, that's a charming picture."

"You'll always be pretty to me. No matter where we are or what we do, you'll always be my baby."

A warm wave of affection overwhelmed her, and her objections washed away. His baby, she'd always be his baby.

When he kissed her again, she relinquished the struggle. She gave herself, mindlessly, to the uncontrollable bliss of their desire.

He swept her off her feet, carried her to the bed. In moments, they were naked, tangled together in the sheets. Helplessly consumed by their lovemaking, her mind went blank.

THE NEXT MORNING, David wakened slowly, luxuriously. The scent of last night's passion still clung to the air in a sultry miasma, and he inhaled deeply before opening his eyes.

Amanda took possession of the whole bed when she

slept. Beneath the navy-blue sheets, her toes pointed to one corner and her body slanted diagonally. She always had to have control.

Except when they were making love. Fondly, he gazed down on her disheveled blond hair. Her eyelashes made dark crescents on her cheeks, and she had a contented look, breathing deeply through her bruised lips. When they made love, she was a tiger, voracious and demanding until he tamed her with kisses, caresses and the final, fierce possession.

David couldn't allow his mind to wander too far in that direction. He'd get hard again. Then he'd have to take her again, and he wanted to let her rest. As a single mother, she probably didn't indulge herself too often by sleeping in. She'd want to be awake with Laurel, giving her daughter as much time as possible.

Rolling out of the bed, he yanked on his jeans and slipped out of the bedroom. Last night came close to convincing him that he and Amanda should be together on a permanent basis. Maybe it was corny to think that when they made love the earth moved, but that was how he felt. No other woman had ever excited him the way she did.

In the kitchen, he started his ritual brewing of coffee. Should he marry her? It wasn't an easy decision. Amanda had already rejected him twice.

Would Stefan get in the way? Someday, that blond jerk might come to his senses, behave like a decent father and claim his rights as a biological parent.

David didn't want that. He wanted Amanda and Laurel all to himself. Life would have been a hell of a lot easier if she'd conceived with him instead of Stefan. She didn't even treat him with respect. She acted as though he were just some guy she dated occasionally, not the father of her child.

Maybe he wasn't. A fresh hope cropped up in David's mind. The timing of their one-night stand had been really close to nine months before Laurel's birth.

Even if Amanda thought Stefan was the father, she could be wrong. They could have DNA tests.

As the freshly ground coffee dripped slowly into the glass decanter, David indulged his imagination. If Laurel was his daughter, he'd give her his heart and soul. He'd surround her with warmth and beauty, nurture her, watch her grow into a woman as remarkable as her mother.

Actually, the biology didn't matter. From working with battered kids at the hospital, David knew that the "real" parents weren't always the best. If Amanda would marry him, he'd adopt Laurel and raise her as his own.

When he opened the blinds in the kitchen, he saw a beige sedan parked across the street. A man in a dark suit coat sat behind the wheel. The presence of the FBI grimly reminded him that they had other problems more immediate than their possible future relationship. Amanda's life was in danger.

Coffee mug in hand, he went around the house opening curtains and blinds. It was almost ten o'clock when he went into the study and checked phone messages.

There was already a call from Frank Weathers, impatiently demanding that Amanda contact him as soon as possible about the repair work being done at Empire Bank.

"I'd appreciate it if you'd come down here," he said on the message. "I'm handling the situation, but I'd like your input on the new carpeting in the office area. Beige or rust?"

He sounded too prissy to be involved in a daring bank robbery, but that might be an act. Little Frankie had a lot to gain if Amanda were ousted as bank president. The sneaking around in her purse and making copies of keys seemed like something he would do.

The next message was a gruff voice. "This is Harry. Amanda gave me this number when she visited me at the hospital. I just wanted to let her know that I'm home and feeling fine. I'll be ready to go back to work as soon as the bank opens."

Why had she given him the number? If she expected to hide out at his house, she couldn't be telling all her friends, family and the media where she was staying.

David rewound the tape so she could play it back for herself. Interesting that she'd had calls from the two men who might have betrayed her. Harry and Frank.

Either one of them could be the inside connection for the bank robbery. Maybe they'd called here to check on Amanda.

He punched in the phone number for his brother's house and talked to his sister-in-law, who raved about how cute and smart Laurel was. Her rambunctious boys were fascinated with the pretty baby girl. Everyone was safe. All was well.

After he hung up, David drained his coffee mug and returned to the kitchen. Looking through the window, he noted that the FBI car hadn't moved, but there was another vehicle that turned into his driveway and parked. A bronze BMW.

Stefan Phillips climbed out. He flexed his shoulders and hiked up the waistband of his khaki shorts. The sunlight glinted off golden highlights in his hair. What the hell was he doing here?

David went to the security pad and punched in the number to deactivate the system. He hurried to open the front door before Stefan could ring the bell and waken Amanda.

"What do you want?" David asked.

"I want to talk to Amanda."

His cool blue eyes bored holes in David's bare chest. "She's still asleep. She needs her rest."

"Don't tell me what she needs, okay? She called me last night. She wants me to take her to my cabin in the mountains." He sneered. "So back off, Doctor. You're through."

Stepping outside onto the porch, David closed the door behind him so Amanda wouldn't be disturbed by what promised to be a loud discussion. "Don't be an ass. Hit the road before you embarrass yourself."

"Amanda and I made plans for today. It's the Fourth of July."

"I'm aware of the month. And the day."

"We're supposed to attend the celebration at the country club. She's excited about it. She loves fireworks."

She certainly did. Last night, there had been Roman candles and starbursts. But that wasn't information David intended to share. "I'll tell her you stopped by. She can telephone when she wakes up."

Stefan planted his feet firmly. "I'm not leaving until I see her."

David took another sip of coffee and considered his next move. Though he wasn't usually a man who resorted to violence, he was tempted to let fly with a quick jab to the face, thereby breaking Stefan's aquiline nose. Or he might grab Stefan by the collar and seat of the pants to throw him off the porch.

"Tell you what, Stefan—I'm going inside and closing the door. You can wait out here as long as you want."

"You tell her. You tell Amanda I'm here."

"By the way, my security system will be on, and it's real sensitive. If you create a disturbance, the cops will be here in five minutes. Not to mention the FBI guy across the street.''

Stefan pivoted and glared at the beige sedan. ''Why are all these people protecting you?''

''They're protecting Amanda. She was in a bank robbery, remember?''

''I don't like this. I want to see her. Now.'' He threw back his head and bellowed, ''Amanda! Amanda, come out here!''

David frowned. He should have opted for the jab to the face.

''Amanda!''

The door behind him opened, and Amanda stepped out. ''Stop it, Stefan. I'm right here.''

She tied the sash of her white satin robe and scowled at both of them. Her hair was a mess, her feet were bare and she was wearing David's T-shirt under her white satin bathrobe. He thought she looked adorable.

Stefan regarded her with less enthusiasm. ''That didn't take long.''

''I was already awake,'' she grumbled. ''How did you know where to find me? I didn't leave an address.''

''David's phone is unlisted, but I got his address from the country club.'' He seemed real proud of his cleverness. ''I figured a doctor—even a doc who works at Denver General—would belong to the club, and I was right.''

Clearly unimpressed, Amanda yawned. ''Well, what's up?''

''Do you still want me to take you up to the cabin? And Laurel, too.''

Finally, David thought. The jerk had finally gotten around to mentioning his daughter.

''I've made other arrangements,'' Amanda said.

''What about tonight? The fireworks display.''

"I'm not going," she said.

"Suit yourself. If I were you, I'd want to put the rumors to rest." He took a step backward. "I want you to know that I still believe in you, Amanda. In spite of what everybody is saying."

His insinuation was a nasty ploy to grab her attention, but it worked. Amanda's poise slipped a few notches. "What are they saying? Who's talking about me?"

"If you don't mind, I'd rather not stand out here on the porch with an FBI guard watching."

"Please come in."

When she held the door wide to let Stefan enter, David felt as if she were inviting a rabies-infected rat into his home. Amanda was an intelligent woman, but she had a soft spot regarding public opinion.

During the wild periods in his life, David had developed a thick hide. He couldn't care less about other people and what they thought of him. But Amanda was different.

She pointed Stefan to the coffeepot in the kitchen and pulled David aside. "I can't believe I slept until ten. Have you heard from Vonnie? Is Laurel all right?"

"Talked to my sister-in-law this morning. Everything's great, and they love Laurel." He peered over her shoulder at Stefan in his kitchen. "I'm going to have to sterilize that mug after he uses it."

"Don't be rude." She pushed her hair out of her eyes. "I need to hear what people are saying."

"It's only gossip."

"In my business, reputation is important."

He tried to understand her concern. But it didn't entirely make sense. "Yet, you chose to be a single mother rather than get married."

She glanced at the blond man who wandered around David's kitchen as if he belonged here. "Do you blame me for not marrying Stefan?"

"What did you ever see in him?"

"He's a good friend of my family."

From what she'd told him about Jack and Shirley Fielding, David would have considered their friends to be people who should be avoided like the black plague. "I still don't want him in my house."

"Nevertheless, I should take advantage of this opportunity to question him. He's suspect number four. And there might be an interesting connection or two."

She led Stefan to the kitchen table, and David decided that he couldn't sit down with this guy and treat him like a guest. But he didn't want to leave him alone with Amanda, either. Instead, he brewed another pot of coffee and milled around in the kitchen.

"I talked to my parents yesterday," she said. "They asked about you, and I told them you were fine."

He nodded. "I like your parents."

"You went home recently for a visit, didn't you?"

"Maybe a year ago. I try to stay in touch."

David admired her casual interrogation technique. Her years as a lawyer prepared her for this subtle gathering of information.

"Dad mentioned something interesting," she said. "Do you know who Jax Schaffer is?"

"He's that criminal who escaped from federal custody," Stefan said. "Why?"

"Did you know him? He used to belong to the same country club as my father. And he had a yacht. Didn't you belong to the Martin Bay Yacht Club?"

"Jax Schaffer belonged to the yacht club?" He appeared to be disgusted. "I can't believe it. Of course, I didn't associate with him. And the yacht club definitely needs a better screening process for members.''

"It's a pretty thorough screen. My parents always wanted to become members, but they could never afford it.''

"Oh, come on, Amanda. Your family is very well off.''

"They aren't as solvent as you might expect.'' She made this admission without apology. "Now, tell me what everyone in Denver is saying about me.''

Though he didn't want to leave Amanda alone with Stefan, David didn't care to participate in a conversation that seemed to revolve around who was saying what about whom. David wandered as far as the first-floor guest bedroom, where he slipped into an old work shirt he found hanging in the closet.

When he returned to the kitchen, Amanda was showing Stefan to the door.

"Thank you so much for stopping by,'' she said, opening the front door. "I'm sorry if I alarmed you. As you can see, everything is just fine. I'm mostly recovered from my injuries.''

He stood in the doorway, reluctant to depart. "What about tonight, Amanda? At the country club. Should I pick you up at seven?''

"I can't make plans,'' she said. "I simply don't know how well I'll be feeling. If I can make it, I'll see you there.''

When he leaned close to kiss her, Amanda ducked. "Goodbye, Stefan.''

She closed and locked the door behind him. With no break in her energy level, she faced David and said, "We're going to that damned country club tonight.''

"Why?''

"Because I'm going to walk in there with my head held

high. I intend to show all those gossips that I have nothing to be ashamed of. I haven't done anything wrong.''

There was fire in her eyes, and her determination made him proud. He stroked her smooth cheek and grinned. "Sounds like a fun time to me."

Chapter Thirteen

At dusk on the Fourth of July, the members of the country club, along with their invited guests and children, were still arriving. The clubhouse, draped with red, white and blue bunting, bustled with an air of all-American patriotism and festivity. Not a single cloud marred the fading blue of the Colorado skies. It promised to be a perfect night for fireworks.

Amanda squared her shoulders and inhaled a deep breath. She was dressed in a designer white sundress splashed with lavender flowers, and her attire showed the correct degree of expensive but casual style suitable for the country club. She knew that her makeup was perfect. Her summer tan was just right. She looked as though she belonged here, but she felt like an impostor.

She would never truly be one of the elite. Her struggle toward success remained too much a part of her. Right now the dire possibility of losing her job was much too close.

"I changed my mind," she said to David.

"Don't you want to see the fireworks?"

"I don't want to see these people. I don't want to hear them whispering behind my back. Looking the other way when I approach."

"You're scared."

"No," she protested. "I just don't see any point in putting myself through this humiliation."

He linked his arm through hers and veered away from the crowd, leading her into the attractively landscaped grounds on the west side of the main building. The fireworks celebration would take place on the other side, and there were only a few people strolling in this area.

"I don't mind leaving," he said. "But I don't want to be chased away because you feel embarrassed."

It seemed like a perfectly valid reason to her. "Why, then?"

"This kind of public exposure could be dangerous. This is a big place with a lot of open space, and it's going to be dark soon."

"Nobody would attack me here. There are too many witnesses."

He led her onto a wooden footbridge above a shimmering ribbon of creek. In the twilight, surrounded by the summer green of the golf course, it should have been romantic.

"Thick foliage and trees," he said. "Good places for a sniper to hide. And don't think there's safety in a crowd. A stranger could come up to you, bury a gun in your ribs and—"

"Stop it, David."

She couldn't allow herself to begin thinking of the potential danger. Staying home all day today at his house when there were so many other things she needed to accomplish had been difficult enough. Amanda simply didn't have the personality to go into hiding.

But David continued, "I think it's fairly certain that the attempted bank robbery was tied in with the escape of this Jax Schaffer character."

"I agree."

"He's a crime boss, a dangerous criminal—even if he is

a personal friend of your family and yachtmate of Stefan Phillips.''

"Not quite,'' she said. "Stefan said he didn't know Schaffer. And Mother hasn't joined the Friends of Arch-Criminals Society, though she probably would if the *right* people signed up.''

"My point,'' David said, "is that Schaffer would fit right in at this country club.''

"I know.''

"Four officers were killed when he escaped, shot down in cold blood. If he wants you dead, he'll keep sending hit men.''

"I don't know what to do.'' She looked toward David for the answer. His black knit shirt tucked into Levi's emphasized his narrow hips and lean torso. Sleek and wiry, he was ready for physical action. The fading sunlight shone in his thick black hair, and his hazel eyes were smoky. "I want to defend my reputation. But I don't want to take foolish chances.''

"Come home with me, Amanda. Instead of this mob scene, spend the night in my bed.''

It was a tempting proposition. Spending the night with David offered safety and another incredible bout of lovemaking, the mere thought of which started a delectable shivering through her body.

If she instead decided to confront her peers at the country club, the result might be unpleasant or even dangerous, but she'd have the chance to cleanse her reputation. A show of bravado would prove that she wasn't taking the FBI's suspicions seriously.

"A compromise,'' she said. "We'll make an appearance, but just for a little while. We'll leave before all the jostling and the fireworks.''

"Fair enough." He leaned forward and lightly brushed his lips across hers. "Let's get this over with."

"Do I look all right?"

"Very pretty."

Still, she hesitated. "Do I look like a bank president?"

"I don't know why you're worried about impressing these people. You're a good woman, Amanda. Intelligent, hardworking and beautiful. You have nothing to be ashamed of."

"It shouldn't make any difference what they think," she said. "I try not to care. But somewhere deep inside, I'll always be the hungry little girl with her nose pressed against the window of a pastry shop full of treats she can't afford."

"The balance in your bank account doesn't matter to anybody who's worth knowing."

He was so sure, so confident. So absolutely correct. Too often, as a banker, she defined people by their net worth. *Don't you know who I am?* The imperious words echoed in her brain. She stiffened as another memory returned. She'd spoken those words during the robbery.

"What's wrong, Amanda?"

"Remembering." She concentrated, hoping for more. In her mind, she saw the dark gleam of automatic weapons and the black ski masks. A sense of panic churned inside her. Out of control. The situation was out of control. The heavyset man approached her. His name was Sarge. He swung the butt of his gun at her head.

Then, her mind went blank again. She blinked furiously, trying to force herself to recall more. But there was no hint of new evidence, no new clues. "It was nothing," she said.

"Tell me anyway. It might help you remember more."

"During the hostage situation, I was trying to impress the robbers with my status and my money."

"Why?"

"Because I didn't want them to hurt Tracy or Carrie. wanted them to use me as their only hostage. They'd already shot that customer, and I didn't want more bloodshed That's when the one named Sarge hit me. Damn it, David Will I ever remember?"

"It's possible."

Her recollections seemed to be important enough for the criminals to send a hit man to assassinate her. How could she have forgotten?

She smoothed her skirt and willed the tremble from her fingers. In a familiar exercise of discipline, Amanda dismissed the dark thoughts from her mind. She clothed her self in regal poise, donned the mantle of an ice princess "Let's do it."

"You look like Marie Antoinette on her way to the guil lotine."

She waved her invisible scepter. "Let them eat cake."

When they entered the clubhouse, Amanda became the focus. Several acquaintances and tennis partners swarmed around her, demanding gory details of her ordeal Smoothly, she answered their questions, always downplaying her role in the attempted robbery and hostage situation As soon as she managed to deflect the topic toward other matters, the interest faded and people moved away.

Finally, she and David were alone. Under her breath, she said, "So, this is what it's like to be notorious."

"How do you like it?"

"It's a bit dehumanizing." And she was glad not to be the center of attention anymore. She grinned up at him "Mostly, it makes me hungry."

As they proceeded to the buffet table, she was reminded why Fourth of July at the country club was different from the revelry taking place in the rest of the city. Instead o

beer, chips and hot dogs, the country-club chef had prepared his famous low-fat barbeque, a culinary treat accompanied by shrimp and crab legs. It was a gourmet feast,
complete with pâtés, Brie and caviar. The salads were fab-
ulous. The ale was imported. It was red, white and cordon
bleu.

She noticed that David stuck to bottled water, and she
did the same.

At the end of the food line, she encountered Frank
Weathers. Though she'd spoken with him on the telephone
several times during the day, he greeted her as if shocked
to see her alive and well.

"Amanda? Should you be out?"

"It's the Fourth of July. I need to celebrate my indepen-
dence."

He reached toward his collar as if to straighten his necktie, but he wasn't wearing one. In a short-sleeved cotton
shirt, he looked vaguely uncomfortable. "It's a mess over
at the bank," he said. "All the papers on the desks were
scattered and trampled. I don't know who goes with what."

"I'll be over to help as soon as possible," she promised.

"I don't suppose this is the right place to discuss business," he said, glancing around. "Although I've seen
nearly all the board members."

"What's the problem?"

"You had a meeting on the morning of the robbery. With
Tracy Meyer. Was there any decision on whether or not
she could access her trust fund?"

Here was a golden opportunity to finally set one thing
right. She wanted to set the wheels in motion before she
lost her job. "Rather than use the fund, I want to arrange
an unsecured signature loan in the amount of ten thousand
dollars. Made out to Tracy Meyer."

"No collateral?"

"None required," she said. She would trust Tracy with her life. What was ten thousand bucks? "Would you put the paperwork through on that as soon as possible?"

"Well, of course," he said. "If you're really in a hurry, we could take care of it right now. The bank isn't far, and I have a key. We could just run over there together, you and I."

"By ourselves? Sounds like a rendezvous, Frank."

"Rest assured," he said with a little sneer, "I have no romantic designs."

Before she could respond, Bill Chessman approached and gave her an enthusiastic hug. "You look fine, Amanda. Just fine."

"Thanks, Bill." Her boss had obviously started celebrating earlier than the rest of them. Even his mustache looked slightly crooked.

He clapped David on the shoulder. "It's good to see you two together again. I always liked your family, David. Haines Construction are good people."

"And we pay off all our loans on time."

"So, my boy, when are we going to play golf?"

"When I'm done with my residency," David responded.

"Don't put it off too long. Every M.D. is required to play eighteen holes a week. It's part of the job." He turned to Frank. "How about you, Weathers? Are you a golfer?"

"No, sir. Tennis is my game."

"Never much cared for tennis," Chessman said.

As the chairman turned again toward David, Frank glared at his back. He was unaware that Amanda was observing, and his bony fingers gnarled into fists. The glint in his eye honed sharp as a slicing blade. Was this prissy little Frank Weathers? He looked capable of murder.

Amanda felt a hand at her waist as Stefan engulfed her

with his presence. "Amanda, I'm glad you could make it. It's good for you to get out and about."

He shook hands all around. The forced camaraderie reminded Amanda of so many other country-club events, both in Denver and Chicago. Bill Chessman was also from Illinois, and she asked, "Bill, were you ever a member at the Martin Bay Yacht Club?"

"As a matter of fact, I was."

"So was Stefan," she said.

"I never actually was a member," Stefan explained. "One of my aunts moored her yacht there."

"Being a member at that club isn't exactly a privilege," Chessman said. "Not anymore."

"What do you mean?" Amanda asked.

"Jax Schaffer was a member."

"Did you know him?" Amanda asked.

"We met. He had a weird voice, but he was a hell of a golfer."

Well, that excused everything. Jax Schaffer could pillage and murder all across the land, but as long as he shot par, he was okay.

"I just heard the police expanded their search for him," Chessman said. "He's supposed to be in the Four Corners area."

That was good news for Amanda. She glanced at David. "Jax Schaffer isn't in Denver anymore?"

"That's what they're saying." Chessman shook his head. "Hell of a golfer."

With her boss taking the lead, the conversation turned predictably to golf, a sport that bored Amanda to tears. However, it wouldn't be politically smart to walk away from a conversation with the chairman of the board. Stoically, she stayed in place, listening with disinterest. Her gaze wandered to the wall behind them. Amid trophy cases and gleaming bronze plaques were row upon row of framed photographs showing winning country-club teams of golfers, tennis players and swimmers. The net worth of those faces on the wall was in the billions.

The conversation swirled around her. Stefan and Bill discussed the merits of Chicago fairways versus those in Denver. It seemed odd that Stefan, an admitted outdoorsman, had never known Jax Schaffer. If he truly was suspect number four, she should explore that connection.

Amanda watched the ebb and flow of the crowd. Because of the promised fireworks, there were more children present than usual at a country-club function. Two little girls dressed in red, white and blue, sneaked truffles off the buffet table and ran away. They reminded her of Laurel. Her daughter was really too young to appreciate fireworks, but she would've loved making faces at the crowd.

She heard her name being spoken. "Pardon me?"

"Your memory," Chessman said. "Have you gotten over your amnesia?"

"I'm still a bit hazy on what happened during the robbery attempt."

"A terrible thing." His expression was fatherly, almost patronizing, as he smoothed the edges of his mustache. "I hope you never have to remember. It must have been frightening."

"I can handle it," she said confidently.

"Sure, you can. I didn't mean to imply—"

"I intend to return to work full-time by Tuesday."

In spite of his jovial social manner and his overindulgence in imported ale, Bill Chessman still had enough intelligence to understand that she was, in effect, issuing an ultimatum. His eyes narrowed as if peering through a jeweler's loupe, searching for flaws.

Other conversations flowed around them, but Amanda

remained focused on Chessman, waiting for his response. Though she doubted that he'd tell her she was fired at a country-club event, he could give a clue as to her current status with Empire Bank of Colorado. A firm handshake and welcome back would be nice.

"Stay home next week," he said.

"I'm perfectly healthy. I want to go back to work."

"Not yet."

Though she maintained her polite smile, Amanda felt hollow inside. Bill Chessman's instructions to stay away from the bank confirmed her darkest fears. The FBI's suspicions had poisoned the confidence of the board. She was on the verge of losing her job.

From outside, she heard the sound of bugles playing "Taps." Though the bugling heralded the beginning of the fireworks display, Amanda thought the music was especially appropriate to her situation. The day was done. The sun was going down on her career.

"Time to go outside," Chessman announced. "By the way, David, how's your brother, Josh? Still living in Evergreen?"

"That's right."

"We'd better hurry," Amanda said in a rush. The mention of Josh and Nancy made her uncomfortable. Laurel would only be safe if no one suspected she was there. "The first burst of fireworks is always the best."

As they filed through the doors, David managed to separate her from the others. Outside, he grabbed her hand and pulled her toward a stand of aspen near the parking lot, far from where anyone else was standing.

Though it wasn't pitch black, night had settled, and Amanda stumbled over an unseen rock on the path. She almost fell but was saved when David caught her arm and supported her. The sudden jolt destroyed her taut control.

She clung to him, too devastated to stand on her own. "Did you hear, David? Chessman said he didn't want me at the bank."

Maybe she was jumping to the wrong conclusion. Her fear of losing her job might have caused her to read too much into his statement. "Maybe it doesn't mean anything. He might just be concerned about my health."

"Sure, it's possible."

"But not likely."

She was going to be fired. Because of the mess with Carrie, the accusations of Sarge and her knowledge of insider banking information, she would lose everything.

A barrage of fireworks exploded, and she looked up. The skies overhead were alive with flame. Starbursts of crimson and blue. Yellow rockets streaked even higher, as high as the stars. Their colors were mirrored in David's eyes, and she looked to him for renewed hope. "There has to be something we can do."

The firecrackers clattered like machine-gun fire, followed by awe-filled oohs and aahs.

"We could go to the hospital tomorrow," he said.

"Why? I thought it was your day off."

"We could look for clues to Temple's murder. See if anybody noticed anything unusual."

"We could investigate," she said. The dying embers of hope fanned brighter. There still might be something she could do to save her reputation and her job. "That's a great idea, David. I know the police have already talked to everybody, but we have something they didn't."

"What's that?"

"Our four suspects," she said. "We could show their photographs to people in the hospital. Somebody might remember seeing one of them."

He nodded. "And where are we going to get these mug shots?"

Lit by the glow from another burst of skyrockets, she pointed toward the clubhouse. "There's a wall of pictures showing country-club teams. I'll bet we can find Stefan and Frank among them. And Bill Chessman, too."

"Is he a suspect now?"

"Don't I wish!" She despised the fact that he hadn't supported her. "He should have backed me up instead of listening to FBI accusations based on testimony from a thug like Sarge."

"I agree," David said. "But it doesn't make him a criminal."

"One can only hope."

He grinned. "You've got your fire back. You're going to be okay, baby."

His arm encircled her waist, and she leaned her head against his shoulder. If he hadn't been here to support her, she would have given up. Her resilience seemed utterly depleted. Only David's unfailing support gave her the strength to carry on.

Heading back toward the clubhouse, they strolled through the parking lot, passing David's Porsche in the farthest row.

A huge boom resounded from the fireworks area on the opposite end of the clubhouse, and a shower of sparkles fell from the heavens.

"When I was a girl," she said, "I used to wish on shooting stars. Do you think this is the same?"

"Make your wish."

"There are three of those stars. I get three wishes."

She pointed to the first. "Number-one wish is for my baby. I wish that Laurel will have a spectacular life. Next,

I wish that all of this would be resolved. The crime will be solved and I will be exonerated."

She stared at the third star winking in the sky. "The third wish is for you, David."

She wished they could get together again, that they would have another chance at happiness. "I wish that you and I—"

A sharp blast interrupted her. It came from nearby. Not from the area of the fireworks. In her peripheral vision, Amanda saw someone dodging between the cars. There was another pop. A gunshot!

David shoved her down between two cars and crouched beside her. "Go to the Porsche," he said. "The doors are unlocked."

There was another blast, either from the fireworks or the gun. "Stay low," he ordered.

Doubled over, she darted through the rows of cars. David was right behind her. She could hear him breathing. Her senses were on superalert. In the semidarkness, she heard the sound of footsteps running on the asphalt.

Were they coming closer?

At the Porsche, she whipped open the door and dived inside. The interior light made her an easy target. Amanda ducked down in the leather seat as David leaped in on the driver's side and closed his door.

There was another pop. The windshield shattered.

He threw the car into gear and pealed out of the lot onto the street. "Are you all right?"

"I think so."

"Damn it, I should have seen that coming. Should have known."

"David, it's not your—"

"Take that cell phone out of your purse and call 911. Tell the cops we'll meet them at the country club."

"No."

"What the hell do you mean? Call the police."

"Whoever the guy was, he's already gone," she said. "I went to the country club to reestablish my reputation. If we mess up their party with a police investigation, it won't be good for me or my career."

"How about your life? If you don't survive, your career doesn't mean a hell of a lot."

"They'll never catch him," she said.

"Maybe not, but a cop investigation would be a damned good dose of reality for that bunch of phonies. Make the call."

Reluctantly, she punched in the numbers for Agent Metcalf and left a message with the FBI. "This is an emergency. I'm Amanda Fielding. Someone shot at me."

She set up a meeting nearby, disconnected the call and turned to David. "I guess I'm going to be notorious again."

"It might look good to the FBI that somebody is still after you. If you're a victim, you can't really be a suspect."

"That's not true, David." She shook her head. "They killed Temple."

IN CONTRAST TO AMANDA, David enjoyed the disruption at the country club. While the fireworks continued, Agents Metcalf and Hess questioned potential witnesses. A cadre of Denver police searched outside in the parking lot. Inside, they stormed the clubhouse and sampled pâté and Brie.

Standing beside the buffet table, David decided that he'd done the country club a service by calling in the cops. Half these people were too drunk to drive home.

Agent Greg Hess joined him. "You and Amanda are free to leave at any time. Sorry about your Porsche, David."

So was he. "Did you find out anything interesting?"

"Nope, and I doubt we will. This place is too big, and

there are acres of landscape to hide the weapon. No good witnesses. Everybody was standing outside in the dark watching the fireworks.''

"Sorry we messed up your Fourth of July."

"I didn't have plans."

Hess straightened his conservative necktie. Even though they were just talking, he looked to be standing at attention.

"You're single, right?" David asked.

"Divorced."

Being an FBI agent had to be hell on relationships. Not only was Hess on call twenty-four hours a day during investigations, but danger was integral to the job.

"I appreciate the information you've been able to give me," David said.

"Metcalf would kick my butt if he knew."

"You're not as uptight as he is," David said.

He nodded. "I don't consider Amanda to be a real suspect, but I've got a gut feeling she's the key to this whole case."

Maybe Hess was acting on his own sympathetic initiative. Or maybe, as David had originally suspected, they were still playing the old good-cop–bad-cop routine. David didn't really care why Hess dribbled out these occasional facts. He'd take any crumb he could if it meant coming closer to a solution. "Got anything else?"

"Two things," Hess said tersely. "We traced the anonymous 911 phone call that alerted the police to the robbery. It was a cell phone. Stolen."

"What do you think that means?"

"The stolen phone suggests that the call was placed by another criminal."

David carried the logic a little further. "If a criminal who was involved reported the robbery to the cops, the point would be to occupy the SWAT teams at Empire Bank. If

hat was the case, the robbery attempt was a diversion so
ax Schaffer could make his escape.''

"Could be.''

"What else?'' David said.

"We viewed the secret surveillance tape that Amanda
ad in her office. The camera was set to activate when
omeone unlocked her desk drawers.''

"Someone was on the tape,'' David said. "Outstand-
ng!''

Whoever had broken into her desk would have access to
he computer codes. Finally, there would be hard evidence
hat could put Amanda in the clear.

"The problem,'' Hess said, "was that they never went
ear the drawer where she kept the computer codes. They
vere digging around in personnel records.''

"Who was it?''

"Frank Weathers.''

Suspect number one. Frankie the ferret had broken into
er desk to peek at confidential personnel information,
probably thinking he could further his career. "Have you
questioned him?''

"We hadn't been able to locate him. Not until now.''

"I thought he was at the bank today,'' David said.

"He's been in and out, but we'll get him tonight.''
Stiffly, he rotated his head to look directly at David. "Have
vou heard anything from Vonnie?''

"She's fine.'' Amanda had called the house in Evergreen
several times during the day. "Are you going to ask her
out?''

His sheepish grin was a contrast to his rigid posture. "Do
vou think she wouldn't mind dating a fed?''

"Only one way to find out.''

David left Hess and went in search of Amanda.

He found her sitting alone in a far corner of the clubhouse, gazing through the polished windows into the night. Though her poise remained unshaken, she showed signs of tension. Her fingers knotted tightly in her lap. When he approached, she cast her gaze downward. She appeared contrite, apologetic for inviting these unwelcome guests to the party.

"We can go now," he said.

"I'm more than ready."

She spoke not another word. Cautiously, she avoided contact with anyone else. David felt bad for her. Her good name was so vitally important to her.

When they drove the Porsche from the country-club parking lot, he was surprised to hear her giggle. "Are you okay?"

"I'm fine, and I really mean it this time." Her voice was rich with energy. "I could learn to like this. Being the center of attention? It's kind of fun. Flashy."

"I'm glad you think so."

"And guess what I stole off the wall in the trophy room?" She dug into her purse and pulled out two photographs. "Here's a photo of the winners of a golf tournament with Stefan and Bill Chessman. And another of the tennis team that won some city-wide tournament. Look at Frank's skinny little legs."

"Suspect number one," he said, thinking of the hard evidence on the secret surveillance camera. "Do you think we're right about him?"

"He's a nerd, all right." She touched his arm. "But I was watching him tonight. Bill Chessman snubbed him, and I saw a look in Frank's eyes that gave me goose bumps. I think he's capable of murder."

Chapter Fourteen

The next morning, with Amanda cuddled in the bed beside him, David lay awake, staring at the long-barreled revolver on the bedside table. The piece had to be over twenty years old, and he didn't even know if it worked. His aunt, who had owned this house before willing it to David, had bought the gun for protection. Once upon a time, when he was a kid, she'd shown him how to use it and told him that she always kept it under the floorboards in the bedroom.

David had always known the gun was there, lurking like a coiled rattler, in a secret cubbyhole under the floorboards in the bedroom. Until now, he'd never thought of taking it out, cleaning it, preparing to use it as a deadly weapon. To kill. What the hell was he doing? He was a doctor. It was his business to save lives.

But he had to protect her. He had to keep Amanda safe.

Her eyes remained closed, and her breathing was steady. He cautiously enfolded her in his arms, careful not to wake her, and he whispered, "I love you, baby."

It felt good to say the words again. Five years ago, they had been in love. This time, it would be better. Perfect.

There was only the small matter of protecting her from professional assassins and clearing her name in a bank-robbery attempt.

David licked his lips. A straight shot of vodka would have been nice. He could use something to take the edge off his tension. Instead, he kissed the tip of her nose.

He threw off the sheets, grabbed a pair of shorts from the dresser drawer and rambled down to the kitchen to make coffee. After the first sip, he went into the office.

The message machine was, of course, blinking. But he ignored it. His first call was to Stella in the emergency room at the hospital.

She recognized his voice immediately. "Glad you called," she said. "I have a message for Amanda."

"Give it to me."

"We found her Guccis," she said proudly. "Those posters I put all over the hospital did the trick. And you can tell her that she was right. It looks like somebody stole the shoes."

He couldn't believe these two women were still obsessing over a pair of shoes in the middle of robbery attempts and shootings. "How can you tell somebody stole them?"

"Because they're being so sneaky. They left one of the posters on my desk. On the back was a note." There was the rustling of paper. "It says, 'I have the shoes. Bring reward. The owner should meet me at noon Sunday on the front lawn. Come alone.'"

Sounded like a ransom note. For a pair of shoes? "I'll tell Amanda."

"Why did you call?"

"I need to come in today." His purpose was to investigate Temple's murder, but he wasn't going to tell Stella about that. "And I wanted to know if Loretta Spangler was scheduled to work."

"Hiding from the big bad neurologist?"

"That would be correct," he said.

"Sorry, Doc. She's already here."

Her presence was inconvenient. He didn't need any more hassles, but he could manage.

Before David could deal with the other phone messages, Amanda sauntered into the den with her daisy coffee mug in her hand. She looked great in the morning.

"Good news," he said. "Stella has a lead on your shoes."

"The Guccis?"

He told her about the note. "Better bring the reward. This shoe thief sounds like a fruitcake."

And he was going to accompany her. This weird ransom note might also be a ploy by an assassin to get her alone. Somehow, he needed to figure out a way to carry his over-size pistol around in the hospital with him.

AFTER THEY'D SHOWERED and dressed, Amanda stood in the driveway outside David's house watching him circle the Porsche and listening to him grumble.

"Bullet holes," he snarled. "Two in the hood. One in the fender. Windshield ruined."

"We can take the minivan," she said.

"You don't understand, Amanda. This car is a work of art."

"Really?" she drawled. "And you had the nerve to give me a hard time about my Gucci shoes."

Her purse rang, and she dug out the cell phone. Standing outdoors with the phone in her hand, she was on the verge of a memory, but it wouldn't quite materialize. "Hello?"

"Agent Metcalf here. I wanted to let you know that our search last night was fruitless."

"I'm sorry," she said. Last night in bed, David had told her about the video of Frank Weathers on her secret surveillance camera. "Have you made any arrests?"

"No, ma'am. Why would I?"

She didn't want to say anything that might get Agent Hess in trouble. "No reason."

"Ms. Fielding, I wanted to emphasize to you that it's important for you to be careful today. Don't leave the house. Our investigation is moving forward, and the people involved might take desperate measures."

Like hiring a hit man? Like shooting at her in a parking lot? "That's good advice," she said.

But she didn't intend to follow it. She and David would be cautious in their investigation at the hospital, and she couldn't force herself to sit on her hands all day.

"Who was that?" David asked.

"Metcalf."

She didn't mention his warning as she climbed into the passenger's side of her minivan. David seemed tense enough already. He stashed a huge, antique-looking revolver in his black doctor's bag and placed it in the back of the van.

"I'm taking Old Betsy with me."

She raised her eyebrows. "Old Betsy?"

"I might not be enough of a marksman to hit the broad side of the Goodyear blimp, but this gun looks like serious business."

"It looks like a relic from the Old West," she said.

"Perfect." He checked his wristwatch. "Because it's almost high noon, and I'm ready for the showdown with the Gucci thief."

Before she buckled her seat belt, she leaned toward him, and he met her halfway for a casual but lingering kiss. She wanted to tell him that she loved him, but last night's lovemaking spoke louder than words.

"I have a good feeling, David. I'll get my shoes. We'll use the photos to investigate and find Temple's murderer. And I'll remember. This will all be over soon."

"I hope you're right."

David started up the engine of the minivan and headed toward Denver General with the taste of Amanda lingering on his lips. She was bright and energetic today. Her clear blue eyes held a touching optimism, and he wanted to believe her when she said this was almost over. After the threats and the danger had passed, they might have a chance to build something wonderful together.

Echoes of her prior rejections resonated in his head, but he ignored the clamor. He knew that she loved him, even if she wasn't ready to admit it. "When this is over, I want to talk about our future. Yours, mine and Laurel's. I don't want you to leave me. Not ever again."

A beautiful smile stretched across her face. It was exactly the response he'd hoped for.

"We'll talk," she promised.

At the hospital, they crossed the patio near the entrance and turned west. Cars and taxis were parked at a long circular driveway. In a grassy area beyond, people were seated at stone tables and benches, innocently eating their lunches.

David was glad he'd taken the black doctor's bag containing his weapon. There was a portent of danger in the air. Something intense was about to happen.

He scanned the crowd, looking for someone alone, someone carrying a shoe box.

Beside him, Amanda gasped. "It's Carrie."

A petite woman with gray hair and eyeglasses strolled toward them. She wore a white lab coat with a stethoscope tucked in her pocket. Her pace was unhurried with hands stuck in her pockets. Though David had never met this woman before, he wouldn't have sworn she didn't work at the hospital.

"A gray wig?" Amanda said.

"I'm really getting into this disguise thing. Lucky for me, I'm nondescript and can blend into a crowd."

But she did have a pleasant, open face and honest eyes. David's first impression of the fugitive Carrie Lamb was positive. She didn't look like a bank robber.

Amanda asked, "Are you the one who wrote the note about the shoes?"

"Yup. I thought this would be a good way to see you. I wanted to say goodbye, Amanda. I'm going to leave town for a little while."

"No," Amanda said. "I won't let you run off with a fugitive bank robber."

David remembered Amanda's panic when she thought the fugitive might find his house and threaten Laurel.

"You've got to trust me," Carrie said. "I have to do this my way. Don't worry, okay? I always land on my feet."

For a long moment, Amanda stared at her friend. A series of emotions played across her face. Anger and fear, followed by acceptance. "I'm warning you, Carrie. If you get yourself killed, I'll never speak to you again."

"Fair enough."

Amanda's eyes shone with unshed tears as she pulled him closer. "I want you to meet David Haines."

"You're David!" She grabbed his hand and pumped. "So, you two finally got back together again. Good. I'm so happy for you both. David, aren't you proud of Amanda and your daughter?"

His daughter? "What did you say?"

"Laurel." Carrie beamed up at him. "You must have known the minute you saw her. She looks just like you."

Laurel Fielding, nine months old, was his daughter, his baby, his own.

Why the hell hadn't Amanda told him? Why had she allowed him to believe Stefan was the father?

She'd lied to him about the most important event that occurred in any man's life. The birth of his child. Cold fury clawed at his heart.

He was a father. This should have been a moment of joy. Not pain. Not rage.

Amanda and Carrie hugged and separated. As Carrie walked away, he was aware of Amanda beside him. He couldn't look at her. He might explode if he confronted her directly.

"I'm sorry, David."

There was no amount of sympathy that could make up for her lies. "I don't want to hear it."

"Please, listen to me. I made my decision—a very wrong decision—based on when we were engaged. I didn't think we could live together."

"You stole the first nine months of my daughter's life." He might have assisted at the birth. He might have been the first person to hold his child in his arms. Now the chance was gone. "It was my right to know."

"If you'd known, you would have insisted that we get married. And I didn't believe it would work out. I didn't know how much I…cared about you."

"The only person you cared about was yourself. Your damned career. Your life."

The anguish in her eyes ripped into him, but he strode away from her, fighting to control his all-consuming rage. His pulse hammered. Every muscle in his body clenched. His fingers, holding the handle on his black bag, were white knuckled.

Then he remembered the danger. The revolver. He came to a stiff and sudden halt. No matter how he felt about what she'd done to him, he couldn't leave her unprotected. He couldn't abandon her now.

"Come with me, Amanda."

"David, I—"

"I made a promise to protect you. In spite of what you think, I keep my word."

AMANDA SEATED HERSELF beside Stella at the counter in emergency. Though she was still able to walk and talk and function, she felt dead inside.

He would never forgive her. He would despise her for the rest of their days. And she couldn't blame him. She should have listened to her heart instead of logically deciding that he wasn't good husband and father material. How could she have been so very wrong? No man would be a better father for Laurel than David.

Stella slammed down the telephone, leaped to her feet behind the desk and shouted, "David, we have a four-car collision and a driveby shooting. Three ambulances. Six victims. Get into your scrubs."

"I don't think so." A tall woman with black hair pulled back in a bun stalked to the desk. "Dr. Haines is under disciplinary review."

"We're shorthanded," Stella said. "Dr. Spangler, we need every available doctor who can—"

The double doors leading to the ambulance area crashed open. Gurneys wheeled inside. Paramedics shouted for help.

And David responded. He shoved the black bag under Amanda's chair. "Don't go anywhere," he ordered.

She nodded.

For nearly half an hour, Amanda sat there. Her knees pressed tightly together. Her shoulders were tense. Her stomach rolled up and down like a yo-yo, but her mind was numb.

Then she caught a glimpse of David. He'd thrown a paper gown over his clothes, and the front was covered in blood. The look of determination on his face wrenched her heart. Her self-control shattered. Tears seeped between her eyelids.

The cell phone in her purse trilled loudly, and she took it out. When she flipped it open and held it to her ear, another memory slammed across her consciousness.

She was inside the bank. Carrie and Tracy were with her. Fear and confusion roiled in her gut. And she looked through the windows. There she saw a man with a cell phone. He stared at the bank, then turned away.

Stefan!

She dropped the phone back into her purse without answering.

Stefan was the man behind the robbery. Suspect number four.

It all made sense to her now. The reason her bank, Empire Bank, had been selected for the robbery was that Stefan had access; he'd used their friendship to get information from her.

He could have easily stolen her spare keys from the apartment and had copies made. Several times, she remembered, he visited her at work. He'd been alone in her office. He could have rifled the desk.

In a strange way, the FBI's suspicions had been correct. Amanda *was* the inside contact for the robbery attempt. But she was only a conduit for Stefan to gain all the codes and procedures the robbers would need.

For another half hour she sat, absorbing this knowledge and trying to decide on her next move. She should have been pleased. Finally, she would be free from suspicion, her job no longer threatened.

More than anything, she wanted to tell David. She wanted to feel his arms around her.

Stella plopped down in the chair beside her. "I don't know why David came in this afternoon, but I'm glad he did."

"What's happened?"

"First, we had the car accident. Then a six-year-old boy was shot in a driveby. Thanks to David, he's going to be all right."

Amanda felt a surge of pride. "I'm glad."

"Your man is a hell of a good doc," Stella said.

The cell phone in Amanda's purse rang again. This time, she connected the call. It was Stefan.

"I want to see you, Amanda. Immediately."

"Sorry, Stefan." The sound of his voice disgusted her. She couldn't wait to turn him in to the FBI. Maybe they'd lock him up for a hundred years. "I'm busy."

"Too busy to see your little baby, Laurel? She misses her mommy."

"What are you saying?"

"Josh and Nancy Haines in Evergreen. I saw their name and address written on a pad beside the phone when I visited you at David's house. But I didn't make the connection until we were all together at the country club and Bill Chessman asked about them. It only took a couple phone calls to confirm. Then I picked her up."

"No," she whispered. Dread and panic choked her.

"Vonnie was only too happy to turn the baby over to me. Did you know? She thinks I'm Laurel's father."

"Where are you?"

"I'm at your place, Amanda. Your condo."

"How did you get in my condo?"

He laughed. "I think we both know that I have a key. Several keys, in fact. Be here in ten minutes, or I'll do to Laurel what I would have done to you."

"If you hurt one hair on Laurel's head, I'll—"

"By the way, if you tell anybody, Laurel dies. You know I'll do it, Amanda. I hate kids."

The phone went dead in her hand. She had ten minutes. She grabbed David's black bag from under her chair and ran for the door.

STELLA POKED HER HEAD into the emergency-room cubicle where David was completing his examination of a teenage boy. "You're going to be all right," he assured the kid. "That's a nice clean break in your arm. And we only had to shave a little place on the back of your head to stitch up the wound. Now, Dr. Spangler is going to take over."

Loretta Spangler nodded to him. "You've done good work today, Haines. I'll consider withdrawing my request for disciplinary action."

"Thanks." He glanced at Stella. "I'm putting in for some serious overtime."

"I'm worried about Amanda," Stella said. "She got a phone call from a guy named Stefan and he—"

"Whoa! Did she tell you this?"

"Well, I was sitting right next to her when she got a call on her cell phone. I couldn't help overhearing."

He wasn't surprised. The only thing bigger than Stella's eyes were her ears. He stepped out of the cubicle. "Okay. So, Amanda got a phone call. So what?"

"She looked really scared. Like in shock. And she said something about Laurel getting hurt."

His blood froze. "Where is she?"

"She ran out of here, really fast. On the phone, she said that Stefan was at her condo."

David took off running. The black bag with his revolver was gone. Amanda must have taken it. She was going to face Stefan head-on. And Laurel was in danger.

In the past hour, he'd saved a child's life. Now he was about to lose his own Laurel, before he'd even had a chance to know her.

He charged out the door to a waiting ambulance and leaped in beside the driver. "Let's roll. We've got an emergency."

IN THE HALLWAY outside her condo, Amanda discarded the bag and held the revolver in her hand. It was huge and heavy, and she wasn't sure that she even knew how to fire the thing. But holding the grip gave her an edge.

On the frantic drive over here, she'd tried calling Josh and Nancy in the mountains, but no one answered. She'd thought of contacting the police, but she didn't dare take the chance. They might overreact. And Laurel's life would hang in the balance.

The cell phone was in her pocket. As soon as she made sure Laurel was all right, she'd call 911. She'd hold Stefan off with the gun and call the police. And Laurel would be safe.

Using her key, she unlocked the door. With the gun behind her back, she stepped inside. "All right, Stefan. I'm here."

Where was he? She walked toward the front room.

An instant before he grabbed her from behind, she heard him. But it was too late to turn around.

He knocked the gun from her hand and crooked an elbow around her throat. "It's about time."

She gasped as he tightened his choke hold. "Where's Laurel?"

"In the mountains where she belongs. I didn't need to

kidnap her, did I? The threat was enough. You're such a good little mommy that you came running.''

"You were bluffing?''

"That's one thing you never figured out about me," he said. "I'm cool. The people who really know me call me the Iceman.''

He released her with a shove, and she fell to the floor. When she looked up, she saw the automatic pistol in his hand. More frightening than the gun was the look on his face. His eyes were wild, unfocused.

"Don't try to run," he warned. "I'm getting pretty good with this gun, and I could probably shoot off your knee-cap.''

He was insane. Why hadn't she seen it before?

Her only chance was to keep him calm. Play for time. Hope that she could reach the gun on the floor. "Okay, Stefan. I'll do whatever you say.''

"Iceman. Call me Iceman.''

"All right. Iceman.''

"You should always be nice to a man with a gun, Amanda. You're going to die, either way. But I can make it fast and painless. Or real slow." He strolled over to the sofa and sat. "Slow would be more fun for me.''

Her gaze flicked to the revolver. Gauging the distance, she knew it lay just beyond her reach. She needed to move closer. "Were you behind the robbery?''

"I organized the whole thing.''

"Pretty smart.'' If she kept him talking, he might get careless. "Have you done this before?''

"A couple of years ago, I depleted my trust fund, and I started doing little jobs for Jax Schaffer.''

"You met him in Chicago.''

"That's right. We ran in the same circles. Like the yacht club. He always paid very well. But the Empire Bank robbery? That was going to be my big score. Half a million bucks, plus a payoff from Jax if his escape succeeded.''

"But the robbery failed," she said.

"Bad luck," he countered. "My men were supposed to be in the process of escaping with the money when the cops showed up, but Temple got shot in the leg, which meant he couldn't be the getaway driver."

"If they escaped, they wouldn't be a diversion for Jax Schaffer's escape."

"Don't be stupid, Amanda. The cops would have been tied up chasing the getaway car. They're really the ones who made a mess of things. They responded too fast."

"Maybe you made your anonymous 911 call too early."

His eyebrows raised. "You knew about the call?"

"I saw you outside the bank with a cell phone in your hand." Subtly, she inched toward the gun. "You really were clever, Stefan. How did you override the computer system?"

"I contracted with specialists. Temple was the driver, and Dallas was the computer genius. He set everything up in advance using the codes I lifted from your desk." He gave her a look of pure disgust. "Sarge was the hit man. He was supposed to kill you during the robbery."

"Why?"

"Because you, Amanda, could point the finger at me. Sooner or later, you'd figure out my connection to Jax. And you'd wonder about my interest in your boring job. Without you, there was nothing at all to connect me to Empire Bank."

"Well, that's not true anymore," she said. She might be able to work a bluff of her own. "I told Agent Metcalf everything. And I called him on the way over here. On my cell phone."

"You're lying."

She forced the tremble from her voice. Slowly, she rose to her feet. In a few steps, she might be able to reach the gun. "It's over. The FBI will be here at any moment. Don't add murder to the list of charges against you."

"You don't fool me, Amanda."

Now! She dived toward the gun. Her hands outstretched. Almost in her grasp.

But he was quicker. An athlete, Stefan beat her to the gun. He lifted it by one finger. "Looking for this?"

Her hopes crashed around her. Escape was impossible. She was going to die.

With his toe, he nudged her hard in the ribs, but she barely felt the pain. She was going to die before she had a chance to make things right with David. She would never see Laurel grown to adulthood.

"Just in case you're telling the truth," he said. "I better not kill you here. I'm not taking any more chances. Let's go."

He grabbed her arm and propelled her through the door of the condo toward the elevator. When the doors snapped open, he threw her inside ahead of him.

Then the doors closed. Though Amanda had ridden up and down in this conveyance a thousand times, this time was different. Panic surrounded her. Her eyes darted frantically as she felt the walls collapsing in upon her. Claustrophobia. Her heart beat faster. A frightened moan escaped her lips.

A cruel grin twisted Stefan's lips. "Poor little Amanda. You don't like enclosed spaces, do you?"

The elevator walls tightened. There wasn't enough air to breathe. She was suffocating.

He pressed the door-closed button and held it. "Did you really tell the FBI?"

"Yes." She clawed at the collar of her shirt, trying to get air. "Yes!"

"And what did you say to them?"

"Don't know." She had to get out of here. She'd go mad if she was trapped here for one more second.

"I'll open the door if you tell me the truth."

Strangled by her own terror, she couldn't speak. Her lungs burned. Frantically, she threw herself against the elevator door. The buttons. She had to press the buttons.

"Tell me!" he demanded.

"I didn't call anybody. Nobody knows!" She hit the button for the first floor and felt the elevator begin to move. "Let me out of here."

She was on fire, unable to breathe. Her head was spinning. She felt herself losing consciousness. Her knees gave way, and she slumped to the floor.

"I think we'll go right back upstairs, Amanda. And then, you're going to die."

On the first floor, the doors opened. She was vaguely aware of David and two policemen who stood waiting.

The small enclosed space exploded with the sound of gunfire. Amanda heard herself scream as Stefan fell to the floor beside her.

"Bitch," he whispered as he aimed the gun at her face.

David grabbed Stefan's hand and threw the automatic pistol away. "Lucky for you, Stefan. The ambulance is already here."

He lifted Amanda to her feet and helped her from the elevator. "It's okay now."

"Air," she gasped. "Outside."

The breeze hit her full in the face, and she inhaled in huge gulps as David helped her to a wrought-iron bench beside the doorway. Sitting, she leaned against him, drawing on his strength. Her heartbeat returned to a more normal level. The terror began to subside, leaving behind an emptiness.

His voice was low and soothing. "It's all over, Amanda. Everything is going to be all right."

She looked up at him. "If everything will be all right, why do I feel so miserable?"

The ambulance driver and one of the cops came past them with Stefan stretched out on a gurney. Another police sedan pulled up in front of the condo.

"David," she whispered, "can you ever forgive me?"

Gently, he lifted her hand, lacing his fingers through hers. "I spent the last hour fighting to save a kid's life. And I realized something. Any minute, any precious minute with a child is a gift. I'd be a fool to throw away one second with Laurel."

"And me? Can you be with me?"

"I don't want to be an absentee father." He kissed her forehead. "You're part of the package."

The blood had begun to circulate in her body again. She felt stronger. Inhaling a deep breath, she said, "I made a terrible mistake. I misjudged you. But know this, David. In all the time we've shared—when we were together and apart—I never stopped loving you."

His lips pressed against hers, and it was the sweetest kiss she'd ever experienced. The taste of forgiveness.

The scene around them had become increasingly crowded with cops and condo dwellers. The concierge argued loudly with one of the uniformed officers.

But Amanda saw only David. His presence filled her.

Epilogue

Two days later, Amanda sat behind her desk at Empire Bank. The broken windows had been replaced, and the air-conditioning system cooled the temperature to a comfortable level. The hammering from an army of workmen sounded like a joyous symphony, promising that the bank would be reopened by next week. She was back in business.

With a final flourish, she completed the loan document that would make ten thousand dollars immediately available to Tracy Meyer.

"Ma'am?" A workman stood in her doorway. "Will it disturb you if I put this new nameplate on your door?"

"It will delight me."

She came out from behind her desk to watch as he affixed a bronze plaque at eye level. It read Amanda Fielding-Haines, President."

What a beautiful hyphenated name! A flight to Vegas and a visit to a justice of the peace, and it was done.

When she saw her handsome new husband coming through the front entrance with Laurel tucked under his arm, pure happiness glowed within her. She wasn't sure how long this perfect joy would last. Forever was a long time, but she expected to come close.

Amanda passed the loan papers to Jane Borelli, former

ead teller whom she had promoted to a position as executive personal banker. "Jane, would you expedite this loan, please? Take the papers downtown."

"I'm kind of busy." Her grin was tentative. "But I'll give it to Frank."

"You're picking on me," he growled from his desk. "Good old Frank. The errand boy."

"Nonsense," Jane said. "I give you extra work because like you."

Amanda couldn't believe it. Jane actually liked the overmbitious little ferret. Frank had caused so much trouble or Amanda, had cast suspicion on her, had seriously reached ethical behavior by going through her desk. She really *ought* to fire him.

But not today, when her mood was rosy and forgiving. As David approached, she happily yielded to the magnetic ull she felt whenever he was near. Gliding into his arms, he thought that perhaps hugging should be official bank policy.

He whispered in her ear. "I love you, baby."

"Love you, too." She shivered with happiness and grinned at Laurel. "And how's this baby?"

Laurel waved her arms and babbled. "Dabba-dabba."

"Hear that?" His face lit up with pleasure. "She said Daddy."

"Obviously a gifted child," she said.

"Laurel was supervising the movers at your condo. Obiously a bossy child. She takes after you."

Distracted by a disturbance at the front entrance, Amanda looked up as Bill Chessman charged through the doors and barked an order to Harry Hoffman, who was back at work s a security guard, "Keep that woman out!"

Fuming, Chessman stormed across the lobby toward hem. "Elaine Montero has been on my tail since Monday,

demanding information about my alleged connection to Ja:
Schaffer. She never gives up.''

"Annoying, isn't it?'' Amanda said. "It's horrid to be
suspected of complicity in a crime you had nothing to do
with.''

She blinked away an unhappy memory. Chessman'
comment had reminded her that Schaffer was still at large
More importantly, Carrie hadn't yet been heard from
Amanda could only pray that her best friend would be al
right.

Chessman's voice held a resigned tone. "Suspicion is a
terrible thing. Insidious. I'm sorry, Amanda, for doubting
you.''

"You're forgiven.'' She glanced toward David. Togethe
they'd learned that forgiveness was a precious gift for both
the giver and the receiver.

David grinned back at her and turned to Chessman. "
know how you can make it right. Give Amanda two week.
off, paid vacation.''

"Done. Why?''

"Honeymoon,'' he said. "I'm thinking of Paris.''

"France?'' Amanda questioned. "Oh, David, I don'
know anything about the day-care situation in Europe.''

"We'll take Vonnie.''

She shook her head. "I don't think she'll want to leave
her new FBI boyfriend.''

"We'll take him, too. I can afford it.''

"But, David, this is too—''

"It's spontaneous,'' he said, leaning forward to kiss he
forehead. "And it's fun. Get used to it.''

"Guess I can't complain about fun, can I?''

"Guess not.''

She passed Laurel to Jane and pulled David into her of

ice for a real kiss. They had a lot of loving to do, making p for the five years they'd been apart, and she passionately nticipated every single moment of responsibility and aughter.

* * *

Look out for Tracy's story in His To Protect, *available in June 2000*

SILHOUETTE

INTRIGUE™

AVAILABLE FROM 19TH MAY 2000

MIDNIGHT CALLER Rebecca York

43 Light Street

Meg Faulkner couldn't remember her accident, her identity or the reason she was stranded with the mysterious Glenn Bridgman. Meg fought to find the memories, and at the same time tried to resist tempting, desirable Glenn. She had to decide—was he her captor or her protector?

HIS TO PROTECT Patricia Werner

Captive Hearts

Tracy Meyer, the scared key witness to a bank robbery, was relying on strong, sexy Matt Forrest to protect her and her young daughter. Matt moved in, but neither expected their long-buried secret desire to erupt… With a dangerous criminal at large, Matt vowed to keep Tracy and her child safe, whatever it took…

UNDERCOVER DAD Charlotte Douglas

FBI agent Stephen Chandler knows he and his ex-partner, Rachel Goforth, are in danger, but he can't remember why. One thing he knows, though, is he's attracted to Rachel. So when Rachel's baby is kidnapped, nothing can stop him from going after her, especially when he learns that Rachel's daughter is also *his*!

SECRET LOVER Shawna Delacorte

Jim Richards found himself inexplicably drawn to Andrea Sinclair—mind *and* body. There was something about the woman. But could he trust her to help him find the killer who pursued him? He didn't have a choice; his heart wouldn't let him leave her…

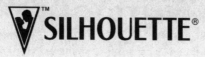

Welcome back to the drama and mystery that is the Fortune Dynasty.

A Fortune's Children Wedding is coming to you at a special price of only £3.99 and contains a money off coupon for issue one of *Fortune's Children Brides*.

With issue one priced at a special introductory offer of 99p you can get it **FREE** with your money off coupon.

Men who can't be tamed by just *any* woman!

We know you'll love our selection of the most passionate and adventurous Sensation™ hero every month as the Heartbreaker.

HEARTBREAKERS

2 Books
and a surprise gift!

We would like to take this opportunity to thank you for reading this Silhouette® book by offering you the chance to take TWO more specially selected titles from the Intrigue™ series absolutely FREE! We're also making this offer to introduce you to the benefits of the Reader Service™ —

- ★ FREE home delivery
- ★ FREE gifts and competitions
- ★ FREE monthly Newsletter
- ★ Books available before they're in the shops
- ★ Exclusive Reader Service discounts

Accepting these FREE books and gift places you under no obligation to buy; you may cancel at any time, even after receiving your free shipment. Simply complete your details below and return the entire page to the address below. *You don't even need a stamp!*

YES! Please send me 2 free Intrigue books and a surprise gift. I understand that unless you hear from me, I will receive 4 superb new titles every month for just £2.70 each, postage and packing free. I am under no obligation to purchase any books and may cancel my subscription at any time. The free books and gift will be mine to keep in any case.

10EB

Ms/Mrs/Miss/Mr ....Initials...................................
BLOCK CAPITALS PLEASE

Surname...

Address...

....

....Postcode ....

Send this whole page to:
UK: The Reader Service, FREEPOST CN81, Croydon, CR9 3WZ
EIRE: The Reader Service, PO Box 4546, Kilcock, County Kildare (stamp required)

Sometimes bringing up baby
can bring surprises —and
showers of love! For the cutest
and cuddliest heroes and
heroines, choose the Special
Edition™ book marked

That's my
baby!

SILHOUETTE
SPECIAL EDITION®